O9-AIF-604

Praise for *USA TODAY* bestselling author Maureen Child

"Maureen Child is one of the foremost names in Americana romance."
—*RT Book Reviews*

"Maureen Child is one of the stars in the ascendant...poised for the next big step."
—*Publishers Weekly*

"Maureen Child has written a beautiful, heartwarming tale of family tragedy, redemption and love in this passionate tale. A keeper!"
—*RT Book Reviews* on *Expecting Lonergan's Baby*

"Filled with heart-wrenching emotions and an unforgettable hero."
—*Rendezvous* on *And Then Came You*

"The ever entertaining Maureen Child warms the cockles of our heart with this sensitive, touching romance."
—*RT Book Reviews*

MAUREEN CHILD

is a California native who loves to travel.
Every chance they get, she and her husband are
taking off on another research trip. The author
of more than sixty books, Maureen loves a happy
ending and still swears that she has the best job in
the world. She lives in Southern California with her
husband, two children and a golden retriever with
delusions of grandeur. Visit Maureen's website at
www.maureenchild.com.

USA TODAY Bestselling Author

Maureen Child

Last Virgin in California

———————

Marine Under the Mistletoe

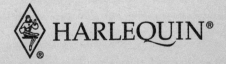

HARLEQUIN®

TORONTO • NEW YORK • LONDON
AMSTERDAM • PARIS • SYDNEY • HAMBURG
STOCKHOLM • ATHENS • TOKYO • MILAN • MADRID
PRAGUE • WARSAW • BUDAPEST • AUCKLAND

Recycling programs
for this product may
not exist in your area.

ISBN-13: 978-0-373-68813-5

LAST VIRGIN IN CALIFORNIA & MARINE UNDER THE MISTLETOE

Copyright © 2010 by Harlequin Books S.A.

The publisher acknowledges the copyright holder of the individual works
as follows:

LAST VIRGIN IN CALIFORNIA
Copyright © 2001 by Maureen Child

MARINE UNDER THE MISTLETOE
Copyright © 1999 by Maureen Child

CONTENTS

LAST VIRGIN IN CALIFORNIA

Chapter One

"You're marrying *who?*"

Lilah Forrest winced and held the phone receiver away from her ear so that her father's voice wouldn't deafen her. Honestly. A lifetime in the Marine Corps had given Jack Forrest such range, he could probably wake the dead if ordered to.

"Ray, Daddy," she said, when she pulled the phone close again. "You remember him. You met him the last time you came to visit?"

"Of *course* I remember him," her father sputtered. "He's the little guy who told me my uniform would look less intimidating if I wore an earring."

Lilah smothered a chuckle she knew darn well her dad wouldn't appreciate. But really, just the thought of her oh-so-proper, career Marine father wearing a tidy gold hoop in his ear was enough to cultivate bubbles of laughter that weren't at all easy to subdue.

"He was kidding," she said when she could speak without a smile in her voice.

"Right." He didn't sound convinced.

"I thought you liked Ray."

"I didn't say I don't like him," he said tightly. "But what do you see in those artsy-fartsy types, anyway?"

Artsy-fartsy, Lilah thought. Translation: Any man who *wasn't* a Marine.

"What you need," her father was saying, "is a man as stubborn as you are. A strong, dependable type. Like—"

"A Marine," she finished for him. For heaven's sake, she'd heard this speech so often, she could give it for him.

"What's wrong with a Marine?" he demanded, clearly defensive.

"Nothing," she said, wishing they weren't having this conversation...*again*.

Lilah sighed and plopped down onto her overstuffed couch. Curling up into a corner of the sofa, she cradled the receiver between her ear and her shoulder and tugged the hem of her dress down over her updrawn legs. "Daddy, Ray's a nice guy."

"I'll take your word for it, honey," he said

grudgingly. "But do you really think he's the right guy for you?"

No, she didn't. Ray's image rose up in her mind and Lilah smiled to herself. Short, with nearly waist-length black hair he kept in a thick braid, Ray was an artist. He wore diamonds in his ears, favored tunic shirts and leather sandals and was absolutely devoted to his life partner, Victor.

But, he was also one of Lilah's closest friends. Which was the only reason he'd agreed to let her tell her father that they were engaged. Victor wasn't the least bit happy about it, but Ray had been an absolute doll.

And seriously, if she hadn't been about to go spend a few weeks with her father, this never would have happened. But she simply couldn't stand the idea of having another parade of single officers thrown at her feet. She didn't much like the idea of lying to her dad, but really it was his own fault. If he'd quit trying to get her married to some "suitable" Marine, she wouldn't have to resort to such lengths, would she?

"Ray's wonderful, Daddy," she said, meaning every word. "You'll like him if you give yourself a chance."

He grumbled something she didn't quite catch and a twinge of guilt tugged at her heart. Jack Forrest wasn't a bad man. He just never had been able to understand his daughter.

As her father changed the subject and started

talking about what was happening on the base, she listened with half an ear as her gaze drifted around the living room of her tiny, San Francisco apartment. Crimson-red walls surrounded her, giving the small room warmth. Sunlight streamed through the unadorned windows, painting the old fashioned, deeply cushioned furniture with a soft golden glow that shimmered on the polished, hardwood floors. Celtic music drifted to her from the CD player on the far wall and the scent of burning patchouli candles filled the air with a fragrance that relaxed her even as her fingers tightened around the phone in her hand.

She hated lying to her father. After all, lying wasn't good for the soul. Besides, she had a feeling it caused wrinkles, too. But as soon as her visit with him was over, she'd call and tell her dad that she and Ray had broken up. Then everything would be fine.

Until their next visit.

But she'd burn that bridge when she came to it.

"I'll have someone pick you up at the airport," he said and Lilah's attention snapped back to him.

"No, that's okay," she said quickly, imagining some poor Private or Corporal delegated to driving the Colonel's daughter around. "I've already arranged for a car. I'll be there sometime tomorrow afternoon."

"You're uh…not bringing Ray along, are you?"

She almost laughed again at the discomfort in his voice. Oh yeah. She could just see Ray on base. What a hoot that would be.

"No, Daddy," she said solemnly, "it's just me."

There was a long pause before he said, "All right then. You be careful."

"I will."

"I'm looking forward to seeing you, honey."

"Me, too," she said wistfully, then added, "'Bye, Dad," and hung up. Hand still resting on the receiver, she stared at it for a long minute and wished that things were different. Wished for the zillionth time that her father could just accept her—and love her—for who and what she was.

But that would probably never happen. Since she was the daughter of a man who'd always wanted a son.

"I'd consider it a personal favor, Gunnery Sergeant," Colonel Michael Forrest said, planting his elbows on his desk and steepling his fingertips together.

Escorting the Colonel's daughter around base a personal favor? Well, how was a man supposed to get out of something like that? Kevin Rogan wondered frantically. Sure, he could turn the man down. He wasn't making this an order—hell, Kevin wasn't sure he *could*. But then again, he didn't have to. Making it a "favor" practically guaranteed Kevin's acceptance.

After all, how was he supposed to turn down a request from a superior officer?

He bit down hard on the words he wanted to say and said instead, "I'd be happy to help, sir."

Colonel Forrest gave him a look that clearly said he was under no misconception here. He knew damn well Kevin didn't want to do this, but would, anyway. And apparently, that was all that mattered.

"Excellent," the Colonel said, pushing up from his desk to step around the edge of it. He walked across the floor of his office and looked out the window onto the wide stretch of the base two stories below.

Kevin didn't have to look to know what the other man was seeing. The everyday hustle and bustle of a recruit depot. Troops marching. Marines. Squads. Drill Instructors shouting, calling cadence, trying to whip a bunch of kids into something resembling hard-nosed Marines.

May sunshine blasted against the window, splintering like a prism as it poured into the room. A wisp of ocean air swept beneath the partially opened window and carried the faint sounds of marching men and women. The distant rumble of a jet taking off from the San Diego airport sounded like the far-off stirrings of thunder.

"I don't want you to misunderstand, Rogan," the Colonel said. "My daughter is a...remarkable person."

"I'm sure she is, sir," Kevin answered politically, though inside, he wondered just how remarkable a woman could be if her own father had to practically force a man to keep her company for the month she'd be in town. He slanted a glance at the other man's desk but found no framed pictures on the cluttered surface. No help there. Already, he wondered just what he'd gotten himself into. Was she nuts? Obnoxious? A one-eyed troll?

But even as those thoughts went through his mind, he reminded himself that he knew *exactly* what she was. The Colonel's daughter. And because of that, Kevin would do everything he could to see to it that she had a good time while she was here.

Even if it killed him.

Dammit. A Gunnery Sergeant in the Marine Corps, reduced to being a glorified baby-sitter.

Lilah sat in her rental car just outside the gates and told herself she was being foolish. But it was always like this. One look at what she thought of as her father's stronghold and her stomach started the ugly, slow, pitch and roll that felt far too familiar.

She slapped her hands against the steering wheel then gripped it tight. Her stomach did the weird little flip-flop that she always associated with seeing her dad for the first time in too long. But then, she should be used to it, right?

"Wrong," she murmured and let her hands fall to her lap. Unconsciously, she plucked at the soft folds of her emerald-green muslin skirt, then lifted one hand to toy with the amethyst crystal hanging from a chain around her neck.

As she fingered the cold, hard edges of the beveled stone, she told herself she was being silly. "This visit will be different. He thinks you're engaged. No more 'suitable' men. No more lectures on finding 'stability' in your life."

Right.

Like *any* Forrest would give up that easily.

After all, she hadn't quit yet. All her life, she'd been trying to please her father. And all her life, she'd failed miserably. You'd think she'd surrender to the inevitable. But no. Lilah Forrest was too stubborn to give up just because she wasn't winning.

And she'd inherited that hardheaded streak from the man waiting for her just beyond the gates.

A flicker of movement caught her eye and she saw one of the Marine guards move out to give her a hard stare. "Probably thinks you're a terrorist or something," she muttered and quickly put the car into gear and slowly approached the gate.

"Ma'am," he said, though he looked younger than Lilah. "Can I help you?"

"I'm Lilah Forrest," she said, and lifted her sunglasses long enough to smile up into hard, suspicious eyes. "I'm here to see my father."

He blinked. Too well trained to show complete shock, the Marine just stared at her for a long minute before saying, "Yes, ma'am, we've been expecting you." He took a look at her license plate number, jotted it down on a visitor sticker and slapped it onto the windshield of her car. Then he lifted one hand and pointed. "Go right on through there and watch—"

"My speed," she finished for him. "I know." She should know the rules well enough. She'd been raised on military bases around the world. And the one thing they all shared was a low threshold of appreciation for speeding drivers. Creep up above the twenty mile an hour limit and you'd get a ticket. Private or General.

He nodded. "The Colonel's house is…"

"I know where it is, thanks," she said, and stepped on the gas. Waving one ring-bedecked hand at the young Marine she left in her dust, she aimed her rental car and headed off to do battle.

She wasn't at all what he'd expected.

And definitely *not* a one-eyed troll.

Kevin shifted on the dining room chair and covertly eyed the woman sitting opposite him. If he'd had to pick the Colonel's daughter out of a group of assembled women, he *never* would have picked this one.

First off, she was short. Not munchkin short, but a good six inches shorter than both he and the Colonel. Kevin had never gone much for short women. Always made him feel like a damn giant. But even he had to admit that Lilah was round in all the right places and her compact body was enough to make a dead man sit up and take notice.

Her long, blond hair hung halfway down her back in a tumble of wild curls that made a man want to reach out and tangle his fingers in it. She had a stubborn chin, a full mouth that smiled often, a small nose and the biggest, bluest eyes Kevin had ever seen.

She also wore silver stars on her ears and ropes of crystals around her neck. She was wearing some soft-looking dress that seemed to float like a cloud of emerald green around her legs when she moved and her bare feet displayed two silver rings on her toes.

Who would have guessed that the Colonel's daughter was a latter-day hippie?

He half expected her to fold her legs into the lotus position and start chanting.

So now he knew why the Colonel wanted his daughter escorted all over creation. He probably didn't trust her to come in out of the rain on her own.

"My father tells me you're a Drill Instructor," she said and Kevin's attention snapped up from the purple crystal lying just above the line of her breasts.

"Yes, ma'am," he said and told himself to pay no attention to the small spurt of interest that shot through him. It was nothing special, he thought. Just the normal reaction of a healthy male to a pretty woman. And she *was* pretty. In an earth mother, hug-a-tree sort of way.

She waved one hand and he swore he heard bells ring. Then he noticed the tiny silver chimes attached to the bracelet around her wrist.

Figured.

"I thought you agreed to call me Lilah?"

"Yes, ma'am," he said.

"Isn't this nice?" the Colonel asked, looking from one to the other of them like a proud papa. "I knew you two would hit it off."

Then the phone rang and the Colonel pushed away from the table and stood up. "Excuse me for a moment," he said. "I have to get that."

He left the room and silence dropped like a stone in a well. Kevin leaned back in his chair, let his gaze wander the elegantly appointed dining room and wished himself anywhere but there.

"Did he order you to be here?"

Guilt charged through him. Kevin shot her a quick look, darted a glance at the empty doorway, then turned back to her. "Of course not," he said, then asked, "what makes you say that?"

Lilah picked up her fork and used the tines to push a stray brussel sprout across her plate. Leaning an elbow on the table, she cupped her chin in her free hand and stared him right in the eye. "It wouldn't be the first time Dad's assigned some poor Marine to 'daughter duty.'"

He shifted in his chair again, but kept his gaze fixed with hers. Hell, he didn't want to embarrass her, but if she was used to this kind of treatment from her father, then who was he to deny it? "All right, I admit, he did ask me to escort you around base while you're here."

"I knew it." She dropped the fork with a clatter and leaned back in her chair. Crossing her arms beneath her admirable breasts, she huffed out a breath and shook her head hard enough to send that fall of blond curls swinging. "I thought this time would be different."

"From what?"

"From the usual."

Just how many Marines had been "requested" to take charge of her over the years, anyway? Curious now, in spite of himself, he asked, "What exactly *is* the usual?"

She shot a quick glance at the empty doorway through which her father had disappeared, then looked back at him. "Oh, he's been throwing you guys in my path ever since I hit puberty."

"Us guys?"

"Marines," she said, giving him a look that clearly said she didn't think he'd been paying attention. "Dad's been trying to marry me off to a Marine for—well, *forever.*"

"Marry?" Kevin repeated, then lowered his voice as he leaned over his now empty plate. "Who said

anything about *marriage?*" He hadn't signed up for *that*. He didn't mind showing her around and in general looking out for her interests while she was in town. But as to marriage...well, he'd been there and done that. And no thank you very much. He'd pass.

"Geez, Sergeant," Lilah said, her big eyes going even wider. "Relax, will you? Nobody's sneaking you off to Vegas."

"I didn't—"

"Your virtue's safe with me," she assured him.

"I'm not worried about my 'virtue.'"

"I just said you shouldn't be."

"I'm not—" He stopped, inhaled and blew out the air in a rush of frustration. "Are we arguing in circles?"

"Probably."

"Then how about we call a truce?"

"It's all right with me," she said, jumping out of her chair to pace the room. Her bare feet made almost no sound at all on the polished wood floor, but her bracelet jingled enough to keep time as she stalked. "But you might as well realize now, that my father won't quit trying. He's obviously chosen you."

"As what?" he asked, even though he had a terrible idea of just what she was about to say.

"As a son-in-law," she said, making a sharp about-face to pace in the opposite direction.

"No way," he said, standing up, not really sure whether to fight or run.

"Yes, way," she said, shooting him a look over her shoulder. "And apparently, the fact that I have a fiancé hasn't changed Daddy's plans any."

"You're engaged?"

"Daddy doesn't like him."

"Does it matter?"

"It does to him," she pointed out all too reasonably. "He likes you, though." The blonde who would soon be starring in his nightmares gave him a brilliant smile. "And in the Colonel Forrest rules of the Universe, who he likes is all that matters."

"Lucky me," Kevin said and wondered if it was too late to volunteer for overseas duty.

Chapter Two

Lilah watched her father's latest attempt at finding himself a suitable son-in-law and couldn't help at least admiring her dad's taste.

Kevin Rogan was tall, broad shouldered and his uniform fit him as if designed with him in mind specifically. He looked like a recruiting poster. Perfect. Too perfect, she thought, glancing from his dark brown hair to his strong, square jaw, lips that were now just a grim slash across his face and narrowed green eyes.

She had to give her father points. At least this one was way better looking than the last few he'd thrown her way. But, she reminded herself, handsome or not, he was still a Marine. And therefore out of the running, as far as she was concerned.

Of course, there was no one *in* the running, but that was a different story.

His hands fisted at his sides and she had the distinct feeling that what he wanted to do was bolt from the house and disappear into the fog—or maybe punch a wall. She couldn't really blame him. After all, he was new to the Colonel's husband hunt.

This was old hat for her.

"Really," she said, shaking her head. "You ought to try to relax. All of that tension can't be good for the spirit. Or the digestion."

"Thanks," he muttered, shoving both fists into his pockets, "but I like tension. Keeps me on my toes."

Well then he should be happy to be around her. Because Lilah had the unenviable talent of making most everyone tense. It was her special gift.

Ever since she was a kid, she'd managed to say the wrong thing at the wrong time.

Still, no point in making him any more miserable than he already was. "Don't take this so personal," Lilah told him and was rewarded with a steely glare.

"I shouldn't take it personal?" he asked, incredulous. "Your father, my C.O., sets me up and I shouldn't take it personal?"

She waved her hand just to hear the sound of the silvery bells on her bracelet again. Very soothing.

"It's not like you're the first," she said. "Or the last for that matter. Daddy's been lining men up in front of me since I was seventeen." Just saying it made her want to cringe, but she curbed the impulse. "You're just the latest."

"Some consolation."

"It should be," she argued.

"And why's that?"

"Well," she pointed out, "it's not as though he isn't picky when he's looking for a man for me. He only chooses from the best. I am his daughter, after all." Not the son he'd always wanted. Just a daughter with a penchant for crystals and toe rings rather than rule books and sensible shoes.

"So I ought to be flattered?"

"Sort of."

"I'm not."

"I'm getting that." She leaned in and studied his fierce expression. "You know, your mirth chakra probably needs work."

"My what?"

"Never mind."

"I don't get you."

"Join the club."

"Are you always this strange?"

"That depends," she said. "How strange am I being right now?"

"Oh, man."

"Sorry about the interruption," the Colonel

announced as he walked back into the room. Both of them turned to face him, almost in relief. They certainly weren't getting anywhere talking to each other.

He stopped just over the threshold and looked from one to the other of them. "Is there a problem?"

"Yes," she said.

"No, sir," he said at the same time.

Lilah turned and fixed the man opposite her with a hard look. The furious expression was gone, replaced now by the professional soldier's blank, poker face. To see the man now, you'd never guess that only moments before he had looked angry enough to bite through a phone book. A thick one.

"Now's your chance, Gunnery Sergeant," she said, urging him to speak up and get them both out of this while there was still time. "Tell my father what you were just telling me."

"Yes, Gunnery Sergeant," the Colonel said, "what exactly were you saying?"

His gaze shot from her to her father and for one brief, shining moment, Lilah almost hoped that Kevin Rogan would stand up and say "no thanks." Then he spoke and that hope died.

"I told your daughter it would be an honor to escort her around the base for the duration of her visit, sir."

She sighed heavily, but neither man appeared to notice.

"Excellent," the Colonel said, smiling. Then he walked across the room, gave her a kiss on the forehead and turned to face the other man. "I have some work to catch up on," he said. "Lilah will see you out and you two can make some plans."

When he left again, Lilah folded her arms across her chest, tapped one bare foot against the floor and cocked her head to one side. "Coward."

He actually winced before he shrugged. "He's my C.O.," was his only explanation.

"But you don't want this duty."

"Nope."

"So why—"

"I didn't want to go to Bosnia, either," he said tightly. "But I went."

Well that stung.

Still and all, it was almost refreshing to talk honestly with one of her father's hopefuls. Usually, the men he handpicked for her were so busy trying to win his approval that they were willing to tell Lilah outrageous lies just to score a brownie point or two. At least Kevin Rogan was honest.

He didn't want to be with her any more than she wanted to be with him.

That was *almost* like having something in common, wasn't it?

"So," she asked, "I'm like Bosnia, huh? In what sense? A relief mission or a battle zone?"

A flicker of a smile curved his mouth and was

gone again before she could thoroughly appreciate just what the action did for his face.

And maybe, she thought as butterflies took wing in the pit of her stomach, that was for the best. She was only in town for a few weeks. Besides, she already knew that she did *not* fit in with the military types.

"Haven't made up my mind yet," he said. "But I'll let you know."

"I can't wait." Sarcasm dripped from her tone, letting him know in no uncertain terms that she knew exactly what his decision would be. She could see it in his eyes. He'd already come to the conclusion that this duty was going to be a pain in the rear.

And a few days alone with her would only underline that certainty.

"Look," he said, crossing the room toward her so he could lower his voice and not be overheard. He stopped just short of her and Lilah caught a whiff of his cologne. Something earthy and musky and what it did to her insides, she refused to think about.

She blinked and tried to focus on the words coming *out* of his mouth, rather than the mouth itself.

"We're going to be stuck with each other for the next month," he said.

Okay, that helped. How charming. "And your point is?"

"Let's try to make this as easy as possible on both of us."

"I'm for that," she said and inhaled deeply again, enjoying the woodsy fragrance that filled her senses and weakened her knees. She looked up into those green eyes of his and now that they weren't scowling at her, she noticed the tiny flecks of gold in them.

Then promptly told herself she shouldn't be noticing anything of the kind. Marine, she reminded herself. Handpicked by her father.

"You're engaged," he said, "whether your father likes the guy or not."

An image of Ray filled her mind and she had to smile. "True," she agreed and mentally crossed her fingers at the lie in a feeble attempt to ward off karmic backlash.

"And I'm not interested in changing that situation."

· "Good." One fake fiancé was about all she could handle at any given time.

"So," he was saying, "we strike a bargain."

She stared at him for a long moment, trying to figure out just what he was up to. "What kind of bargain?"

He folded his muscular arms across a chest that looked broad enough to be a football field. "We play the roles the Colonel wants and at the end of the month, we say goodbye."

Hmm.

"Sounds reasonable."

"I'm always reasonable," he said and darned if she didn't believe him.

He looked so straight-arrow, gung ho Marine, he wouldn't know a bend in the road if he fell on it. Completely the wrong kind of man for her. Exactly the kind of man she'd avoided most of her life.

In short, he was perfect.

They could get through this month and make her father happy and neither of them miserable. She smiled again as she considered it. For the first time, she and a Marine could be honest with each other. They could form a friendship based on mutual distaste.

This idea actually had merit.

"Well?" he prodded, apparently just as impatient as her father. "What do you say?"

"I say you've got a deal, Gunnery Sergeant," Lilah told him and held out her right hand.

He enveloped it in his much bigger one and gave her a gentle squeeze and shake. Ripples of warmth ebbed through her, much like the surface of a lake after a stone's been tossed into it. She blinked and held on to his hand a moment longer than was necessary, just to enjoy the sensation. Tipping her head back, she thought she noticed a like reaction glinting in his eyes, but she couldn't be sure.

When he released her, she still felt the hum of his touch. And she was pretty sure that wasn't a good thing at all.

* * *

Twenty minutes later, Kevin was gone and Lilah was sitting in the living room alone when her father walked into the room.

He moved straight for the bar and poured himself a short drink, then asked, "Would you like something, honey?"

"No, thanks," Lilah said as she studied her father. A tall, handsome man, he had streaks of gray at his temples, smile lines at the corners of his eyes and the solid, muscled frame of a much younger man. Not for the first time, she wondered why he'd never remarried after her mother's death so many years ago. But she'd never asked him. And now seemed like as good a time as any. "Dad, why have you stayed single all these years?"

He set the decanter down carefully, studied the amber liquid swirling in the bottom of his glass, then turned and walked to the couch. Sitting opposite her, he took a sip, then said, "I never met another woman like your mom."

Her mother had died when she was eight years old, but Lilah still had a few memories. Snatches of images, really. A pretty woman with a lovely smile. A soft touch. A whiff of perfume. She remembered the comforting sound of her parents laughing together in the darkness and the warmth of knowing she was loved.

And then there were the lonelier years, when it

was just she and her father and he was too busy to notice that his daughter had lost as much as he had.

She shifted, curling up in a corner of the overstuffed love seat. "Did you try?"

Again, he looked for answers in his glass before saying, "Not really." Another sip. "I just decided I'd rather be alone than be with the wrong person."

"I can understand that," she said, meaning every word. In fact, she thought that if they'd had this conversation a few years ago, she might have been able to avoid the series of matchmaking attempts he'd been foisting on her regularly. "But what I don't understand is," she added softly, "if it's all right for you to be single, why is it so important to you that I get married?"

Her father sat up, leaned forward and set his unfinished drink on the table in front of him. Folding his arms atop his knees, he looked into her eyes and said quietly, "Because I want you to be settled. To find someone to—"

"Take care of me?" she finished for him and felt a spurt of frustration shoot through her veins. To him, she'd undoubtedly always be his slightly flaky daughter. But it might surprise him to know that in some circles, she was actually pretty well thought of. "Dad, I'm a grown-up. I can take care of myself."

"You didn't let me finish," he said and stood up, looking down at her with a fond expression on his face. "I want you to have what I had. What your mother and I had for too short a time."

Hard to be angry at something like that. But it was his methods she objected to.

"If that's what I want, I can find it myself," she pointed out and gave herself points for not raising her voice. After all, he meant well.

"I'm not so sure." He looked at her bare ring finger and Lilah curled her hands under the hem of her shirt. Blast, she should have bought herself a ring to wear. Lifting his gaze to hers, he said, "You picked Ray, didn't you?"

"What's wrong with Ray?"

"Probably nothing," her father allowed. "But he's the wrong man for you."

In more ways than one, she thought, but only asked, "Why?"

Her father reached out and cupped her cheek. "Honey, you'd run him in circles inside a week. You need a man as strong as you are."

"Like Kevin Rogan?"

"You could do worse."

"I'm not interested, Dad," she said, preferring not to think about the flicker of attraction that had licked at her insides when Kevin Rogan was too close. Rising, she stood up straight, though she was still nowhere close to being on eye level with him. "And neither is he."

One of his eyebrows cocked up and then he played his ace in the hole.

"He's a little down on women right now."

"Gee, then thanks for setting him up with me."

He smiled at her. "You'll be good for him, honey. His ex-wife cut quite a swath through his life a couple of years ago."

Instantly, Lilah felt a tug of sympathy she didn't want to feel. And she knew darned well her father had been counting on her natural inclination to want to mend broken hearts. "How do you know?"

"Gossip travels on base as easily as it does in the civilian world."

True. Hadn't she been the subject of enough base gossip to know that for a fact?

"So take it easy on him, huh, honey?" he asked, and bent down to kiss her forehead.

Before she could answer, he left the room and she was alone. Wrapping her arms around her middle, she wandered over to the wide front window and stared out at the encroaching fog. Despite the fact that she didn't want to care, Lilah couldn't help wondering just what Kevin's ex-wife had done. And what she, Lilah, could do to help.

Bright and early the next morning, Kevin reported for "daughter duty." He parked his car in front of the Colonel's house and turned off the engine. Silence crowded him, as for a few minutes, he just stared at the place.

Windowpanes gleamed in the morning sunshine. The lawn was neat, the house tidily painted. And inside, waited a woman who was, he knew, going to be the bane of his existence for the next few weeks.

There was just something about her, he thought, remembering that almost electrical charge he'd felt when he shook her hand the night before. He hadn't been expecting it, and for sure hadn't wanted it. But damned if he hadn't felt something inside him tighten up and squeeze.

Hell. He'd been too long without a woman, that was all. Obviously. If one touch of a hippie's hand could send his hormones into overdrive, he was due for some R and R. Fast.

But, for the next month, his personal life was officially on hold. Although, he admitted silently, his personal life wasn't exactly jumping, anyway. Except for stopping by his sister's house to visit his niece, Kevin pretty much centered his life around work.

Concentrating on his job and the recruits in his charge made for a nice, orderly life. He'd learned the hard way that he just wasn't the "relationship" type. He liked his world to proceed in a precise, military fashion.

And a woman was the surest way he knew to blow that all to hell.

His back teeth ground together and he swallowed

the bitter taste of bad memories. It was over and done, he told himself, his hands tightening on the steering wheel until he wouldn't have been surprised to see it snap in two. Deliberately, he forced his grip to relax and reminded himself that ancient history had nothing to do with today. Except of course as a warning to not repeat it.

A flash of movement at one of the front windows caught his attention and as he watched, the curtains were pulled back. Lilah's face appeared and she gave him a quick smile before dropping the curtains back into place and disappearing from sight.

He didn't much care for the jolt of awareness that stabbed at his gut, so he ignored it. Taking the key from the ignition, he opened the car door and got out just as she stepped out onto the front porch.

Today, she was wearing a deep crimson shirt that hugged her curves, tucked into a brown suede skirt that hit just below her knees. A silver chain draped around her narrow waist and dangled about halfway down the front of that skirt. As she waved, the silver swayed and caught the sunlight, flashing in his eyes like a warning beacon.

Warning, he told himself. Good thing to keep in mind.

"So?" she called out, her voice carrying to him on the morning stillness, "do you want some coffee before we head off?"

"No thanks," he answered. Hell, he didn't need

coffee. He needed a drink. Or his head examined. "You ready to go?"

She set both hands on her hips and cocked her head to one side as she watched him. That hair of hers fell like a golden curtain to one side of her body and drifted lazily in the soft wind. Kevin's insides did a slow lurch before he had the chance to remind himself that this was the Colonel's daughter for God's sake.

Not only that, she was completely the wrong kind of woman for him even if he was interested.

And he *wasn't* interested.

Dammit.

He kept telling himself that as he watched her walk across the lawn toward the car. That long skirt swayed around her legs and even though he knew damn well that he shouldn't be thinking the things he was thinking, he couldn't seem to stop. His gaze moved over her, from that incredible smile right down to the tips of her black, low heeled, slouchy boots.

Want dug into the pit of his stomach and he did his best to ignore it.

Stepping up alongside the car, she planted both hands on the hood and leaned forward. "My dad's already left for his office."

"Not surprising," Kevin said, deliberately keeping his gaze locked with hers. Way safer than looking at the rest of her. "Half the morning's gone."

She glanced down at a silver-and-turquoise

watch strapped to her left wrist. "Gee, you're right. It's almost seven forty-five. Practically afternoon." Lifting her gaze to him again, she said, "Early rising is definitely something I don't miss about living on base."

"I'll remember that," he said. Tomorrow he'd pick her up a little later. The less time spent with her, the better. Hell, at this point, he'd take anything he could get.

Chapter Three

"You cold?" he asked.

Lilah nearly jumped, startled at the sound of his voice. For the last hour, they'd been walking aimlessly around the base and he'd hardly said more than a word or two. And she was pretty sure that if he'd been able to get by with a grunt, that's what he would have done.

"No," she answered a moment later, "I'm fine. You?"

He looked at her like she was crazy.

"Sorry," she said, lifting both hands, palms out. "I forgot, Marines don't get cold."

His lips quirked, but otherwise, there was no shift of expression. It was like taking a walk with a mobile statue. Any sympathy she might have been feeling for him last night dissolved in the bubbling stew of frustration simmering inside her. Not being one to suffer silently, Lilah, as usual, let it erupt. "What's the deal here, Gunny?"

"What?" he gave her another look, then absently took her elbow and steered her around a parked car.

Lilah ignored the flash of warmth that the slightest touch from him ignited inside her. On top of everything else, she didn't need the distraction of fluttering hormones. Plus, at twenty-six, she was a little too old to be developing crushes that were destined to go nowhere.

Besides. They'd had a deal, hadn't they?

"Excuse me," Lilah said, flipping her windblown hair back out of her eyes, "but aren't you the guy who just last night offered me a bargain?"

"Here I stand."

"Uh-huh." Did he ever, she thought, with a purely feminine glance of admiration. Well over six-feet tall, he looked like a khaki brick wall. With gorgeous green eyes. And that had absolutely nothing to do with anything, she told herself firmly. Taking a deep breath, she continued. "So, what happened to the part about how we're going to get along and get through the month without making each other miserable?"

One dark eyebrow lifted into an arch.

Impressive.

"You're miserable?"

"Gee, no," Lilah told him, sarcasm dripping from every word. "So far, this is better than Disneyland."

He stopped walking, heaved a dramatic sigh and turned to face her. "What's the problem?"

"The problem, Gunny, is that I might as well be by myself, here."

"Meaning?"

"Meaning," she snapped, "you could actually speak occasionally. Or were you ordered to keep quiet?"

A cold blast of air swept past them, ruffling the hem of her skirt, lifting her hair into a tangled mess and sending goose bumps racing up and down her arms. And it was still warmer than the chill she saw in his eyes.

But in a moment or two, that coolness was gone, replaced with a frustration she understood all too well. Heck, she'd been seeing it most of her life. She never had fit in and once again, that was being pointed out to her.

He shook his head, lifted his gaze to a spot inches above her head and stared out into the distance. From overhead, came the distinctive roar of a jet taking off and the sun slipped behind a bank of clouds.

"No," he said, lowering his gaze briefly to hers. "I wasn't ordered to keep quiet. It's just—"

"I know. You don't want to be a tour guide."

"Not particularly," he admitted, and looked directly at her.

"Well," she said, "that's honest, anyway."

"It's not your fault," he muttered, "but this whole thing really goes against the grain."

"Tell me about it," Lilah said, shoving her hair back out of her face. "You think I enjoy being handed off from one Marine to another? I'm like a human hot potato!"

"So why do you put up with it?"

"Have you ever tried to say no to my father?"

"Can't say that I have," he said.

"I don't recommend it." Not that her father ever lost his temper or anything. But he just sort of steamrolled over a person's objections. Especially, she told herself with just a touch of shame, when you didn't speak up and be honest. Heck, she'd called Kevin Rogan a coward for not telling the truth. Yet she hadn't either, when given a perfect opportunity. She pushed that thought aside for the moment. "Don't get me wrong," she added, "Dad's terrific. He's just…how do I say this?"

"A Marine?" he inquired wryly.

"Exactly," she said.

Kevin stared at her. That smile of hers should be classified as a weapon. Top grade. It had the wattage of a nuclear bomb and probably had the same results on most men. Able to leave them flat and whimpering.

He, however, was a different story. Oh, he wasn't blind. And since he was most definitely male, he could appreciate her package. Just like he'd appreciate a beautiful piece of art. That didn't mean he wanted to take her home and hang her on his walls.

And he'd been down this route before, he reminded himself. He'd taken one look at a woman and seen everything he'd wanted to see and nothing he didn't. He wouldn't be making the same mistake again.

"I don't really need a tour of the base anyway, you know," she was saying and he told himself to pay attention. He had a feeling that *not* paying attention around Lilah Forrest could be a dangerous thing.

"Why's that?" he asked. Not that he minded cutting the tour short.

"Because," she said, shrugging, "all bases are pretty much the same." Turning in a tight circle, she lifted one hand and pointed as she counted off, "Headquarters, Billeting, Provost Marshall, beyond that, the PX, Post Office, Commissary. And," she said, turning back to him with another one of those smiles, "let's not forget the theater, rec center and oh, yeah. There're the clubs, enlisted, officers and Staff NCOs, and last but not least, the all important Recruit Receiving."

When she was finished, she looked up at him and gave him another one of those smiles. "Same church, different pew."

She was right, of course. Hell, she'd been raised

on bases around the world. She probably knew her way around as well as he did. Which led him back to the one question that was flashing on and off in his brain like a broken neon light. Before he could stop himself, he asked, "So what are we doing here?"

"You've got me."

A simple phrase. So why did it snake along his spine like a red-hot thread? Because *having* her implied all sorts of things that his body clearly approved of wholeheartedly. Unfortunately, though, there would be no having of any kind. Not only was she the Colonel's daughter and Kevin's responsibility for the next few weeks…but she wasn't the one-night-stand kind of woman and he wasn't the happily-ever-after kind of man.

So that left them square in the middle of "no touch" land.

Then she touched him. A simple touch, she leaned into him and laid one hand on his upper arm. Heat skittered through him, but he drew on every ounce of his formidable will and told himself to ignore it. It wasn't getting any easier, though.

"It's weird," Lilah muttered more to herself than to her strong, silent type companion.

"What is?" he asked, but she had the feeling he didn't really care.

"Being back on a base."

"How long's it been?"

Not long enough, she thought. But all she said was, "A year or so."

"Why's that?"

She slanted a look up—*way* up—at him. "Do you always talk like that?"

"Like what?"

Lilah sighed. "In short, three-to-four-word sentences. I mean you don't say much and when you do, it's almost over before you start."

"You talk enough for both of us."

She did tend to babble when she was nervous, she admitted silently. Which brought up the question of just *why* she was nervous. It wasn't being on base. Or being around her father. Those things she was used to dealing with. She just plastered on a smile and went out of her way to point out her unsuitability herself to avoid having others do it for her.

An old trick, Lilah had been using it for years. Rather than wait for someone else to make fun of her, she poked fun at herself. Then everyone was laughing *with* her. Not *at* her.

So, if she wasn't nervous about where she was… she must be nervous about who she was with.

Uh-oh.

"Hmm. Talk too much. Where have I heard *that* before?"

"From everyone you've ever met?" he asked, one corner of his mouth lifting.

"Wow." Lilah stared up at him. It was truly

amazing what that smile did to his face. No wonder he didn't do it often. The bodies of women would be littering the parade deck. But she didn't have to let him know that. "A smile. This is a real moment. Too bad I don't have my journal with me, I could make a note of it."

"Funny."

"Thanks." She laid one hand on his forearm and felt that jolt of heat again. Okay, she hadn't counted on that. Instantly, she let her hand drop again and took a step back, just for good measure. Couldn't hurt to keep a little distance between herself and the surprising Gunnery Sergeant.

"Well," he asked, "if you don't want the tour, what would you like to see?"

Before she could answer, someone shouted, "Gunny! Hey, Gunny!"

Kevin turned around and Lilah looked past him at the man hurrying up to them. Judging by his Smokey the Bear hat, he too was a Drill Instructor. He came to a stop in front of Kevin and spared her a quick glance.

"Excuse me, ma'am," he said, "but I need to borrow the Gunny for a minute."

"Sure," she said.

Kevin frowned slightly. "Staff Sergeant Michaels, this is Lilah *Forrest*."

The Marine's gaze widened in surprise. "As in Colonel Forrest?"

Lilah nearly sighed. Happened every time she met one of her father's troops. They looked at her, imagined him, and just couldn't seem to put the two of them in the same family. But she'd long ago quit trying to be what everyone else expected her to be, so she just smiled at him. "He's my father, yes."

"Pleased to meet you, ma'am," he said. His gaze swept over her and as he took note of the crystal around her neck and the silver chain around her waist and her boots, she could almost hear him feeling sorry for her father. A moment later though, he was all business, and turning his gaze on Kevin.

"I need your help tonight."

"I'm off for the next couple of weeks," Kevin told him and Lilah noticed for the first time how rough and gravelly his voice sounded. Must be from all the shouting the D.I.'s did at the recruits. But whatever the reason, it scraped along the back of her neck and felt like sandpaper rubbing against her skin.

"I know that," Sergeant Michaels said. "But Porter's wife is in the hospital. Their first one's about to be born and I've got a busload coming in tonight."

"A busload?" Lilah asked.

"Recruits," Kevin told her with a glance over his shoulder.

"Ah…" Of course. She'd been around the Marine Corps long enough to know that when new recruits arrived at the depot, they arrived in the middle of the night. Bringing them in on a bus in the dark was sort of a psychological thing, she supposed. Kept them from knowing exactly where they were. Enforced the feeling that they were all in this together. Made them start looking to each other for comfort, for strength.

Because that was the whole point of boot camp. To take individual kids and build them into team player Marines. The military wasn't exactly big on individualism. Which is exactly why she'd always had such a hard time fitting in.

Free spirits in the Marine Corps? She didn't think so.

"You won't have to do anything," Michaels said, talking faster now, "just be there as backup."

She'd never seen the recruits arriving and as long as she was here, it seemed like a good idea. "Can I come, too?" she asked.

Both men turned and glared at her.

"No."

She pulled her head back and stared at them. "Why not?"

"You said you didn't want a tour," Kevin reminded her.

"That's not a tour. That's just observing."

"No observers allowed," he said.

"Staff Sergeant Michaels just asked you to be an observer."

"He asked me to be backup."

From the corner of her eye, she noted that Sergeant Michaels was watching the two of them with fascination. But she paid no attention to him. Instead, she concentrated on the huge man glowering at her.

"And if you're not doing anything but being backup," she pointed out, "what exactly will you be doing?"

"Watching."

"Ah-hah." She folded her arms across her chest, leaned back and gave him a victorious smile. "In other words, *observing*."

She watched him grind his teeth together. Every muscle in his jaw clenched and unclenched several times before he trusted himself to speak.

"Whatever I'm doing, it's my job," he said. "These kids don't need an audience."

"Hardly an audience. One woman. In the background. Watching."

"No."

"Look," Michaels interrupted, apparently sensing that there was going to be no time limit at all to this argument, "all I need to know is if you can do it."

Kevin, still scowling, said, "Yeah. I'll be there."

"Good, thanks." Touching the brim of his hat with his fingertips, he glanced at Lilah and said, "Ma'am, enjoy your stay."

"Thank you," she said, but he had already done

an about-face and was striding away, leaving she and Kevin alone again.

Before she had the chance to open the discussion again though, he was looking at her. "Forget about it," he said tightly.

One thing Lilah had never been able to stand was being told what to do. Another reason why she'd never have made it in the military.

"I could pull rank on you," she said.

"You don't have a rank," he reminded her.

"My father does."

"He'd be on my side."

Hmm. She suspected that was true. Her father was a stickler for the rules. Poor man.

"What harm could it do?"

"None, 'cause you won't be there."

"You know," she said, walking again, headed across the grounds toward a patch of grass where several squads were drilling, "I don't need your permission."

"Actually," he said, falling into step beside her, "yeah. You do."

"What?" She looked up, and her hair flew across her eyes. She clawed at it, then reached around, grabbing a handful of hair and holding it in place at the nape of her neck. Hard to argue with a person when your own hair was working against you.

"I'm a senior D.I.," he said and darned if he didn't look like he was enjoying himself, saying it. "I train the instructors. They answer to me. I look after the new recruits. I say who comes and goes." He bent down again, bringing his gaze in a direct line with hers. "And I say you don't go anywhere near the new recruits tonight. Understand?"

Lilah ducked back into the shadows as the bus pulled around the corner and came to a stop. Two in the morning and the faces she could make out through the windows were wild-eyed. "Probably scared to death," she muttered, then slunk farther back into the darkness as the sound of footsteps rose up from close by.

Staff Sergeant Michaels, with Kevin Rogan just a step or two behind him, headed for the bus. The driver slammed the double doors open with a "thunk" that seemed to echo in the otherwise stillness.

Lilah went up on her toes and wished she was five inches taller. She'd never liked being short. People never took short people seriously. They always thought you were "cute." Besides, she'd rather reach her own cereal down from the top shelf at the grocery store, thank you very much. But she'd never been as frustrated with her height as she was at the moment.

"Not bad enough I have to hide like a criminal," she whispered, "but I go to all the trouble of coming down here and now I can't see anything."

Sergeant Michaels vaulted up the three steps into

the bus and started his long walk down the narrow aisle. She caught glimpses of pale faces and she could only make out the Gunny's silhouette, but she had no trouble at all hearing him.

"Listen up!" he thundered in a roar that was designed to capture everyone's attention. "When I give you the word, you *will* get the hell off this bus. Then you *will* stand in the yellow footprints painted on the pavement. You *will* then wait for further instructions. Do you hear me?"

"Yes, sir," came a desultory answer from only a handful of the kids trapped on that bus.

"From this moment on," Michaels screamed and Lilah was pretty sure even *she* flinched, "you will begin and end every answer to every question with "sir." Is that clear?"

"Sir, yes, sir!" A few more voices this time.

"I can't hear you."

"Sir, yes, sir!"

With that, he strode back down the center aisle, left the bus and stood just at the bottom of the steps. "Move, move, move, move…" he shouted and instantly, dozens of feet went into action.

Clamoring to hurry, racing to follow instructions, a bunch of kids who only the day before had only to worry about which hamburger joint to have lunch in rushed toward destiny. Lilah winced in silent sympathy for what she knew they'd be going through soon. Boot camp was rough, but if they made it through, each of those kids would be stronger than they ever would have believed possible. Heaven knew she had never really felt as though she belonged, but she respected what the Corps could do. What they represented. What was possible with the kind of teamwork taught in the Marines.

A flash of pride swelled inside her as she listened to those feet hustling off the bus. They were scared now, but in a few short weeks, they'd be proud.

"I should have known," a voice came from right beside her and Lilah jumped, just managing to stifle a screech of surprise.

Grabbing the base of her throat, she half turned and looked up into now familiar green eyes. "Good God, you almost killed me," she said.

"Don't tempt me."

She straightened up to her full, less than impressive height. "Hey, I'm not one of those kids, you can't order me around."

"That seems pretty clear," he muttered, then grabbed her upper arm in a grip that told her his temper was carefully leashed. "Why are you here?"

Lilah flashed him a grin. "Because you told me I couldn't be."

"You know," he said, with a shake of his head, "I never thought I'd feel sorry for an officer. But damned if I don't feel some sympathy for the Colonel."

"I'll pass that along for you," she said.

Chapter Four

"Do you ever do what you're told?" he asked, voice tight.

"Almost never," she said softly.

And damned if she didn't sound proud of that little fact.

Standing here in the dark with her, Kevin wasn't sure if he wanted to strangle her or kiss her. Either way would only lead to trouble though, so he resisted both impulses.

Still, he felt her warmth, felt it drawing him in. And after being so cold for so long, the temptation to step closer was a strong one. Warning bells went off in his mind, but unfortunately, his mind wasn't in charge at the moment.

Moonlight barely reached into this one little darkened corner of the base. But even in the dim light, he had no trouble making out her delicate features, the paleness of her skin or that wild tangle of hair lying about her face and well past her shoulders. He caught a whiff of her perfume and it tantalized him, making something inside him clutch up tight and hard. And he damn well resented it.

What was it about this one tiny woman that seemed to be getting past every defense he'd erected over the last couple of years?

"How'd you know I was here?" she asked, keeping her voice low enough that no one else would hear her. Especially over Staff Sergeant Michaels's shouting.

How to explain that, he wondered. He wasn't about to admit that he'd sensed her presence. He would cheerfully stand up against a wall and smile at a firing squad before confessing that he'd actually been *looking* for her. So he picked up her left wrist and gave it a gentle shake.

Silvery music tinkled into the darkness from the chimes she habitually wore.

"Ah," Lilah said. "I knew I should have dressed a little more covertly."

"A *little* more?" he asked, letting his gaze drift down her compact, curvy body. Even in the dark, he could see that she wasn't exactly dressed for espionage. She wore some light-colored full-length sweater over yet another swirly skirt and a pale blouse. She couldn't be more noticeable if she were doused in glow-in-the-dark paint.

"So I'm not spy material," she quipped. "Besides, I don't look good in black."

He was pretty sure she'd look good in whatever she wore, but he had no intention of saying so.

"C'mon," he said, still keeping a grip on her wrist. "I'll take you home."

She dug in her heels. "I could just stay here and—"

"Forget it," he said, glancing over his shoulder to where the new recruits were being hustled in out of the damp fog and into the receiving center. "Show's over."

She looked past him, then lifted her gaze to his. "Okay, I'll go. But you don't have to walk me. Sergeant Michaels is probably expecting you inside."

True, he thought, looking from the tiny woman beside him to the well-lit glass doors to his left. But there were more Marines inside who could help out. And he didn't think the Colonel would appreciate his daughter left to walk across the base alone in the middle of the night.

Decision made, he said, "Wait here." Then he dropped her hand and marched off to receiving. It only took a moment or two to tell Michaels that he was taking off and then he was stepping back into the damp night, peering into the mists of fog drifting across the yard.

He glanced at the spot where he'd left her with orders to stay put. Naturally, she wasn't there. Knowing her, she could be anywhere on base by now. "Dammit," he muttered.

She laughed from somewhere just ahead of him. "Have you ever tried meditation?"

"No," he said, narrowing his gaze to stare into the fog, looking for her.

"You should. It would help with that temper."

"You know what else would help?" he asked as he moved forward quietly, scanning the area, searching for a glimpse of that pale sweater.

"What's that?"

"People doing what I tell 'em to do."

"Like giving orders, do you?"

"Better than you like taking them, apparently."

Then she was there. Right in front of him. Materializing out of the fog as though she were a part of it somehow. Mist clung to her hair and body and shone in damp patches on her cheeks. She tilted her head back, smiled up at him and he felt a cold, hard fist close around his heart.

"You should keep that in mind then, huh?"

Oh, there were a lot of things he'd have to keep in mind about her, Kevin told himself firmly. Not least of which was the fact that she was the *engaged* daughter of the Colonel and only here temporarily.

"Doesn't it look eerie out here?" she whispered

and her voice was softened even further by the heavy mist surrounding them.

"Yeah," he said. "It does."

"Sort of like a horror movie."

He'd never really noticed that before, but got into the spirit of things. "Just before something comes lurching out of the fog?"

She took a step closer to him and let her gaze sweep across the shrouded base. "Okay, bad idea to go down that road."

"Scaring yourself?" he asked, surprised. Hell, he would have been willing to bet that nothing scared her. Certainly not her father. Or him. But apparently, the boogeyman could do it.

She linked her arm through his as he started walking. He knew this base like his own backyard. Foggy or not, he could get her back home with no trouble.

"Not a big fan of scary movies," she admitted. "I get too involved, too drawn into the plot, then it's like I'm the one being chased by a knife-wielding maniac." She shivered. "Nope. Give me romantic comedies."

The fog acted like a blanket, keeping them wrapped in a small cocoon of silence. Only their own footsteps sounded out, like twin heartbeats, thumping in time. The grip of her hand on his arm was strong and warm and damned if Kevin wasn't enjoying it. It had been too long since he'd taken a walk with a woman. And even though this was strictly business, so to speak, that didn't mean he couldn't enjoy it.

"Me," he mused aloud, "I'm more of an action-adventure movie person."

"Gee," she said with a half laugh, "there's a surprise."

He chuckled, too. "Nothing better than a few good explosions and a couple of firefights."

"Ah, the romance."

"Ah, the glory."

They walked on in a companionable silence for another minute or two and then she spoke. Kevin had been wondering just how long she could go without talking. Clearly, not very long.

"So what do you do when you're not being Gunnery Sergeant Rogan?"

"When am I not?" he wondered aloud.

"Vacations," she supplied, "days off. R and R."

It had been so long since he'd taken any personal time, he couldn't remember what he'd done. Of course, before the divorce, he'd had plenty of plans for vacations and even retirement. Maybe buy a boat and run a charter fishing service off one of the islands in the Caribbean.

But then, his neat little world had dissolved and so had the plans.

Her question was still hanging in the damp air between them though, so he found an answer that would satisfy her curiosity. "I go see my sister and brothers. And my new niece."

Lilah heard the pride in his voice and smiled wistfully to herself. As an only child, she would never get to be Aunty Lilah. And at the rate she was going, she'd never get to be "mom" either. Suddenly, she saw herself thirty years from now, curled up in her same apartment in San Francisco, surrounded by cats and peering through the curtains at the world going on without her.

Not a pleasant prospect, by any means.

"You know," he said, "when you're quiet, it's a little scary."

She chuckled. "A Marine? Scared? I don't believe it."

"Worried more than scared. What are you thinking about?"

Since the image of her older self alone with cats sounded a little too "pity-party," she said, "Just wondering what it was like to grow up with brothers and sisters."

"Loud," he said.

"And fun?"

There was a long pause while he thought about it. Then he said, "Sometimes. Most times, it was work. I'm the oldest, so I was usually left in charge and—"

"So giving orders really comes naturally to you."

"All right…"

"Sorry," she said. "Go on."

"Not much more to tell." She felt him shrug. "I have one younger sister and three brothers. Triplets."

"Triplets. Wow. Identical?"

"Oh, yeah. Almost no one can tell them apart."

"But you can," she said, enjoying that hum of pride in his tone again.

"Sure. They're my brothers."

"And your niece?"

"Ah," he said, his voice warming, "Emily's a heartbreaker. And since she's walking now, she's driving Kelly, my sister, nuts."

Lilah enjoyed hearing about his family. Love filled his voice when he spoke about them and as he painted word pictures, she drew their images in her mind. The brothers looked like Kevin, she guessed, although she was willing to bet they weren't as handsome. After all, what were the odds of having four gorgeous men in one family?

She imagined Kelly and her baby and—

"What's Kelly's husband like?" she asked, assuming the woman was married. She couldn't imagine Kevin Rogan, master of all he surveyed, allowing his sister to be a single mother.

Beneath her hand, the muscles of his arm tensed slightly before relaxing again. Hmm. Not too fond of the brother-in-law, was he?

"Jeff's a Marine. He's on duty now. Some-where."

"Somewhere?"

"He's Recon. Kelly doesn't even know where the hell he is."

"And you're not happy about that," she said.

He shrugged again and Lilah wished she could see his expression, but the fog was still too thick, sliding past them like phantom fingers.

"Marines make lousy husbands, that's all."

"Kind of a generality, don't you think?"

"Personal experience."

Ah. She remembered what her father had had to say about Kevin's ex-wife leaving him a mess, so Lilah trod carefully. She didn't want him to know she'd heard anything about his past. He didn't seem the kind of man to enjoy knowing that his private life was still being talked about.

"So you were a lousy husband?"

His footsteps faltered slightly, then he went on and if she hadn't been paying such close attention, she might not have noticed the hesitation at all.

"My ex-wife must have thought so," was all he said.

"Was she a good wife?" She probably shouldn't have asked that, but Lilah's nature was something she couldn't fight. She didn't mean to be nosey, exactly. It was simply that she couldn't keep herself from trying to help. Whether that help was wanted or not.

"I'd rather not talk about it."

"It might help," she said. "Sometimes telling a stranger your problems makes them easier to solve."

"There's nothing to help," he said, his voice low and sharp as a knife. "It's over. My marriage ended a couple of years ago."

Maybe, she thought. But there seemed to be a part of him that hadn't let go. Though she doubted he'd admit that under threat of torture. And, since she'd been enjoying herself up until this minute, she let the conversation end. No point in starting a fight.

She stumbled over something in the dark and would have pitched face forward into the dirt if he hadn't caught her.

His hands at her waist, he held on to her while she steadied herself and Lilah tried not to feel the heat from his hands pouring into her body.

This was ridiculous. She was twenty-six years old. The last living virgin in California. She had a pretend fiancé and absolutely no business being swept away by a good-looking Marine with a bad attitude and a glorious smile.

And yet…

She stared up at him and the mist enveloping them parted, drifting away on the sea air and leaving them in a patch of moonlight. He hadn't let her go and Lilah felt every imprint of his fingers, right through her sweater and the shirt she wore beneath it. His pulse beat seemed to hammer into her, accelerating her own heartbeat and twisting her stomach into knots.

"This is a bad idea," he said, his gaze moving over her face as if seeing her for the first time.

"Terrible," she agreed.

"We have nothing in common."

"Absolutely zip." She ran her tongue across her bottom lip and watched his gaze follow the action. Her stomach pitched again as though she were on some high-flying roller coaster and taking the long dip in a rush of speed.

"You're only here for a month."

She nodded. "Maybe less."

"You're engaged."

"Oh, yeah."

"And," he whispered as he lowered his head toward hers, "if I don't kiss you right now, I just might lose what's left of my mind."

She went up on her toes, rising to meet him. "Can't have that," she said on a sigh.

Lilah kept her eyes open and watched him come closer. But when his lips came down on hers, her eyes closed and breath left her body. If he hadn't been holding on to her, she would have dropped, because her knees gave out the instant his tongue touched hers.

She groaned and leaned into him. His arms came around her like an iron vise, pressing her to him, holding her length along his. His hands swept up and down her back, stroking, caressing.

His mouth tantalized her, his breath dusted across her cheek and she felt the pounding of his heart slamming against her chest. He explored her mouth, tracing the tip of his tongue along her teeth, her cheeks, drawing the last of her breath from her. She gave as good as she got, returning his caresses while she clung to his shoulders in an effort to keep from puddling on the ground at his feet.

Never, she thought wildly, as sensation after sensation coursed through her body. Never had she felt anything like this. It was as if sparklers had been set off inside her. Her blood dazzled and bubbled in her veins as a low down, deep-seated throbbing pulsed to life within her.

He growled. Actually growled. And tightened his hold on her. His kiss deepened until she was sure he was trying to devour her and Lilah was so afraid he wouldn't.

She wanted more. Wanted to feel his hands on her. Wanted to slide, skin to skin and relish the experience of having Kevin Rogan be the man to finally broach her body's last defenses.

She felt as though she'd been waiting all her life for this one moment. Here in the moonlight, with the patchy fog drifting like gossamer threads around them, she'd found the skyrockets that all the romance novels she'd ever read had promised.

The question was, what was she going to do about it?

Chapter Five

Reason pushed its way into his brain and instantly, Kevin released her and took a step back. His arms felt empty without her. He still had the taste of her in his mouth and he knew that had been a big mistake. And even knowing that, it was all he could do to keep from grabbing her again and having another taste.

He slapped one hand across the back of his neck and rubbed hard enough to scrape skin off. It didn't help.

"Wow," she said softly, her voice reaching out for him as surely as her scent did. "That was some kiss."

"Yeah," he muttered thickly and was more than grateful for the sporadic moonlight. In the darkness she wasn't likely to see exactly how much he'd enjoyed that kiss. But he could for damn sure feel it. And the discomfort was enough to make his tone a little harsher than he would have liked. "I apologize," he said formally. "That was out of line and— Look Lilah, it'd probably be best for both of us if we just forget that ever happened."

Silence.

Oh man, she was probably ready to cuss him out, or punch him or best yet, he thought grimly, report this to her father. Great. Just what he needed. What had he been thinking? His Commanding Officer's daughter. An engaged woman.

A nut.

In an instant, he saw the end of his career, or being transferred to some far-flung, ice-covered base, or being busted down to Private. There was no telling what she'd do once the shock wore off.

"I think my toes curled."

He blinked. "What?"

"Seriously," she said. "That was an amazing kiss, Gunnery Sergeant Rogan."

"Thanks." What else could he say? Hell, he should have known she wouldn't react as he'd expected her to. Any sane woman would be either furious or— well, just furious. But then, he told himself, Lilah Forrest didn't even *dress* sane.

"I mean to tell you," she said, admiration clear in her voice, "you could give lessons."

He didn't speak. Didn't trust himself to.

"Forget the Marines," she added, "you could probably make a bundle being an escort."

"What?"

"Just checking," she said with a short laugh that sounded nearly as musical as the bells she wore on her wrist. "You were so quiet there for a minute, I thought maybe you were the first person to ever slip into a coma while standing up."

"You're out of your mind, you know that?" Big surprise there, he thought.

"Why?" she asked. "Because I didn't kick you or run off to daddy to complain? Would you be happier if I was angry?"

"Well," he said, "yeah. At least that I'd understand."

"Sorry to disappoint you," she said and started walking toward home again.

He fell into step beside her.

Even without the fog, the air was damp and carried the scent of the ocean. Shadowy clouds scuttled across a black sky, covering and then displaying the stars as if some giant hand were playing hide-and-seek with diamonds.

"Not disappointed," he said, weighing the words mentally before speaking them, "just…confused."

"I don't know why," she said, drawing the edges of her sweater closer around her. "You kissed me, I kissed you and it was terrific."

More than terrific, he thought, but didn't say.

"And that's it," he said. "No big deal."

She glanced up at him and in a snatch of moonlight, he saw the smile curving her delectable mouth. "If you want to run get a sword, I'll fall on it for you."

"That's not what I meant," he said tightly and wondered why in the hell it bothered him so much that she wasn't bothered.

"Just what did you mean then?" she asked as they came up on the low, three-foot-high brick wall that surrounded the backyard of the Colonel's house.

He grabbed the regulation cover off his head and ran the flat of one hand across the top of his high and tight haircut. For the first time in too many years to think about, he almost wished his hair was longer. At least then, he'd have something to grab hold of and yank.

"I don't know what I meant. All I'm sure of is, I don't get you at all."

"Ah," she said and he heard the smile in her voice. "The mystery that is Lilah Forrest."

"You are that."

"Because I didn't swoon or run off screaming into the fog because of one kiss?" Lilah shook her head and stared up at him. Her knees had quit shaking and she was pretty sure her heart wasn't going to climb out of her throat. But her stomach was still pitching and quivering with excitement and it felt as though every one of her nerve endings was standing up and shouting, "Ooh-rah!"

She shook her head. "If that's the case, then you think either very highly of yourself or very little of me."

"Neither," he said. "You're just…surprising, is all."

"Is that a good thing or a bad thing?"

"Not sure about that, either."

"You'll let me know when you figure it out?"

"You'll be the first," he promised. "But don't hold your breath. You're only going to be here four weeks and something tells me it'd take years to understand you."

"And sometimes," she said softly, thinking now of her father, "not even then."

A moment later though, she pushed those thoughts aside. They were old aches and there was no need to reexamine them again tonight. Besides, she'd much rather think about what had happened to her only a few minutes ago.

Granted, she wasn't exactly the most experienced woman around, but Lilah had the distinct feeling that even if she had been, Kevin Rogan's kiss would have stood out from the crowd. The man was an absolute master at lip manipulation. She ran her tongue across her bottom lip as if she could still taste him there and just the thought of that sent a shiver of expectation shooting down the length of her spine.

She wanted to kiss him again and even admitting that silently, she knew just how dangerous this was. After all, he was career military. A Marine, for pity's sake. A man, for all intents and purposes, exactly like her father. The two of them were like peas in a pod as far as their views, their goals and no doubt, the kind of woman they approved of. And that kind of woman was definitely *not* her kind. She'd been the bane of her father's existence for as long as she could remember. She had no reason to think that Kevin Rogan would be any different.

How could she be interested even slightly in a man hand-chosen by her father? This had never happened before. Every other time her dad had tossed a Marine in her path, she'd either frightened them off or been bored silly.

Wouldn't you know that the one time she'd come prepared—armed with a pretend fiancé—*that* would be the time she'd meet a man who set off alarm bells throughout her body? The key word in that sentence being *alarm*. If she had any sense, she'd go inside and tell her father that she couldn't stay after all. Then she'd pack up and go home to San Francisco. Back to the world where she felt comfortable and wanted and respected.

But she knew darn well that she wasn't going anywhere.

Not after a kiss like that.

She wanted another one and then, maybe, another one after that.

And giving in to that thought, she looked up at him, went up on her toes and slanted her mouth against his. He went rigid, as if suddenly called to attention. But electricity hummed between them, lighting up Lilah's insides and pushing her to go for more. She wrapped her arms around his neck and tilted her head to one side, giving him more and silently asking him to return the favor.

Moments ticked past and still she waited for a response. When it finally came, it was more than she had hoped for. His arms went around her middle, his hands fisting at the small of her back, pulling her tightly to him. She felt his need pulsing through her as he parted her lips with his tongue and reclaimed her mouth.

Lilah sighed into him and she heard him swallow a groan that rumbled up from deep in his chest. He yanked her flush against him and instantly she became aware of the rock-hard proof of his desire for her. A flicker of something damp and hot and unbelievably exciting settled and pooled deep within her and Lilah wanted nothing more than to give in to it.

His breath puffed across her cheek, his warmth and strength surrounded her. The silence of the night crept close, making their rapid heartbeats and ragged breathing the only sounds she heard.

Then he tore his mouth from hers and stared down at her with wild-eyed, deep-rooted shock. But despite the denial she knew was coming, he couldn't disguise the passion she saw in his gaze. Not to mention the fact that his body was telling her all she needed to know about whether or not he wanted her.

"Why'd you do that?" he demanded, sliding his hands from her back to her upper arms. His fingers pushed into her flesh, but in spite of his strength, or maybe because of it, his grip was still gentle. "Didn't we just say that it would be better if we both forgot about that other kiss?"

"Actually no," she said, and took a deep breath in a futile attempt to slow down her heartbeat. "*You* said that."

"Whatever."

"And," she went on as if he hadn't spoken at all, "I figured if you're going to forget something, might as well make it memorable."

"Memorable? If it's memorable, you *don't* forget."

"Good. I don't want to."

"What kind of game are you playing?" he asked, releasing her and taking a long step backward.

"Who's playing?" she asked and locked her knees to keep them from liquefying.

"Look," he ground out, "you're here for a few weeks. You're my Commanding Officer's daughter *and* you're engaged to some poor guy who probably thinks you're missing him."

She imagined Ray, no doubt at home, having dinner with Victor and not giving her a second thought. Ah, the old "tangled web" parable about deception had just risen up to bite her in the rear.

If she told him that she wanted him, then she was a cheating fiancée. If she told him the truth, that she wasn't engaged to Ray, then she was a liar. Hmm. No way to win there.

Which was probably for the best, she told herself as her blood cooled and her brain cleared. No matter how good a kisser Kevin Rogan was, the plain fact was that there could be nothing between them. He was military and she just didn't do military very well.

Nodding to herself, she said, "You're right."

"I am?"

"Don't sound so surprised," she quipped. "Even a blind squirrel finds an acorn once in a while."

"Thanks," he said dryly.

"So we're agreed then?"

"On?"

"On the fact that there's going to be no more kissing between us."

He nodded shortly. "Yeah, we're agreed."

"Okay then."

"Fine."

"Fine." She looked up at him, then shifted her

gaze to the house behind her. "I guess I'd better go inside."

"Yeah, you probably should," he said.

She was freezing on the outside and bubbling hot on the inside. It just didn't seem fair. But then, this was probably just punishment for allowing herself to get so turned on in the first place.

After all, she should know better. She'd long ago accepted her unofficial title of the Last Virgin in California.

She sat down on the edge of the low wall, swung her legs over and stood up in the middle of her father's rose bushes. A stray thorn or two tugged at the folds of her sweater, but she ignored them.

"I'll see you tomorrow?"

He took a step back from the wall. "I'll be here."

"All right then. Good night." Lilah turned, paused, then looked over her shoulder at him. In the indistinct wash of moonlight, with the fog stretching out behind him, he looked impossibly gorgeous and as unreachable as the stars overhead. So she couldn't resist saying, "Just for the record, you're a great kisser."

He scowled at her and she headed for the house. She could feel Kevin's gaze locked on her. Heat blasted through her as surely as if she'd been standing with her back to a roaring fire. It was all she could do not to shiver again.

She was in some serious trouble, here.

So it was a good thing she didn't hear Kevin mutter thickly, "You're not a bad kisser yourself."

One week.

She'd only been on base one lousy week and Kevin's world was pretty much shot to hell. He wasn't even getting any sleep. Every time he closed his eyes, he saw her face, heard her voice, listened to the faint sound of those blasted bells that were as much a part of her as that long blond hair.

Scowling fiercely enough to keep all but the bravest souls at arm's length, Kevin stepped into the PX. He nodded to the cashier, then walked straight to the back of the room. He opened the refrigerator door, pulled a soda off the shelf and turned to leave.

"Hello. Gunnery Sergeant Rogan, isn't it?"

He froze, looked to his right and managed to give the older woman striding up to him a tight smile. If not for Lilah, Frances Holden wouldn't have known him from Adam. But because the Colonel's daughter had insisted on touring the child-care facility on base, he was now acquainted with the gray-haired woman in charge of the place.

She had a no-nonsense walk, a twinkle in her eyes and a short, square body that the base children seemed to love to cuddle up to.

"Ma'am," he said, gripping the neck of his soda bottle in one tight fist, "it's good to see you again."

She laughed, a booming sound that he swore

rattled some of the glassware on the nearby shelves. "Liar." She held out her right hand and he took it in a firm grip. When she let him go again, she said, "Right now you're thinking, 'what does this old bag want and how long will it take.'"

"No, ma'am," he argued quickly, though he was wondering if the nursery school teacher did a little mind reading on the side.

"I won't keep you but a minute," she said, lifting one hand to wave away his objections. "When I saw you, I just had to say something."

"Ma'am?"

"The next time you see Lilah, will you thank her for me again?"

"Again?" he asked, before he could help himself.

"Oh, yes," she said. "I thanked her once, but it just isn't enough, though she'll argue with me on that point, I'm sure."

Oh, he was pretty sure Lilah would argue with *anyone* about *anything,* but that wasn't the point here, was it?

His grip tightened on the soda bottle until he wouldn't have been surprised if the glass had shattered in his hand. Why was it women talked *around* something instead of simply spitting out what they wanted to say? Now a man would have stepped up to him, said what needed saying and been on his way.

Much simpler.

The woman in front of him was still talking and to dam up the flow of words, he held up a hand. When her voice trailed off, he asked one question. "What exactly are you thanking her for?"

The older woman blinked up at him. "She didn't tell you? Isn't that just like her? Such a sweet girl. The Colonel can be proud of that one, I'll tell you. So thoughtful and she didn't have to do it, frankly I don't even know *how* she did it, though Lord knows—"

"Ma'am," Kevin interrupted the flow again and smiled to take the sting out of his cutting her off. "Just what exactly did Lilah do?"

"Oh, for heaven's sake," she said, shaking her head, "didn't I tell you? She went to a local children's store and somehow convinced them to donate new winter jackets for the children. *All* of the children. Most of their parents are enlisted and don't make much money." The older woman beamed at him. "She really is a wonder, isn't she?"

Before he could answer, Mrs. Holden was off, leaving him standing there wondering what else he didn't know about Lilah Forrest.

Chapter Six

"Do you know I've *never* seen you out of that uniform?" Lilah said, giving him a quick look up and down while he stood on the front porch.

His eyebrows shot straight up and she realized just how that had sounded. And though she was intrigued by the notion, she had the feeling he was not.

"I *meant,*" she said, stepping out of the house and closing the door behind her, "I've never seen you in civvies."

He took her arm and led her down the short flight of steps to the path leading to the driveway. "Yeah, well, I'm more comfortable in the uniform."

Lilah shot him a look from the corner of her eye. She didn't believe him one bit. She'd never met a

Marine who didn't wear civvies off the base if he could. A uniform always attracted attention and most Marines would rather blend in than stand out. So it wasn't comfort Kevin was looking for, here.

It was a barrier.

A fabric wall standing between them.

He probably figured that if he wore that uniform, it would serve as a reminder that he wasn't with her by choice, but because her father had asked him to be there. As if she needed reminding.

Heck, Lilah'd never exactly been at the top of the dating food chain. Even in high school, she'd been just a little too weird in a world where everyone else was trying to fit in. College had been no better. She'd actually gone to class rather than the latest fraternity bash, so she'd pretty much been on the outs there, too.

Which really explained the whole "virgin" issue.

Hard to lose something nobody wants.

A brisk wind shot across the base and tugged at the hem of her sapphire blue skirt, rippling it around her calves. She wore a knee-length blue sweater atop the white cotton blouse that was tucked into the waistband of her skirt. Pulling the edges of that sweater around her more tightly, she glanced at Kevin and asked, "Don't you ever get cold?"

"Nope," he said, his grip on her elbow firm, but

gentle. "But if I ever do, you suppose you'll be able to find me a jacket?"

"Huh?" she asked, watching him instead of where she was going. She didn't see the rise in the sidewalk and the toe of her boot caught it just right. She stumbled and would have fallen except for the strength of his hold on her. Once she had her feet steady beneath her again, Lilah asked, "What are you talking about?"

He led her to the car, released her and opened the door. Then leaning both forearms atop it, he kept his gaze on her and said, "I just ran into Mrs. Holden at the PX."

"Ah…"

"She said to say thank you again."

Lilah smiled. "Tell her she's welcome." She gathered up her skirt, preparing to slide onto the front seat.

"Why'd you do it?" he asked.

She stopped and stared up at him. "Do what? Get the jackets for the kids?"

"No," he said dryly. "Invent penicillin."

"Funny."

"Thanks. So…why?"

Lilah shrugged, trying, unsuccessfully, to make light of the situation. "The kids needed the jackets and it was a good deal for both sides. The store gets a tax write-off and is able to do something for the community and the kids get new winter jackets. Everybody wins. Why wouldn't I do it?"

"Most people wouldn't have gone out of their way to go and talk some department store into donating clothes."

She smiled at him. "As you've already pointed out more than once, I'm not 'most people.'"

"Point taken," he said and watched her as she sat on the seat and swung her legs inside. He closed the door, walked to the driver's side and got in himself before looking at her again and saying, "All I wanted to say was, it was a nice thing to do."

Just a little uncomfortable, as she always was when being thanked for something, Lilah pulled her head back and stared at him in mock amazement. "Gee… is this a compliment I hear?"

"Could be."

"And me without my journal again."

"You keep surprising me," he said.

"Good. I do hate being predictable."

"I *like* predictable," he said and fired up the engine.

"Now why doesn't that surprise me?" she murmured. Quickly, she hooked the seat belt then turned her head to look out the side window. He put the car into gear and backed out of the drive onto the road.

Lilah barely paid attention to the passing scene. Instead, her mind rattled along at its own pace, dredging up one thought after another. She'd been happy to arrange for the new jackets for the kids. It hadn't taken much effort—if there was one thing Lilah was good at, it was talking to people—and after all, it had worked out well for both sides.

But she never had been comfortable with compliments. She preferred doing her volunteering and then slipping away into the mist—like the Lone Ranger, she thought with an inward smile.

They drove through the main gate, and waited for a break in the cars to join the traffic. Once they were a part of the streaming line of lemmings, Kevin spoke up, breaking the silence in the car.

"At least Sea World shouldn't be crowded. This time of year and all, there aren't many tourists."

Grateful that he'd apparently decided to drop their earlier conversational thread, Lilah looked at him and smiled.

He was right. When they pulled into the parking lot twenty minutes later, they had their choice of slots. The weather probably had something to do with that, she thought. Leaden skies and a cold, wintry wind would keep even the locals away from the park. It was almost as if they'd been given the place to themselves for the day.

Kevin watched her as she studied the pamphlet and decided what she wanted to see first. Something inside him shifted uncomfortably. She was just so damned…tempting.

She always had a rumpled, tousled look that made him think of rolling her around on silky sheets—and as that thought strolled through his mind, it was all he could do to keep from reaching for her. But it wasn't just what she did for his body. He liked how her mind worked. Even when it frustrated him. Talking to her was like walking in circles and her sense of humor was a little unsettling at times, too. But the sound of her laughter was enough to set off sparklers in his bloodstream.

And now he knew that she was thoughtful enough to arrange for kids to get brand-new jackets. And that she was selfless enough to be embarrassed about it when he found out and faced her with it.

She couldn't be more different from his ex-wife. Alanna couldn't see further than her own reflection. She'd tossed him over without a thought, to get the one thing she'd wanted and wasn't able to get without him.

Entrance to the United States.

Old hurts rippled through him, but he buried their memory into a dark hole in the corner of his heart and hoped they'd stay there for a while. It wasn't often he thought about Alanna. And he liked that she was becoming more and more a part of his past. Though even he had to admit that she'd influenced his present and certainly his future. Never again would he trust that "head over heels" feeling. Never again would he believe a woman when she told him that she loved him more than life itself.

And most important, never again would he allow himself to be as vulnerable to pain. If that meant living alone, then that's just how it would have to be.

Grumbling to himself, he pushed thoughts of Alanna aside and concentrated on the woman standing in front of him. Lilah tossed her head to one side, swinging that long, glorious fall of hair back over her shoulder and he studied the line of her throat, the delicate curve of her jaw. Air jammed up in his lungs and he had to fight for his next breath. Not a good sign, he told himself, but didn't know how to keep from feeling that nearly electrical jolt of awareness.

Especially when memories of that kiss kept plaguing him.

She turned those big blue eyes on him and gave him one of her damn near nuclear smiles. And Kevin knew for sure that he wanted her more than his next breath. His entire body was practically humming with a kind of need he'd never experienced before. Not even with Alanna.

And that fact worried him.

"What time is it?" she asked.

Why wasn't she wearing a watch? Crystals, yes.

Silver bells, of course. But a simple watch? No way.

"Ten hundred," he said with a quick glance at his left wrist.

"Ten o'clock," she said and checked the pamphlet again. "Good." She lifted her gaze to his and dazzled him with a smile bright enough to start a fire. Then she grabbed his hand and tugged at him. "We just have time to make it to the dolphin show."

Obediently, he followed after, trying to keep his gaze from settling on the curve of her behind or the damn near delicious sway of her hips.

Dolphins.

And that's how it went all day. They hurried from one show to another, stopping only for lunch. He'd never seen a woman so completely entranced by the little things. She loved cotton candy and hot chocolate. She dipped her French fries in ranch dressing and ordered a diet soda with an ice-cream sundae. She laughed easily and teased him mercilessly and he enjoyed it all.

By late afternoon, Kevin had seen enough fish and sea-going mammals to last him a lifetime. But Lilah showed no signs of slowing down. Damned if she wasn't as fresh and enticing as she had been at the beginning of the day. With her endurance, she'd have made a helluva Marine.

And she wasn't about to leave until she'd seen what she laughingly referred to as "The Big Guns."

Shamu.

The arena was practically empty, but still she insisted on sitting down on the azure benches—despite the clearly painted warning that the first five rows might get wet.

The water was incredibly blue. Nearly as blue as her eyes and as Lilah applauded and laughed and oohed and aahed at the whale and its trainers, Kevin was watching her. Everything she felt registered on her face. Her expressions shifted constantly and he felt as though he could watch her forever.

Such a contrast, he thought. She fired his blood and kept him on his toes when she argued with him. Yet here she sat, as excited as any of the kids in the arena. There were so many sides to Lilah Forrest, he had a feeling that even if he knew her for years, she'd be able to keep him guessing.

Years, he thought and waited for the inward shudder that usually accompanied such thoughts, but it didn't come. That alone should have worried him.

"Look at him," she said in an awed whisper. "Isn't he amazing?"

Dutifully, Kevin tore his gaze from her to look at the huge tank in front of him. The huge black-and-white whale did a quick circuit of its tank, creating waves that crashed and broke in its wake. The trainer was treading water in the middle of the pool, shouting instructions and slapping his open palm on the surface of the churning sea water.

Lilah's excitement was damn near contagious. Even he got caught up in watching that mammoth creature swimming so gracefully. But a moment later, Kevin saw it coming. Knew what was going to happen the minute the killer whale made its first leap out of the water. On the far side of the tank, it lifted its huge body clear of the pool, then slammed home again, sending a wall of water swooshing over the clear side of the tank and onto the benches.

Before he could grab Lilah and make a run for it though, Shamu was upon them. Again, the whale rose from the depths, seemed to pause briefly in midair, then crashed back into the water. Instantly, a regular tsunami swelled over the lip of the clear tank wall and slammed down onto Lilah and Kevin, drenching them both instantly.

Sputtering and blinking, Kevin stood up and looked down at the laughing woman beside him. Her hair was absolutely soaked, hanging down on either side of her face like blond seaweed. She laughed and the pure, warm sound of it slid down inside him, taking the chill from his blood and lighting up his soul.

Then his gaze slipped from her face to her chest and just that fast, his body went on full alert. Her plain, white cotton blouse had suddenly become transparent. And the white lace bra she wore hid nothing from him. He saw her every curve. Her erect nipples peaked against the fabric and it was all he could do to keep from reaching out and cupping her breasts in his palms. He wanted her more than he'd ever wanted anything in his life.

His mouth went dry and when he lifted his gaze to hers again, he saw knowledge in her eyes. She knew just what he was thinking. But even better, she seemed to be thinking the same thing.

"You're all wet," she said.

"Yeah," he said, his voice sounding rusty even to himself. "You, too."

She glanced down at her shirtfront briefly, then swung her hair out of her face as she looked back up at him. "Guess you can pretty much tell I'm cold, too."

"Pretty much," he admitted, though her being cold was making him hotter than he'd ever been before.

Then she shivered and his hormones slipped a notch. Wrapping one arm around her shoulders, he pulled her in close to his side.

"You're as wet and cold as I am," she said, looking up at him even as she snuggled in, looking for warmth.

"Oh, I'm wet," he said, then muttered, "but cold? I don't think so."

He led her down and out of the arena, and instinctively headed for the front gate. The sun was already sinking behind a low-lying bank of clouds on the horizon. Streaks of rose and violet burst along the edges of those clouds and spread across the sky like a spill of paint. A cold, ocean wind blew past them and Lilah pressed herself to his side, wrapping one arm around his waist.

"It'll only take a minute to get to the car. We'll get the heater on and thaw out."

"Heat," she repeated, her teeth beginning to chatter. "Good."

His hand rubbed her upper arm, and held her tightly to him and Lilah felt the ice chips in her bloodstream beginning to melt. She ran her hand up and down his back, pretending to help keep warm, but really, she was simply enjoying the feel of his back. Hard, muscled flesh lay just beneath a soaking wet uniform blouse, and Lilah wanted more than anything, to slip her hands beneath that shirt and feel his skin against hers.

A feeling that had been building inside her for days erupted with his nearness and she gave in to it, enjoying the hum of desire pulsing within. There was just something about this man. Something strong enough to have her thinking about him at odd moments, dreaming about him at night and worrying about the dreaming during the day.

A flicker of emotion flashed inside her and Lilah wondered just what it was. More than passion. More than simple desire. This was something she'd never felt before. And rather than try to put a label on it, to try to understand it, she decided to simply nurture it.

He stopped alongside the car and reached into his pocket for the keys. The instant his arm left her shoulders, the cold slipped into her and Lilah hugged the edges of her sodden sweater across her middle.

Glancing at her, he opened the door and said, "Get in. Quick, before you freeze."

Lilah nodded and slid onto the seat. He closed the door after her and as he walked around the back of the car toward the driver's side, she told herself that here was her chance. With this man. At this moment. She was finally going to lose her title as the Last Virgin in California.

He climbed in, settled behind the wheel and turned the key in the ignition. Flipping a few dials, he had the blower going and the rush of air quickly shifting from cool, to warm, to positively toasty.

With the engine purring, she turned toward him and found him staring at her. Those green eyes of his looked stormy, dark with a desire she recognized and shared.

A muscle in his jaw clenched and released. He swallowed hard and said, "Get your seat belt on."

"In a minute," she said, leaning closer.

His gaze shifted from her eyes to her mouth and back again. He shook his head. "Don't be starting this, Lilah. We both know it would be a mistake." He was saying all the right things, but hunger colored his tone and boiled her blood.

"And we both want it anyway." She tilted her head and leaned in farther, closer to him. She could almost hear his heart pounding.

He reached up, stroked her cheek with the tips of icy fingers and reaction shimmered up and down her spine. Then he speared his fingers into her hair and pulled her to him.

His mouth came down on hers and stole the last of her breath. Her heart hammered in her chest, her stomach did a quick jig and when he released her, Lilah looked into his eyes and knew without a doubt that this was right.

Even if it was wrong.

Chapter Seven

Outside, the wind was cold and fierce. Trees along the highway twisted and danced in the ocean gusts, bending low, their leaves breaking free and pelting the passing cars like oversized raindrops. But inside the car, heat roared into life and had nothing to do with the blast of forced, warm air rushing from the heater.

Lilah's heartbeat quickstepped until breathing became a near Olympic sport. Her hands fisted in her lap, she kept her gaze locked on the view through the windshield and told herself she was being foolish. None of this made sense. She wasn't the type to fall for a Marine, for pity's sake. Hadn't she proved that over the years with a succession of failed attempts?

Hadn't every Marine who'd ever crossed her path eventually run for the hills?

Oh, this was a mistake.

And any minute now, she'd say so.

Or he would.

She slanted a glance at him from the corner of her eye and felt her heart beat even faster. That strong jaw of his, those green eyes. The full curve of his mouth. She licked her lips in anticipation of another kiss and wondered when it had all come to this. When had she become so attached to this normally stoic, hard-lined Marine? Was it his seemingly unbendable nature combined with a smile that tugged at her insides and promised intimate secrets and shared laughter? Was it his generous heart contrasted with his love for rules?

What was it about this one man that had allowed him to slip past her well-honed defenses to lay siege to a heart that hadn't been touched in years?

And what was she going to do now that he had?

"Lilah?"

She turned to face him and felt her breath catch in her throat. His gaze flicked to her briefly, then shifted back to the road in front of him.

"What?" she asked, when she could get her voice to work.

He opened his mouth, then shut it again, as if he'd wanted to say something, then changed his mind. But a moment later, he asked, "Still cold?"

That wasn't what he'd wanted to say. She knew it. Felt it. But maybe he, too, was suffering pangs of doubt. That would be about right, wouldn't it?

"No," she said, shaking her head. "Not cold."

He nodded as if she'd just said something profound.

And after another long silent minute passed, he added, "I'm taking you back to your father's house."

A small curl of disappointment unwound inside her. Going back to the base and her dad's house meant that nothing was going to happen between them. He *had* given in to his second thoughts. He had decided that the two of them surrendering to the fire building between them would be a colossal error in judgment.

She wasn't even surprised.

But the jab of hurt caught her off guard.

"I don't want to," he said and his voice sounded tight and harsh, strained nearly to the breaking point. She watched his hands clench and unclench on the steering wheel until his knuckles went white. "You've got to know that. What I want is to take you back to my place."

His place. Her insides thrummed with a low, pulsing need that threatened to swamp her with a desire that rushed up to choke her breath and strangle her heart. Instantly, images clouded her mind and filled her thoughts. Kevin, bare chested, leaning over her, running his hands up and down her naked body. She could almost feel the gentle scrape of his calloused hands on her skin. Almost taste his kiss. Almost smell the soft, male scent of him as he leaned in closer, closer.

Her body flickered into a life that was, she knew, doomed to wither away into the unsatisfied, incomplete state with which she was all too familiar.

"But I can't do that." He didn't sound any happier about it than she did, but at the moment, that was small consolation.

"Oh, naturally you couldn't do that," she said. "That would be breaking some kind of rule, wouldn't it?"

"You're engaged, dammit," he said.

Ah, she thought, Ray. She should have known that lie would come back to haunt her. It wasn't even her status as the Colonel's daughter that was keeping Kevin at arm's length—instead it was the pretend fiancé she'd invented as a safeguard.

"I almost wish you weren't," he added.

Her gaze shot to him. "You do?"

"Hell, yes," he snapped.

"And if I wasn't?" she asked, and probably shouldn't have. After all, why torture herself?

"If you weren't—" He shook his head. "No point in going down that road, is there?"

"I suppose not," she admitted, and had to grind

her teeth together to keep from blurting out the truth. Because it wouldn't get her anywhere. If he knew the truth now, he'd think her a liar or worse and race her back to the base.

She laughed shortly and he heard her.

"What can you possibly find funny in any of this?"

"Are you kidding?" she asked, leaning her head against the seat back. "Here we are, two consenting adults, hot as a couple of teenagers and instead of doing anything about it, we're running for safety."

"We're supposed to be smarter than teenagers."

"Yeah, well, maybe *smart's* not all it's cracked up to be."

Not when she was feeling like this, anyway. She didn't want to be logical. What she wanted, no. What she *needed,* was to feel. To feel everything. To finally and forever lose her virginity crown to a man she was willing to bet would make the losing of it memorable.

He made a sharp left turn and she looked at him. "What are you doing?" Lilah stared out the side window at a residential neighborhood, noting the lamplight glowing from behind windows and the children playing on neatly manicured lawns.

"Being stupid," he muttered.

"What happened to being smart and you taking me back to Dad's house?"

"Yeah, well," Kevin said, telling himself what

an idiot he was, "I changed my mind. We'll go to my apartment first. Get you dried off before you get pneumonia." Damn. Even *he* didn't believe him. But he had to say something. Engaged or not. Colonel's daughter or not. He wasn't ready yet to take her back.

So he'd torture himself just a bit longer by taking her to his place.

"That's probably a good idea," she said and her voice reached down into the depths of his soul and warmed him through.

Dammit.

"No," he said, keeping his tightfisted grip on a steering wheel that somehow kept from shattering, "it's probably a lousy idea. But I'm not taking you home dripping wet, either."

"Sounds smart to me." Easing back into the car seat, she kept her gaze locked on the passenger-side window until he pulled into the driveway of the duplex he rented from Mrs. Osborne. Nosiest woman on the planet.

This should just make her week.

Him showing up with a soaking wet woman.

No help for it, though.

"I kind of expected something a little more red, white and bluey," she said. "Or maybe khaki."

"I don't own it," he said. "I just rent the back apartment."

He barely glanced at the single story, white wood-framed bungalow. But he knew what she was seeing. A small place, with green shutters and two emerald-green doors. Mrs. Osborne was proud of her Irish heritage and didn't mind showing it off at every opportunity.

"It suits me," he said simply, not bothering to tell her that it gave him a break from the world that was his life. He loved the Corps, couldn't imagine living any other kind of life, but at the same time, he enjoyed having a home off base. "Come on."

He hopped out of the car and walked around to her side. Before he got there though, she had the door open and was climbing out. He told himself not to glance down at her white shirt, still wet in patches that seemed to be strategically placed to drive him insane. His gaze dropped anyway though and his body went hard and tight.

Kevin swallowed a groan and ground his back teeth together. This was asking for trouble, he knew. Being alone with her right now was definitely not a good idea. He was hanging on to his self-control by a ragged thread that was disintegrating with every passing second.

A blast of wind slapped at them, Lilah shivered and Kevin called himself a thoughtless bastard. Here he was thinking about getting her into his bed while she was turning into a gorgeous blond icicle right in front of him.

"You're freezing," he muttered and laid one hand against the small of her back.

"Not too bad," she said.

"Yeah, right. And your teeth chattering? That's just for show?"

"A turn-on, huh?" She flashed him a smile and just that quick, his hormones kicked into overdrive again.

"Oh, yeah," he muttered, guiding her up the drive to his front door. "Nothing I like better than a blue woman."

"You're a strange and twisted man," she said.

"Tell me about it."

"I like it."

Oh, man.

She stood closely to him while he shoved the key in the lock and turned the knob. He hustled her inside and as soon as he had the door closed, he reached over and adjusted the thermostat on the wall. The far-off, subtle roar of the heater jumping to life was a comforting sound, but they needed more heat. Fast.

"Take that sweater off," he ordered as he crossed the small foyer into an equally small living room. Walking to the fireplace, he knelt beside the hearth, snatched up the nearby matches and set fire to the kindling he always had ready. In a few minutes, the newspaper and wood shavings had caught and were already licking at the log lying across the grate.

Satisfied, he turned around and saw her standing

just as he'd left her. "You keep that soaking wet sweater on and you'll never get warm."

"I'd love to accommodate you, especially since you're so used to having your orders followed." She shrugged and laughed shortly. "But my hands are so cold, I can't get the darn thing off."

Dammit. Rising, he walked back to her side and stood behind her, scooping the sodden wool off her shoulders and down her arms. Instantly, she shivered again, wrapping her arms around her middle and hanging on tightly.

This wasn't going to be enough, he told himself. "All right." He took her by the shoulders, turned her around and pushed her through his bedroom. "The bathroom's in there. Go inside, and take a shower. There's a robe hanging on the door that you can wear until your clothes are dry."

"Uh…" She stopped dead and looked from him to his bed, neatly made and way too inviting and back again. "Is this some kind of roundabout seduction? Give a freezing girl a shower, just to get her naked?"

"No."

"Rats."

He gave her a gentle nudge toward the waiting bathroom, reminding himself that the most important thing at the moment was simply to get her warmed up again. "Just take a hot shower, all right? And when you get those clothes off, toss 'em to me. I'll throw them in the dryer."

"Smooth talker."

"Knock it off."

"Thought you wanted me to 'take it off.'"

Kevin gave her one of his best D.I. glares and she didn't flinch. "Are you *trying* to make me nuts?"

"Apparently I don't have to try," she said, smiling despite her chattering teeth.

"Look, I'm not trying to seduce you. Trust me, you'll know when I am."

Both blond eyebrows lifted. "*When,* huh? Not *if?*"

Definitely not "if." He knew as well as she did exactly where they were headed. All he could hope for at this point was to put it off as long as possible and pray that he regained his senses before it was too late.

Slim hope, but he'd take it.

"Get in the damn shower, will ya?"

She nodded and laughed, though he was pretty sure he heard a thread of nervousness in the sound. And that surprised him. Hell, he would have bet that *nothing* made Lilah Forrest nervous.

He watched as she headed for the green-tiled bathroom and listened, though it pushed every one of his already too sensitive buttons, as she fought her way out of her wet clothes. Then what seemed just moments later, she poked her head around the side of the door and held out those wet things. "Here you go."

Kevin stepped up close and took her clothes in one tight fist, trying desperately not to think about the fact that only one small door was separating him from her naked body. His fingers curled into the wet fabric and squeezed.

And just like that, the memory of that kiss they'd shared slapped into his brain with the force of a train wreck. He recalled her taste, her smell, her breathy sighs and those memories fanned the flames licking at his insides.

"I'll be out in a few minutes," she said.

He looked right into those big blue eyes of hers and said, "Take your time."

For both their sakes, he hoped she stayed in there, under a spray of hot water, for at least an hour. And even then, it probably wouldn't be long enough.

When she stepped out of the bathroom, Lilah paused briefly to look at his bed. Neat. Tidy. Like the rest of the small space. She was willing to bet that she'd be able to bounce a quarter off his mattress, too, since the bedspread was tight and wrinkle free. Yep. He was Marine to the bone. He kept his apartment clean enough to pass a surprise inspection.

But then, it probably wasn't hard to clean a place that held almost no personal items. Oh, he had the necessities. But nothing extra. No pictures hanging on the wall. No extra rugs. No throw pillows.

He lived as though ready to walk out the door and never come back.

And darned if she didn't find that a little sad.

Pushing that thought aside, she yanked the belt on his too big, blue robe tighter around her middle and headed for the living room. Here at least, she spotted a few framed photographs lining the mantle. Above the fireplace, hung a mounted, ceremonial sword, with a small, brass plaque beneath it.

But it was the man kneeling in front of the fire that caught her attention. Kevin had changed, too. In jeans and a red sweatshirt, he looked less formidable and Lilah knew instantly that she'd been right about why he wore his uniform around her all the time.

He heard her come into the room and stood up, turning to face her.

She pushed her damp hair back behind her shoulder and said stupidly, "I'm finished. Shower's all yours if you want it."

"No. I'm fine."

Yes, he certainly was, she thought, her gaze sweeping up and down those long legs of his. Her stomach jittered nervously, but she ignored it. "Well, the hot water felt great," she said. "Thanks."

"No problem." He shoved his hands into the back pockets of his well-worn jeans and said, "Your stuff's drying. Shouldn't be long."

"No hurry." She was warm and cozy and completely naked under her borrowed robe, but no hurry.

She walked around the edge of the sofa and took a seat in the corner, curling up, tucking her bare feet beneath her. Then looking up at him, she noted his gaze and followed it. The edges of the robe had gapped, giving him a tantalizing peek at her breasts. Lilah swallowed hard and pulled the gap closed.

"I made you some tea," he said, pointing to the cup waiting on the low table in front of her.

"Thanks." She reached for it, took a sip, then gasped, blinking. "Wow. That's some kind of tea."

"Rum. To take the last of the chill off."

"That ought to do it," she assured him as a fire crept down the length of her throat to settle in the pit of her stomach.

"We should probably talk," Kevin said and Lilah lifted her gaze to his.

She knew that tone, Lilah thought. And the words. It was the beginning of the "Gee, I think you're swell, but let's just be friends" speech. Heck, she'd heard it so often, she could deliver it for him and save him the effort.

Just for a little extra courage, she took another healthy sip of the rum-laced tea, then set the cup down on the table again.

"Sure, why not?" she said, then added, "what say I get you started?"

"What?"

She folded her hands at her waist, tipped her head to one side and staring at the ceiling, said, "You're a terrific woman, Lilah. But I'm (a) not good enough for you, (b) seeing someone else, (c) being transferred to Greenland, (d) all of the above."

"What are you talking about?"

"The speech," she said, shrugging as if it didn't mean a thing to her. "I've heard it all. Whatever you're about to say has already been covered. Trust me when I say that no matter what excuse you have lined up, I've heard it. Up to and including, 'You're just too weird.'"

Suddenly, she couldn't sit still. Hopping up from the couch, she walked toward him and stopped just in front of him. Lifting one hand, she poked his broad chest with the tip of her index finger and said, "A little while ago, you were talking about seducing me. And now you want to back off fast." She threw her hair back when it fell across her eyes. "Well, trust me, Marine. I've seen sparks fly from the heels of guys getting away from me. So you can't surprise me."

And then he did.

Grabbing her, he pulled her to him, planted his mouth across hers and gave her a kiss that singed the ends of her hair. His fingers dug into her upper arms and he literally swept her off her feet, lifting

her from the carpet and drawing her close enough
that her heart pounded against his.

She couldn't breathe.

And even better, she didn't care.

Chapter Eight

Kevin wrapped his arms around her and held on tight. His good intentions fell by the wayside as he felt her breasts push into his chest. He parted her lips with his tongue and at the first taste of her, his blood boiled and his heart staggered.

Better, he thought. Better than he remembered. Kissing Lilah was enough to feed and sustain a man for the rest of his life. Groaning, he shifted his hold on her and swept her up into the cradle of his arms. He held her fiercely as if someone might rush into the house demanding that he let her go.

And just now, with his mouth on hers, with her breath brushing across his cheek, he knew he couldn't do that. If a full battalion came crashing through that front door, he'd find a way to stand them off.

He had to touch her. Had to have her.

Walking to the sofa, he sat down and settled Lilah on his lap. Her arms came up around his neck and held on tight. She gave as good as she got, kissing him with an abandon that threatened to rock his world. And still it wasn't enough.

He tore his mouth from hers only to trail his lips down the line of her throat. He paused at the base of her neck to taste the rapid thump of her pulse beat, then went on, moving down into the V of fabric caused by the parting robe.

She sucked in a gulp of air as he slid one hand beneath the blue terry cloth to cup one of her breasts.

"Kevin," she whispered, her voice straining, rising.

"I'm right here, baby," he assured her, then took her nipple between his thumb and forefinger, tweaking, tugging, pulling gently at the sensitive flesh until she was squirming on his lap. Her bottom ground against his arousal until Kevin was nearly afraid he'd explode like some hormone-driven teenager. Finally, he held her still, clamping one arm around her waist and hips. The delicious pressure of her body nestled so closely with his drove him wild even as he dipped his head to taste her nipple.

The moment he took her into his mouth, she groaned and pushed herself into him.

"Kevin, yes," she said, swallowing hard after choking the words out. "Oh, yes, do that some more."

He planned to. He planned to taste and lick and suck on her flesh until neither one of them could think rationally again. But the best-laid plans were bound to come undone.

Her eager responses raged inside him, making him impatient and too hungry for her to wait another moment.

Sweeping one hand down her body, he found the juncture of her thighs and with his fingertips, gently parted the delicate flesh there. She planted her feet on the sofa cushion and rocked against his hand. He watched her eyes glaze, her mouth open, her tongue dart out to lick her bottom lip.

He slipped a finger into her warmth and almost came undone. So hot. So wet. So tight. Her legs parted, granting him access and he looked down, enjoying the sight of his hand on her body. She rippled in his arms like a ribbon cut free of its spool. He dipped in and out of her body, teasing, taunting, pushing her to the edge of sanity and then pulling her back, refusing to let her find the release she was chasing.

"Kevin, help me…oh, my…it's so…"

"Come, baby," he said, slipping inside her again,

rubbing that one small, sensitive nub with the pad of his thumb. "Let go and come."

"I can't—" Her head twisted from side to side. "I can't—oh!"

He knew it the moment the first tremor claimed her. Her interior muscles clamped around his fingers and he felt each tiny convulsion as it rolled through her. Her breath gasped in and out of her lungs, she clutched at his shoulders, her fingers digging into his body like talons.

Emotion, raw and rich filled him and Kevin realized that he was finding as much pleasure in giving to her as he would have in taking. That fact stunned him. He'd never felt this before. Never enjoyed so much bringing a woman to a staggering, mind-numbing climax.

But Lilah was different, as he'd already guessed. Her emotions, her feelings were right out there for all to see. She held nothing back. There was no coyness. No false embarrassment. No shyness. No lies. There was only her and the incredible fascination he had for her.

And just when he thought he could watch her pleasure forever, it was over and she lay limp and spent on his lap. Gently, he shifted her in his grasp and tugged the edges of the robe together across her body. Lilah turned into him, burying her face in his chest.

"That was…"

"Good?" he asked, running his fingers through the soft, silky strands of her hair.

"Oh, there's got to be a better word than that." He smiled down at her and she tipped her face up to his. Passion colored her eyes. "I'll let you know when I think of it."

"You do that," he said and bent to kiss her. As his lips came down on hers, she ran the flat of her hand up his chest and even through the red sweatshirt he wore, he felt the heat of her touch. Her palm settled over his flat nipple and he crushed her to him, to ease the flash of need that rose up inside him.

Breaking the kiss, he stared down at her and knew he'd never wanted a woman more. He had to have her. Had to be inside her.

"Make love to me," she whispered, reaching up to cup his cheek in her palm.

"Oh, yeah," he said. All doubts, all worries were banished to a dark corner of his mind. There'd be time enough later for recriminations. For regrets. But for now, all he needed was to be able to feel her skin against his. Feel her warmth surround him, and take him into her depths.

And he needed it more than air.

The phone rang and Kevin swallowed hard, muttered a curse and shot a glare at the damn thing lying on the table beside him. He thought about ignoring it. But duty was too well ingrained.

He snatched it up and brought it to his ear.

"Hello?" he barked, just a shade more aggressively than usual.

Lilah had scooped her hands beneath his sweatshirt and he felt her touch singing along his skin like tiny electrical pulses. He fought to concentrate, when all he wanted to do was pitch the phone through a window and carry her off to his bed.

Then the voice on the phone registered and it was as effective as a bucket of cold water crashing down on his head.

"Colonel Forrest, sir," he answered sharply, sitting up straight.

"Gunnery Sergeant Rogan," the other man said and his voice was like a buzzing in Kevin's ear. "I don't mean to disturb you at home, but I was wondering if Lilah might be there with you."

Dammit.

Easing Lilah's bare legs off his lap, Kevin stood up, putting as much distance as possible between him and the nearly naked woman.

"We had a dinner reservation at the club tonight and—"

The Colonel's voice droned on, but Kevin hardly heard him. His gaze fixed on Lilah, he watched as she tugged the robe into place and stood up in front of him, smiling. How in the hell she could smile was beyond him, though. Hell, it felt to Kevin like the Colonel was right there in the room with him. That he could see them both. And knew damn well what Kevin had been doing to his daughter.

There was a thought.

"Yes, sir," Kevin said, letting his gaze slide from Lilah to something a lot less hot. The fire. "She's here. I was just about to bring her home and—"

"Fine, fine," the Colonel interrupted. "Just wanted to make sure. I'll see you both soon, then."

"Yes, sir, Colonel." Kevin hung up, setting the receiver back into place then turning to face the woman watching him.

"That was your father."

"I got that much."

"Something about a dinner reservation?"

"Oh, my," she said and shot a look at the clock hanging near the front door. "We're going to be late."

"That's the impression I got."

She turned back to him and gave him a slow, secretive smile that he would have been willing to bet one female taught another, generation to generation. It was a powerful thing, that smile, designed to bring even the strongest man to his knees.

"It was worth it, though," she said and walked up to him, sliding her arms up until she could wrap them around his neck. She went up on her toes and brought her mouth to within a breath of his own.

He figured she knew what she was doing to him.

And by the looks of it, she was enjoying it.

He set his hands at her waist, lifted her and then set her down again, at a distance. "Your clothes should be dry by now," he said, hoping to God he was right. A few more minutes with naked Lilah and he would forget all about the dinner reservations, the Colonel, and anything else that wasn't soft, warm, Lilah.

Dammit.

"Just like that, huh?" she asked, tipping her head to one side and looking at him.

He shoved one hand along the side of his head, mainly to keep his brain from exploding. "No, not 'just like that.'"

"Seems that way to me," she pointed out. "You darn near saluted the phone."

"It was your father."

"On the phone," she told him. "Not actually here."

"Don't even say that." He was having a hard enough time as it was.

"You're amazing," she said, tossing her hands high, then letting them fall to her sides. "How do you do that?"

"Do what?" he muttered, wishing she'd just go get dressed and put him out of his misery.

"Go from hot to cold so fast," she said.

"Trust me," he managed to grind out, "I'm a long way from cooled off. If you think it's easy for me to just stop what we were doing," he snapped, "you're wrong."

"Then why stop?"

"Because," he pointed out as he stalked across the living room toward the kitchen, "none of my sexual fantasies include having an armed Colonel break in and shoot me for sleeping with his daughter."

"What kind of fantasies *do* you have?"

His steps faltered, but he didn't turn around. If he looked at her now, he was a goner. "Never mind."

"No, there's something else going on here besides my father calling."

"Nope. That's it," he called, opening the dryer and rummaging around inside. Her clothes weren't completely dry yet, but they were better than they had been and they'd just have to do.

"Are you sure this isn't about your ex-wife?"

"What?" Stunned, he stood up and looked at her, the clothes momentarily forgotten.

She picked up the terry cloth belt and worried it between her fingers. Dipping her head briefly, she looked up again quickly and watched him as she said, "I, uh, heard that you and your wife, well—"

Bitterness charged through him, but he choked it off almost instantly. "I can imagine what you've heard."

"I don't listen to gossip."

"Really?"

She ignored the ring of sarcasm in his tone and said, "I was just wondering if maybe you're pulling away from me because you're not entirely over your ex-wife."

"Alanna and I were over a long time ago," he said flatly. "This has nothing to do with her."

She stared at him for a long, silent moment before nodding. "Okay then," she said, and Kevin was grateful that she was apparently going to drop it.

Bending down, he grabbed her clothes and walked back to the living room. Tossing them at her from a safe distance, he said simply, "Get dressed."

She clutched the pile of warm clothes to her chest, snapped him a salute and clicked her bare heels together. "Sir! Yes, sir!"

Then she laughed and left the room. And he was alone with a rock-hard body screaming for release and no end in sight.

A week later, Lilah was still kicking herself.

She never should have mentioned his ex-wife. She still wasn't sure why she had. But it had seemed pretty reasonable at the time. Although looking back now, she could admit that her brain had been so fuzzy, she wouldn't have known "reasonable" if it had strolled up and bit her.

She sat at her father's dining room table, cradling a cup of coffee between her palms. Staring out at the windswept base and the gunmetal-gray sky hovering over it, she really wasn't seeing any of it. Instead, she saw a strong jaw, narrowed green eyes and a mouth that looked stern until you kissed it.

Taking a sip of her coffee, she let it slide down her throat and ease away some of the chill within. He hadn't called. Hadn't come by. And was probably determined to stay far, far away from her.

And a part of Lilah knew that would no doubt be for the best. Unfortunately, a bigger part of her wasn't about to let that happen. She'd found something in Kevin Rogan. Something she hadn't been looking for. Something she'd given up hope of *ever* finding. She'd be a fool to turn her back on it now. She had to at least take it as far as she could, discover if there was more out there just waiting for her.

For them.

"'Morning, honey," her father said as he came into the room.

She jumped, startled, then turned her head to give him a smile. "Hi, Dad."

Taking a seat opposite her, he glanced at his wristwatch, then looked at her. "So what's on your agenda for today?"

Well, she was thinking very seriously about hunting Kevin Rogan down like a dog. But she didn't think her father would want to hear that. So instead, she said, "I thought I'd go over to the base school. Look around."

"Uh-huh," he scanned the stack of papers in front of him and took a gulp of his coffee. "And

Gunnery Sergeant Rogan? Will he be taking you to the school?"

"I don't know. Haven't seen him in a few days." Look at me, she thought, willing her father's gaze to shift to her. A moment later, she was almost convinced she had psychic powers when he did just that.

"You two have a disagreement?" he asked, frowning. "Already?"

Already. Naturally, he'd have expected trouble. Hadn't every Marine he'd ever set her up with eventually run for cover? But this time it was different. This time, the Marine in question wasn't running because he couldn't stand being around her—this time it was exactly the opposite.

"No," she said, setting her cup down onto the table, she wrapped her arms around her up-drawn knees. "Surprised?"

He drew his head back and looked at her. "Why would I be surprised? You're a lovely woman."

Just a little flaky, she silently finished for him. And once again, she wished he could love her for who she was, not who he wanted her to be. She wished she didn't feel the sting of his disappointment in her. She wished she had the guts to come flat out and ask him what she had to do to make him proud of her.

But she didn't. So instead, she stood up, crossed to him and kissed his forehead. "Thanks for the vote of confidence, Dad."

As she left the room, she heard him say, "Have a good day, honey."

When she glanced back at him though, she saw he'd already turned his attention back to the work in front of him.

Chapter Nine

One week and he hadn't been able to get her out of his mind. Request from the Colonel or not, Kevin had steered clear of the man's daughter, figuring they both needed a cooling-off period. Not that it had worked. In his case, anyway.

Hell, for all he knew, Lilah Forrest hadn't given him a second thought. But he didn't believe it. After the way she'd come undone in his arms, he knew she too would be remembering those stolen moments in his apartment. She too would be hungering for more.

Which is exactly why he'd kept his distance.

Until now.

From the inside of the PX, he watched her walk

past. Chin up, that long hair of hers blowing in the same cold wind that whipped her sapphire-blue skirt around her short, shapely legs. A flash of sunlight dazzled off the silver stars in her ears and he could almost hear the tinkle of bells at her wrist.

How had this happened? he wondered. How had he allowed himself to become *attached* to her? She'd somehow sneaked up on him, like an attack at midnight. Blowing past his guards, infiltrating his inner circle, she'd slipped beneath his defenses and left him wide open for assault.

All with a smile and a toss of her head.

Dammit.

He was supposed to be immune to this sort of thing. Would have bet cold, hard cash that Alanna's betrayal had wiped the ability to love right out of his soul.

Love?

That one little word brought him up short.

Did he love Lilah?

No. Even the possibility of such a thing was too hideous to contemplate. He wasn't going back down that road. Not again. He wouldn't give a woman everything he had just to watch her throw it in his face. He wouldn't trust anyone again the way he'd trusted Alanna. Hell, maybe he learned the hard way—but he learned. He felt something for Lilah, but it wasn't love. It was lust, pure and simple. He wanted her. No, needed her. And that was it.

For the first time since Alanna, Kevin had found a woman who interested him. One who challenged his mind even while tormenting his body. He could enjoy it, he told himself, without making more of it than it was. They were two consenting adults.

One of whom was the engaged daughter of his Commanding Officer, but that was a different story.

The point here is, he told himself as he walked closer to the window to get a better look at her as she went past, they both had itches that needed to be scratched. Now all he had to do was figure out if he was going to allow the scratching to pick up again.

Allow. He chuckled to himself and walked to the shop entrance. Pushing through the door, he stepped into the bite of the wind and ducked his head slightly. As he started after her, he reminded himself that anyone trying to "allow" Lilah anything had better be girded for war.

Lilah heard him approaching. Well, she heard the heavy click of footsteps behind her. It could have been anyone. But the rush of her blood told her instinctively that it was Kevin.

Strange that just by being near, he could light up her insides and set a rumbling need rolling through her body. Instantly, memories came crashing back. She remembered lying across his lap, naked. She remembered vividly the feel of his hands on her. The heat of his mouth on her nipples. The soft slide of his fingers as they entered her.

Her mouth went dry and a dull, throbbing ache settled between her legs.

"Lilah."

She stopped and tried to work up enough saliva to make it possible to talk. Of course, when she turned around, all it took was one look at him and she was practically drooling. Problem solved.

"Hi, stranger," she said and silently congratulated herself on her mature, adult behavior. Especially when all she really wanted to do was throw herself at him.

He squinted down at her and she wished she could read his emotions. But like all good Marines, he kept them hidden behind a mask of professionalism.

"Where you headed?"

"To the school."

"I'll walk with you."

Avoid her for a week and then show up out of nowhere and offer to escort her to the school. If she wasn't so glad to see him, she'd tell him to take a hike. But since he looked way too good to send on his way, she glanced around furtively as if searching for eavesdroppers, then tipped her head back and met his gaze. "Are you sure that's safe?"

"What?"

"You know," she said, beginning to enjoy herself. Really, the man's sense of humor was buried so deep it would probably be a full-time job to resuscitate it. Not a bad job, she thought as she continued, "Being alone with me. I mean, I might just throw you to the ground and have my way with you."

One corner of his mouth tilted. "Good one."

"Don't think I could do it?" Nothing she liked better than a challenge.

He shook his head, took her elbow and turned her around, pointing her in the direction in which she had been walking a minute ago. "I wouldn't put anything past you," he admitted. "But I'm willing to take my chances."

"Gee," she said, concentrating on the warmth of his touch on her arm, "and they say there are no heroes anymore."

He laughed and Lilah luxuriated in the sound. "You really ought to do that more often," she said.

"What? Laugh?"

"Yeah," she said, glancing up at him, "it does great things for your face."

Instantly, the easy smile faded away to be replaced by a flicker of desire that shot across his features so fast, she would have missed it if she hadn't been studying him so closely. And if she hadn't been so affected by the hunger in his eyes, she probably wouldn't have said, "I've missed you."

His grip on her elbow tightened. "I thought it would be easier if we had a little space."

"Easier for whom?"

He glanced down at her. "Damned if I know."

Good. Then it hadn't been easy for him to stay away from her. He'd missed her, too. Small consolation, but at this point, she'd take anything she could get. And somehow, it helped knowing that he'd been as affected by her as she had by him.

"So," she asked, wanting to actually hear him admit it, "you missed me?"

His back teeth ground together and his squint narrowed so tightly, she would have thought he couldn't see at all.

"Yeah," he said on a grunt of sound. "I guess I did."

"And you sound thrilled about that."

He looked down at her briefly again and his green eyes shone like streetlights from beneath the shaded brim of his Smokey the Bear hat.

"It shouldn't make either one of us happy."

"Why the heck not?" she asked, waving her hand, making the bells at her wrist jangle noisily.

"Because we have nothing in common, for one," he pointed out.

"Oh, I think we were doing pretty well a few days ago," she said and instantly felt a renewed flush of heat swamping her.

"Yeah, too good." His fingers tightened on her elbow until she squeaked in protest and he relaxed his grip. "Sorry."

"No problem," she said. "I bend, I don't break."

"I'll remember that."

"I probably shouldn't ask," she said, knowing she would anyway, because she needed to know, "but did you stay away because I mentioned your ex-wife?"

He actually went even stiffer than usual. She felt tension crowd him and spill over onto her. "No."

"Hard to believe, judging by your reaction."

He sighed, glanced at her, then shifted his gaze forward again. "Look, I don't know what you heard, but—"

"I didn't hear much."

"Surprising," he said, "since it was the talk of the base a year ago."

"I'm sorry. I know what it's like to be gossiped about."

He gave her a quick look and a half smile. "Yeah, I guess you do." Then speaking quickly, he said, "The short version is, I met Alanna in Germany when I was doing embassy duty. She knocked me off my feet, I married her and as soon as we got back to the States, she split."

"What?" Worlds of hurt were crouched behind his words and Lilah was almost sorry she'd brought it up. Almost.

"She wanted to get into the U.S. and couldn't. So she married me and when we got back here, she disappeared."

"So she's here illegally."

"Yeah. But that's her problem."

"And she's yours," Lilah said thoughtfully.

"What's that supposed to mean?"

"That she still haunts you."

"No way."

"Just talking about her makes you all snarly."

"I'm *not* snarly."

She laughed. Couldn't help it.

He scowled at her, then gave her a grudging smile. "Okay, maybe I am a little,"

Lilah pulled her elbow free of his grasp, then linked arm with his. "You're allowed, I guess," she said, looking up at him and holding his gaze with hers. "But you shouldn't waste too much time and effort on such a stupid woman."

"Stupid?"

"She left you, didn't she?" A flicker of pleasure lit his eyes and one corner of his mouth lifted in a half grin. Lilah answered that grin with one of her own. "And look on the bright side. Maybe she'll get caught and deported."

"I like the way you think," he said in a low, rumbling tone.

"Thanks," she said as they turned into the school yard.

Crowds of kids played on the grass and blacktop. The noise level was incredible and Kevin told himself if they could only find a way to bottle the sound, the Marines would never have to invade another country. All they'd have to do was put these kids on a loudspeaker and any enemy in their right mind would surrender.

Lilah though, didn't seem to mind the cacophony a bit. She smiled at the kids, paused long enough to toss back a stray dodge ball, then headed right through the crowd of children toward the front door. She grabbed hold of the doorknob, then looked back at him over her shoulder. "You could wait for me out here."

"Are you nuts?" he asked, appalled at the idea. "It's got to be quieter inside."

She thought about it for a moment, chewing at her bottom lip. "Okay, come on."

Once inside, he removed his cover and tucked it beneath his left arm. Following behind Lilah, he couldn't help noticing the sway of her hips or the way her hair moved with every toss of her head. The sounds of their heels on the floor were the only sounds and as she stepped into the principal's office, Kevin took up a post just outside the open doorway.

While she did whatever it was she'd come here to do, Kevin let his gaze sweep down the length of the hallway. Bulletin boards were tacked up to the wall and crowded with notices of bake sales and movie nights and parents' night and PTA meetings. Kevin shook his head and thought for the first time in a long while that if Alanna hadn't betrayed him, then left him, he might have felt more at home here. In this school. He might have, one day, had a child himself enrolled in a base school.

As it stood now though, he'd forever be an outsider in halls like these.

Still, he thought, thanks to Lilah, the last of the cold, hard knot he'd been carrying around in his guts since Alanna's betrayal was gone. He sucked in a gulp of air and enjoyed the sensation of freedom that coursed through his veins.

Meeting this woman had changed him in ways he hadn't expected. Who would have thought that doing a favor for his Commanding Officer would lead to this? Shaking his head, he stepped across the threshold into the office in time to hear a woman saying, "Miss Forrest, it's amazing."

"It's nothing," Lilah assured her. "Honestly. I was happy to do it."

"It's much more than nothing," the woman, whose picture hung on the wall and identified her as Katherine Murray, Principal, went on. "When Computer Planet called this morning and told me they would be donating three of last year's models, well I—" the woman held up both hands in surrender, apparently unable to think of anything else to say.

Lilah smiled, reached across the wooden counter and took one of the woman's hands in hers. "Trust me, Mrs. Murray, it's a good deal for them. They get a write-off and get to make room for newer models they can sell for more money."

The older woman shook her head. "I still don't

know how you managed it, but I thank you for it. This will mean so much to the computer lab class."

Kevin looked from one to the other of the women as they chatted, and he felt a swell of pride fill him. Lilah Forrest was really something. She continued to surprise him and that ability intrigued him. Too often, he was able to look at a person and pretty much sum up who and what they were. But Lilah… she was so much more than the flighty, flaky woman she appeared to be.

Hell, she wouldn't even take credit for doing something incredibly generous. First, the jackets she'd had donated and now apparently she was playing computer fairy. But she seemed bent on brushing these things aside as if they were nothing. Yet how many people, he asked himself, went out of their way for others? Not many. Lilah, he was beginning to realize, was one in a million.

Mrs. Murray caught his eye and smiled before looking back to Lilah. "It seems you have someone waiting for you, so I'll let you go. But I do want to thank you again."

"Enjoy the computers," Lilah said, looking at Kevin with twin spots of embarrassed color staining her cheeks. Amazing. Not only did she run around acting like Santa, she didn't want anyone to know about it.

When she turned and left the office, Kevin was right behind her. Her soft leather boots barely made a sound on the linoleum floor. Her spine was so stiff, it was a wonder it didn't snap. And knowing her, Kevin was pretty sure this awkward silence between them wouldn't last.

He was right.

She stopped suddenly and turned around. He was so close, she almost smashed her nose into his chest. She backed up a step, planted her fists on her hips and looked up at him. "Not one word, Kevin."

"Not even if it's a compliment?"

"Especially then," she said and paused to take a long breath. "I didn't arrange for those computers so people would thank me."

That he believed, but it led to another question. "Why then? Why did you do it?"

She tried to shrug off the question, but he wouldn't let her. She'd delved into his life, now it was his turn to ask the questions.

"Why, Lilah?"

She blew out a breath and shifted her arms to fold across her middle. "Because I could. Because the school needed the computers."

"So you just went out and got them?"

"It's easy for me," she said and almost sounded apologetic. "I like talking."

"God knows that's true."

She smiled a little. "And most people are more than willing to help if you tell them exactly *how* to do it. That's my job. I run fund-raisers and arrange donations and well…" She finally ran out of the steam and shrugged.

Oh, he'd be willing to bet that she excelled at that part of the job. She had a way of talking to a person and somehow reaching down inside them to find things they hadn't known were there. She'd probably gotten donations from companies who had policies *against* charitable donations.

"Somehow, you convince them that they wanted to do it all along, don't you?"

"Sort of." She reached up and fingered the amethyst crystal hanging from around her neck.

"You do this all the time?"

"Is there something wrong with that?" she asked just a bit defensively.

"Not wrong," he said. "Just…unusual. Jackets, computers, anything else you're arranging for?"

"Turkeys for Thanksgiving, Toys For Tots, blood drives, Make-A-Wish Foundation…" She shrugged and asked, "Anything you need?"

He grabbed her and pulled her around to face him. His gaze swept over her features, her eyes, her mouth and when he looked again into her gaze, he actually heard himself say, "You, Lilah. I'm beginning to think I just might need you."

"Wow," she whispered. "I do believe we're having another journal moment."

Chapter Ten

Something indefinable had changed.

Kevin could almost *see* his words hanging in the air between them. Too late to call them back—even if he wanted to and he wasn't altogether sure he did want to. It had been so long since he'd felt this…*alive*. Just looking at Lilah Forrest was enough to fan the flames inside him.

The way she moved, the way she thought, intrigued him. Her touch, her laughter, aroused him like no one ever had. Being near her and not being able to hold her, kiss her, taste her, was a sweet kind of torture that kept his body humming and his blood racing.

And he didn't know what in the hell he could do about it.

Lilah pulled in a deep breath and blew it out before saying, "Would you like to come to dinner tonight?"

Dinner. With her and her father. Instantly, he imagined sitting across the table from Colonel Forrest, while trying to hide the desire he felt for the man's daughter. Not exactly his idea of a good time.

But he couldn't go anyway. "I can't," he said, "have to be at my sister's house for dinner tonight." Disappointment flickered across her expression and before he could stop himself, Kevin blurted, "Why don't you come with me?"

Surprise widened her eyes and he enjoyed seeing it. Nice to be the surpriser for a change instead of the surprisee.

"I'd like that," she said.

"Good. Pick you up at six."

His words were still echoing in Lilah's mind hours later. Her heart quickened every time she recalled the look in his eyes and the soft strength of his touch.

He needed her.

But did he love her?

Well, he'd brought her here, hadn't he? That had to mean something.

The Rogans, taken in a bunch, were a little overpowering.

Even Kelly, the only girl in the family, more than

held her own in the pitched battles that passed for dinner table conversation. Kevin and his brothers took turns passing Kelly's daughter Emily around, each of the big men becoming cooing imbeciles as soon as the little girl smiled up at them.

The dishes were washed and put away by everyone, with all of them bumping into each other in the small kitchen. Laughter and arguments punctuated the air and Lilah felt, oddly enough, completely at home.

She envied the easy love the siblings shared and wondered if they'd ever really stopped to appreciate the closeness that was so clearly a part of them all. As an only child, Lilah had longed for brothers and sisters and now she could see how much she'd missed in her solitary childhood.

And seeing Kevin in his element only made her admire him more. With his family, he became the man that she'd only caught glimpses of in the last couple of weeks. Here, the starch came out of his spine and he was open, reachable to these people he obviously loved so much.

An ache settled around her heart as Lilah realized that she wanted to be important to him, too. She wanted to be a part of this family. And yet, in less than two weeks, she'd be leaving. Going back home. To her apartment. To her job at Charity Coalition. To loneliness.

Her gaze shifted, moving over the Rogan brothers until it stopped on Kevin. One look at him and her blood simmered in her veins. Every nerve ending stood straight up and screamed. He laughed at something one of his brothers said and her breath caught. He cradled his niece in his arms and Lilah's insides melted. He gently ran one hand up and down little Emily's back and all Lilah could remember was his touch on her skin. His hands. His mouth. And she wanted him so badly, it was all she could do to stay in her chair.

"I know that look," Kelly said and took a seat close by.

"Hmm?" Startled, and just a little embarrassed to be caught drooling, Lilah turned her head toward Kevin's sister. "What look?"

"Oh, the one you get every time you stare at Kevin."

So much for a poker face. "No, I…"

Kelly shook her head. "I get that same look on my face whenever Jeff comes home."

"I didn't realize I was being that obvious."

"Don't worry," Kelly said smiling, "you're not. I doubt if any one of the guys noticed. Including Kevin."

"Swell."

"Hey, don't get me wrong," Kelly said, reaching out to pat Lilah's hand. "There's definitely something up. Heck, this is the first time my big brother's brought any woman to meet us since—"

Her voice trailed off and she paused uncomfortably.

"Alanna," Lilah finished for her. "He told me about her."

"He did?" Kelly grinned and sat back, giving Lilah a look of approval. "The plot thickens."

"She hurt him."

"Big time," Kelly agreed. "But he got through it. And I can't tell you how glad I am he's dating you."

Dating? Well, they were doing something, but she didn't think dating was the word to describe it. Still, she didn't correct the other woman, mainly because she enjoyed the notion of *really* belonging with Kevin.

He's so much more than she'd suspected when she first met him. Not just a D.I., he's patient, even when she flabbergasts him. He's gentle with his niece and protective of his family. He's loyal and kind and despite the stern expression he habitually wears, he's a marshmallow inside, where it counts.

But on top of all that, the irritatingly logical side of her brain reminded her, he's a Marine to the core. He's responsible and organized and dutiful. He's as orderly as she is chaotic. And a part of her, despite the wild yearnings of her heart, wonders if he wouldn't, one day, be as impatient with her flakiness as her father generally was.

"Telling lies about me?" Kevin asked as he walked up to join them.

Lilah forced her mind away from the train wreck of her thoughts and looked up into forest-green eyes that sparked with a desire that churned up the embers carefully banked inside her.

"Hah!" Kelly said, taking her daughter from him. "No need for lies. The truth is hard enough." Then she went up on her toes and kissed his cheek.

"And very interesting," Lilah teased.

"Okay," he said, his gaze shifting nervously between the two women before settling on Lilah. Holding out one hand to her, he helped her up and said, "Think I'll take you home before Kelly has the chance to talk too much."

She stood up, but kept her grip on his hand. Grinning, she said, "But we were just getting to the good stuff."

"Uh-huh," he said. "Maybe next time."

"Oh, definitely next time," Kelly said, reaching out to give Lilah a hug.

And as they said their goodbyes, Lilah hugged the words "next time" to her. They implied a longer relationship than the next couple of weeks. And for now, that was good enough.

Kevin walked her to the car, unlocked the door and opened it. But before she could slide onto the seat, he stopped her, one hand on her forearm.

"Gonna make me walk?" she asked, looking up

at him. Moonlight dazzled her skin, making it glow like fine porcelain. Her long blond hair twisted in the wind, and her big blue eyes fixed on him. Kevin felt their impact even in the dim light. He dreamed about her eyes every blessed night. All day every day, he carried her image in his mind. And now, he would have other pictures there as well. Mental snapshots of her with his family. Laughing, joining in the arguments, holding Emily while she slept. He would think of his brothers' approving smiles and Kelly's instant rapport with her.

And from this night on, whenever he was with his family, if Lilah wasn't a part of it, he would miss her. He would notice her absence and wish she were there.

So much had changed for him the last two weeks, he hardly recognized his own life. But the need inside him, he knew. It had become a living, breathing thing that threatened to consume him. And the only way to conquer it was to surrender to it.

"I don't want to take you home," he said and he had to force the words past a throat nearly too tight to breathe.

She licked her lips and he followed the motion with his gaze. His body tightened even further and he flexed his fingers on the car door, to keep from snapping.

"I don't want to go home," she said. "Not now. Not yet."

"Not yet," he agreed and snaked one arm around her waist, pulling her to him, pinning her body to his. She tipped her head back and he swooped low, taking her mouth in a kiss designed to push them both over the edge of the cliff they'd been dancing on for a week now.

She gasped into his mouth and he swallowed her breath, exchanging it for his. He tasted her, sweeping his tongue into her mouth and caressing her warmth with long, deliberate strokes. And it wasn't enough. He needed more. Wanted more. Wanted to touch her, hold her, explore every inch of her body with the tips of his fingers. And when he was finished, he wanted only to begin again.

Lilah leaned into him, relishing the hard, solid strength of him. The night air pushed at them, damp fingers trying to pry them apart, but the heat they shared withstood it. She kissed him, tangling her tongue with his, enjoying the rush of desire, the heart pounding thrill of being in his arms again. She didn't want to think about tomorrow. Or next week. Or the week after.

All she wanted now, was to be beneath him. To feel him join his body with hers. She wanted to at last know what every other woman her age had long since discovered. The magic of becoming one with the man you loved.

And as that word rose up in her mind, she clutched at it. True, she thought. Love had happened where she had least expected it. A Marine, of all things, had stolen her heart. Now she wanted to give him her body.

He broke the kiss and gulped for air like a drowning man rising to the surface of a freezing lake. His gaze swept over her features, then zeroed in on her eyes. Voice ragged, he asked, "My place?"

Lilah swallowed hard, nodded and said, "Fast."

It wasn't fast enough.

As if fate was taunting them, Kevin hit every red light on the drive to his apartment. Lilah's nerves jangled like the bells on her wrist and she squirmed in her seat in a futile attempt to ease the throbbing ache settled between her thighs.

"I don't believe this," he muttered thickly as he came to a stop again. One hand fisting around the steering wheel, with the other, he reached across the seat for Lilah. She grabbed his hand and held on, her fingers threading through his.

A short, tight laugh shot from her throat. "Think someone's trying to tell us something?"

"If they are," he said, throwing her a glance, "I'm not listening."

"Good to know," she managed and gave him a smile that felt as tight as the knot lodged in the pit of her stomach.

He disentangled his fingers from hers and reached up to briefly cup her cheek. "You do something to me, Lilah. Something I never expected. Something I'm not real sure what to do about."

A long breath staggered into her lungs and she wasn't sure if it was his touch or his words having this effect on her. And she didn't care. "I know," she said, swallowing hard. "I feel the same way."

His jaw clenched and his finger curled into his palm. Then he let his hand drop to her lap and Lilah groaned, closing her eyes, concentrating only on the feel of him. Even through the fabric of her emerald-green skirt, his hand was warm, strong. His fingers played on her thigh and she leaned her head against the seat back, trying not to move.

"Finally," he whispered and she opened her eyes long enough to see the light had turned green. Instantly, the car jumped forward and while Kevin steered the car through traffic with one hand, he used the other to begin the seduction they'd both waited for.

His fingers inched up the hem of her skirt and she felt the soft fabric sliding up her calves, across her knees and up her thighs. And when he stroked her bare flesh, she almost came off the seat. The lightest of touches, the gentlest of caresses, tingled her skin and set off a string of fireworks in her bloodstream.

"How much farther?" she asked and thought she sounded pretty good, considering the fact that she couldn't breathe.

"Couple of blocks."

"Too far."

"Yeah." His hand came down on her thigh and she felt as though his palm had branded her with the heat pouring from his body into hers. Then he slid his hand higher up, to the very heart of her. Her own heat seemed to call to him and he cupped her, pressing his fingers tight against her center. Lilah fought the constraints of the darn seat belt, lifting her hips into his touch, wriggling against his hand, creating a delicious friction that shimmered along her nerve endings.

"Soon, baby," he ground out tightly.

"Soon," she said, clinging to that one word as if it were a life raft bouncing on a churning sea. Her mind raced, her heart pounded and then he touched her again, this time dipping his fingers beneath the elastic band of her panties.

She gasped and let her legs fall apart, opening for him, welcoming him. She wanted to feel it all again. Experience that wild rush to completion that he'd shown her just a few days ago.

Cars flowed past them. Streetlamps became a blur of yellowish light flying by the car like streamers in the wind. The night crowded in around them, making the inside of Kevin's car a refuge—a private retreat where only they mattered. Only the next touch. The next kiss. The next unspoken promise.

His fingertips stroked her and Lilah felt herself

quickening. Just like the last time, it wouldn't take long. She grabbed hold of the armrest and braced herself for the explosion she felt coming.

But Kevin pulled his hand free with a muttered curse and before she could moan her disappointment, he turned his car into the driveway. "We're here," he said, and shot her a quick, desperate look.

"Then why are we still in the car?" she asked and yanked at the door handle, swinging the door wide.

"Right." He climbed out of the car and was to her side before she'd righted her skirt. Holding out one hand to her, he helped her up, slammed the door and stalked toward his front porch, keeping a tight grip on her hand.

Lilah's breath felt strangled in her chest. Her heartbeat thudded painfully against her rib cage. Her legs were weak and her insides seemed to be pitching and rolling. She'd never felt so wonderful.

He had the door unlocked and open in a matter of seconds and still it wasn't fast enough. He drew her inside and just as the front door swung closed again, Kevin pulled her close and claimed her in a back-bending, mind-boggling kiss.

His hands were everywhere. She felt surrounded by him, enveloped in his strength, his warmth. Desire swamped her, dragging her down even as he took her higher, higher.

"I have to be inside you, Lilah," he whispered

and his words dusted across her skin, spilling goose bumps along her spine.

"Oh, yes," she said, tearing her mouth from his and tipping her head to one side, inviting his kisses along her neck. His lips trailed across her flesh, tasting, exploring, driving her closer to the brink of madness and she didn't want him to stop. She never wanted him to stop.

"Come with me," he murmured, close to her ear.

She nodded and stumbled after him as he drew her down the hall and into his bedroom. She didn't see the room. Couldn't see anything beyond his eyes, looking at her, devouring her.

Hands moved in a blur of motion and in a breath of time, they were naked, flesh to flesh, strength to slim, hard to soft. Her breasts ached for his touch and when he lifted her, scraping her nipples gently against his chest, she moaned softly before meeting his kiss again.

He laid her down on the mattress and covered her with his body. Her body hummed for him. Her legs parted and he came down between them, positioning himself to take her and Lilah held her breath. At last, she thought. At last, she would leave the virgin crown behind her and know what it was to be with a man completely.

And all she could think was thank heaven she'd waited. Thank heaven that this moment, with this man, was as special as she'd always dreamed it would be.

"I need you, Lilah," he said, through clenched teeth.

"Now, Kevin," she whispered brokenly, staring up into his eyes, willing him to see her need. "For pity's sake, now."

"Yes," he assured her and pushed himself home.

Instantly, Kevin felt as though he was drowning in her heat. She filled him up, easing away the dark shadows inside him, lighting up every corner of his heart and soul. He felt invincible and yet humbled. Here, in her arms, was the world. A world he'd never thought to find again and now that he had, he never wanted to lose it.

He rocked his hips against hers, relishing the sweet torture of her body cradling his. He looked down into her eyes and saw the past, present and future and wondered if it had always been there. If he simply hadn't seen it before because he'd been too afraid to look.

Then she reached up, entwining her arms around his neck, pulling him down, offering her mouth for his kiss and he took all she offered. Giving her all he had.

Lilah felt the first tremor rock her soul and it was more, so much more than what she'd felt that day in his arms. It built slowly, wonderfully, teasing her with its nearness and then backing away again, continually urging her on. She labored for it. Worked for it, moving her body with his, finding a rhythm and keeping it. She luxuriated in the feel of his body actually *inside* hers and silently told herself to remember it all. Every touch. Every kiss. But she knew she would remember. This night would be etched in her memory for all time. Even when she was old and gray, she would be able to reach back and remember exactly what it had been like to feel Kevin's body pushing into hers.

And then it was upon her and all thought ended. Tiny splinters of light and heat rocketed throughout her body as she clung to him, riding the wave of sensation that carried her beyond anything she'd ever known.

Kevin sent her over the edge, and when the tremors eased and her eyes glazed, he surrendered to his own need and found a completion he'd never felt before in the arms of the one woman he couldn't have.

Chapter Eleven

When her brain unfogged, Lilah said the first thing that popped into her head. "Wow. That was *way* better than I expected."

Kevin rolled to one side, bringing her with him until she lay stretched out atop him. "Just what I was thinking," he said and pulled her head down for a kiss. After a long, satisfying moment, he said, "But that was just for starters."

Lilah's heart skipped. "There's more?"

"Oh, yeah."

Instantly, heat flooded her and she was more than ready to go on that wild ride again. Boy, once the whole virgin thing was behind you, a person could really catch on quick. "Well don't just lay there,

Marine," she said, "if there's a job to be done, get on with it."

"Ma'am, yes, ma'am," he said with a grin and flipped her over onto her back.

A whoosh of air escaped her at the unexpected movement, and a moment later, she was breathless for an entirely different reason. He bent his head to her breasts and as she watched, he took first one, then the other nipple into his mouth.

Her stomach twisted and her lungs collapsed. Over and over again, his mouth worked her erect nipples. His lips and tongue tormented her, sending her on a roller coaster ride of sensation. His left hand swept down the length of her body, his calloused palm scraping gently against her skin. She gulped for air and when he suckled her, she groaned and arched into him.

"Oh, my," she said on a sigh. Holding his head to her breast, she writhed beneath him, giving herself up to the amazing feelings he evoked within her. Bright colors flashed behind her eyes and she felt as though the world was exploding around her. Too many sensations. Too much pleasure. She fought for breath and when it didn't come, she didn't even mind. All she needed—all she wanted—was Kevin's mouth on her breasts.

Moonlight dusted the room with a silvery light that seemed to shimmer around them. Except for the ragged sounds of their breathing, the world was silent. As if it belonged only to the two of them. And in the dim light, Lilah almost believed it did. There was only Kevin, looming over her, taking her places she'd never dreamed existed. There was only this night. This place. This wonder.

His hand swept lower, across her abdomen, beyond the triangle of soft, blond hair to the secrets beyond. And with his first touch, she felt herself dissolve. She puddled on the bed and wouldn't have been surprised if she had simply oozed off the mattress.

Love rose up inside her, strangling her with its sweet, unexpected beauty and she held him even tighter, hoping to keep him with her always. She wasn't sure when it had happened. Didn't care to figure it out. All she was sure of, was the fact that she loved him.

Kevin took his time with her. He reveled in the taste of her, the feel of her beneath him. He felt as though he'd been waiting for this moment a lifetime and now that it was here, he didn't want to waste any of it. Their first joining had been fire and frenzy. This time, there would be tenderness.

He felt her tremble and knew her body was as ready as his. He lifted his head to look down at her and saw the glazed sheen of passion clouding her blue eyes. Something inside him shifted, twisted, creating an ache that tore at his heart and raged at his soul.

She was so much more than he'd thought. So wild and open and beautiful. His heart trip-hammered in his chest and he knew for the first time that despite his reservations—despite the defenses he'd erected and defended so zealously—he loved her.

"Please, Kevin," she said, lifting her hips into his touch. "Please." She licked dry lips, caught his face in her hands and whispered, "Be inside me. Complete me again."

A hard, tight fist clenched at his heart and Kevin couldn't speak. Didn't trust himself to be able to form words. Instead, he only nodded and moved over her, positioning himself between her legs, covering her body with his and laying siege to her one more time.

He entered her on a soft sigh of fulfillment. This is where he belonged. With her. In her. A part of her. Always. He felt the *rightness* of it and sent a silent thank you to whatever Fate had brought them to this point.

There was no past, no future. There was only now. And Lilah.

Her legs and arms came around him, enveloping him in her warmth. He held her tightly, watching her eyes, staring down into her soul and as the first tremors began to course through her, he surrendered to the inevitable himself. Cradling her, he went with her as she took that long plunge into oblivion.

She cried out his name and Kevin clung to the sound of her voice as the world around him fell away.

* * *

When the room stopped spinning, Lilah stared up at the darkened ceiling and smiled to herself. Running her hands up and down his back, she realized that he was as unmovable as a dead man.

"Strange," she said quietly, "you're exhausted and I feel like I have enough energy to run a marathon. If I enjoyed running, that is. Which I don't, because really, what's the point? Why would anyone run unless someone was chasing them with a knife or something?"

He laughed shortly, the sound muffled against her throat. Then slowly, he lifted his head, looked down at her and asked, "Absolutely nothing shuts you up, does it?"

She grinned. Hard to be insulted when you were just feeling so darn good. "Nope."

"Didn't think so," he said, still smiling.

Lilah studied his face and lifted one hand to trace the line of his jaw with her fingertips. He turned into her touch, brushing his lips against her hand and she shivered just a bit. "I have to say this," she said, meeting his gaze and holding it. "Even if your ego blows up to the size of Cleveland."

He propped himself up on one elbow, but made no move to disentangle their bodies. And she was glad of that. She wasn't quite ready yet to lose the feel of his weight atop her.

Staring down at her he said, "Well now, I'm intrigued."

"Thought you might be." She shifted just far enough so that she could rub one foot up and down his leg, enjoying the closeness. "It's just that, I waited a long time for this night and I want you to know that you made losing my virginity a real event."

"What?"

She sensed the change in him more than felt it. He hadn't moved. Hadn't even shifted position, and yet, it suddenly seemed that he was far out of her reach.

"Well heck," she said, "I didn't mean that as an insult."

"You were a virgin?"

She blinked up at him. "Yep. You and me. The Drill Instructor and the Doomed Virgin. Well, until tonight, that is. You mean you couldn't tell?"

"No, I couldn't tell."

"Well that's disappointing." In every book she'd ever read, the hero *always* noticed a thing like that.

"Disappointing?" His voice was a low rumble of sound and as he rolled off of her, she felt the coldness begin to seep into her bones. "It's crazy. What the hell's the matter with that fiancé of yours?" As soon as he said that word, he groaned. "Fiancé. Dammit, you're engaged. Engaged *and* a virgin. This never should have happened."

Guilt pooled inside her and Lilah cringed. She'd known this moment would have to come, but now didn't seem like the right time for it. On the other hand, what better time?

"Actually," she said, sitting up and reaching for the blanket he'd tossed to the end of the bed. Clutching it to her, she swung her hair out of the way and said, "There's something else I should tell you."

He shot her a look from the corner of his eye. "What else could there possibly be?"

"I'm not really engaged," she blurted and watched his face to judge his reaction. Funny, but she'd expected anger—followed by the pleasure of knowing that she was free and able to love him. She hadn't expected the cold fury that slowly crept over his features, obliterating any lingering tenderness.

"You're not—"

"Engaged, no." Then she started talking, instinctively knowing that she had to get it all said. Quick. Before he stopped listening altogether. "See, I was just trying to get my father off my back. Get him to quit trying to set me up with Marines." He didn't speak, so she went on in a rush. "So I told him I was engaged to Ray. But Ray isn't my fiancé. He's my friend. And actually he's gay, too."

A muscle in his jaw twitched. "You have a gay fiancé?"

She nodded. "And Ray's partner, Victor, wasn't any happier about the idea than you seem to be."

"So you lied."

"Lied seems harsh."

"But true."

"All right, yes." She flinched at his harsh tone. A bitter pill to swallow. Ordinarily, she didn't believe in telling lies. She lifted one hand to push her hair back again and the faint, tinkle of bells broke the silence before she said, "I want you to know, I never lie. Usually. It's bad for the karma and besides, it just gets too tiring, trying to remember which lie you told to which person. Much easier to just tell the truth." She blew out a breath and sucked in a new one. "I feel so much better now that you know."

"Great," Kevin muttered, and rolled off the bed, energized by the rush of anger pulsing inside him. Emptiness opened up inside him and the warm glow of completion he'd felt so brief a time ago was gone. Crushed under the knowledge that he'd done it again. Picked another woman who was ready to lie and cheat to get what she wanted. Damn he was an idiot. Even monkeys learned from their mistakes.

"Kevin?"

Her voice sounded small, distant. Only moments ago, he'd been ready to admit his love for her. Now all he could think to do was get her dressed and the hell away from him.

"I'm glad you feel better," he said, turning for a look at her even as he grabbed his pants up from the floor. Even now, even knowing that she'd lied, he still felt a hard, solid jolt just looking at her. Her hair tumbled around her shoulders and in the drift of moonlight spilling through the window, it looked nearly silver. Her eyes were wide and even in the half light, he read the hurt glimmering there. It jabbed at him, but did nothing to ease the ache that seemed to sink right into his bones.

His hands clenched on the waistband of his jeans and as he stepped into them, he kept his gaze fixed on her. "Get dressed. I'm taking you home."

"Home? But I thought we—"

"Look," he snapped, reaching for a sweatshirt lying on a nearby chair. "Let's just forget all about tonight, all right?"

"Forget about it?" she repeated, clambering off the bed, still holding the stupid blanket to her chest like some sort of shield. "I don't want to forget about it. I lo—"

"Don't." He cut her off, holding one hand up to keep her from finishing that sentence. Man, if she said she loved him, he wasn't sure what he'd do. He'd been close. So close to something he hadn't thought he'd find. Now that it was gone, the ache of it tore at him. And he wanted to hurt her in return. Wanted her to know the pain that was rising and falling inside him with every breath he took. "I don't want to hear it." Wouldn't hear it. He towered over her, leaning in until she had to tilt her head back to keep from slamming her forehead into his. "You lied to me."

"Yes, but—"

"You used me. Just like Alanna." A short, harsh

laugh shot from his throat and the sound of it stabbed at Lilah's heart. Pain rippled through her as she watched him look at her as though she was a stranger.

"I'm nothing like her," she argued.

"No?" He pulled the sweatshirt over his head and jammed his arms through the sleeves. "She lied to me to get into this country." He paused for the greatest effect, then said the one thing he knew would cut at her. "You lied to me to get laid."

Lilah sucked in a gulp of air that fed the outrage and guilt erupting inside her. Before she could say anything though, he went on.

"I've been suckered again," he said and reaching out, chucked her chin with one finger. This pain went so deep, cut so wide, he didn't think he'd be able to draw breath much longer. Strange, he told himself. This kind of thing should get easier with practice. But it didn't. His only defense now was to act as though it didn't matter. To not let her know just how badly this hurt. He steeled himself, forced a smile that felt as cold as it looked and said, "Thanks, honey, for reminding me what a lousy judge of character I really am."

He should have known she wouldn't take this lightly.

Lilah smacked his hand away, stepped up to him and jabbed her index finger into his chest as if it were a bayonet and she could simply skewer him. "I resent that. Don't you dare compare me to that treacherous bitch you married. All I did was tell a simple lie to placate my father. Somehow, you got drawn into it and for that, I'm sorry. But I am *not* Alanna."

"And lying to your father makes you a great person?"

"No, but—" she swallowed hard. "It doesn't put me in the same class as your ex-wife."

"Close enough."

"If you think that, then you are an idiot."

"Lady," he said, bending down to scoop up her clothes from the floor, "we finally agree on something." He tossed her stuff at her and headed for the bedroom door, snatching up his shoes as he went. "I'm taking you home. Now. And by the way, maybe it's time you talked to your father like the adult you claim to be. Tell him the truth for a change. Then you won't end up suckering the next poor Marine who gets stuck with escort duty."

Tears stung the backs of her eyes, but she blinked them back, refusing to let them fall. Instead, she lifted her chin and watched him as he stepped through the doorway. So she saw the look of disgust on his face when he glanced back at her and added, "If you need any more escorting the rest of the time you're on base, find someone else. I'm through being used by the Forrest family."

She stepped into her father's house and slammed the door, but it didn't help. And she was pretty sure nothing would.

"Lilah?"

The Colonel came around the corner of the living room and stopped just in the foyer, looking at her. His gaze narrowed and he frowned. "Are you all right?"

"No." Shaking her head, she wondered if she'd ever be all right again. Pain splintered through her, like broken glass, sending millions of tiny shards of misery to every corner of her body and soul.

Hard to believe that only an hour ago, she'd been wrapped in Kevin's arms silently planning their future.

"What is it?"

Lilah looked at her father and said the words she'd wanted to say to the man who'd practically pushed her out of his car a moment ago. "I love Kevin Rogan."

A grin touched his face briefly then disappeared. "And yet you've been crying. Am I going to have to kill Gunnery Sergeant Rogan?"

"No," she said on a half laugh at the ridiculousness of the idea.

"Then everything's all right," her father said. "You'll be breaking up with the little artsy guy, right?"

"Oh, Dad," she said, walking up to him and taking both his hands in hers. "I was never engaged to Ray. He's my friend. Plus," she added, "he's gay."

Confusion flashed across his features, followed

quickly by a dawn of realization. "So you lied to me," he said tightly.

Disgusted, she said, "Boy I can't hear enough of that tonight." She let him go and wrapped her arms around her middle. Shaking her head, she swallowed hard and said, "Karma. I knew that lying wasn't healthy. But who knew it would create such a hideous mess?" Lilah grabbed the amethyst hanging from the chain around her neck and held on tight, squeezing the stone as if she could eke out any healing powers that might be locked in the cool, purple quartz.

"What are you talking about? Why did you lie to me about Ray?" He took her hands in a firm grip. "What's going on around here?"

Lilah flashed him an irritated glance. "It's really your fault, Dad."

"Excuse me?" Both eyebrows lifted into high arches and he gave her a look she hadn't seen since she was sixteen and had crashed his car into the garage. "You lie to me and it's *my* fault?"

Tears blinded her momentarily, but she blinked them back and stood her ground. "Kevin was right about one thing anyway," she said. "It *is* time to tell you the truth."

"I'm all for that," he said, drawing her into the living room. He took a seat and said, "Talk."

So she did. She told him everything. How she'd felt his disappointment over the years. How she knew that she wasn't the kind of daughter he wanted. She let him in on every one of the fears and insecurities that had dogged her for years and by the time she finally ran down, Lilah was exhausted.

Lying wasn't good for the soul, but truth could be very grueling.

"I love you so much, Dad, but I'm tired," she finished, and heard her voice break. There'd been too many emotions tonight, she thought. Too many heartbreaks. "So tired of you always trying to make me something I'm not. Why can't you just love me the way I am—crystals, incense, scented candles and all?"

A long minute of silence passed with her father staring at her as if he'd never seen her before. Lilah braced herself but was still shaken when he spoke.

Pushing himself out of the chair, he crossed to her, placed both hands on her shoulders and said, "Lilah, I do believe that is the *dumbest* thing you've ever said to me."

Her mouth dropped open but before she could speak, he continued.

"I have loved you from the moment the Navy doctor laid you in my arms," he said, his gaze boring into hers, willing her to believe. "You looked up at me with eyes so much like your mother's, you stole my heart and you've had it ever since."

Lilah actually felt years of secret sorrows melting away, but she had to say one more thing, no matter what it cost her. "Daddy, I know you always wanted a boy. A Marine."

He laughed and shook his head, reaching out to take her face between his hands. "I wanted a Mustang convertible, too, but that doesn't mean I didn't like driving a jeep."

"What?"

"Oh, Lilah, honey," he said, pulling her into the circle of her arms and holding her as he had when she was a child, "I wouldn't trade one of your silver toe rings for a son. You're all I ever wanted, sweetie. I love you."

Finally, the tears that had threatened all night spilled free and she let them come. For the first time in years, Lilah felt completely secure in her father's arms. Completely loved. And as his hands smoothed up and down her back in comforting stroked, she nestled in close, held him tight and asked, "Dad, how am I ever going to convince Kevin that I love him?"

His sigh ruffled her hair. "Ah, honey, I just don't have an answer for that one."

Neither did she.

Chapter Twelve

Three days.

Three days without her and it felt like a year.

Kevin cursed under his breath and told himself to keep his mind on the recruits. His gaze scanned across the different squads drilling on the field and while one corner of his brain kept time with them and their instructors, another corner was somewhere else entirely.

As it had so often in the last few days, his mind turned to that last night with Lilah. Instantly, memories of holding her, loving her rose up inside him and damn near strangled him with their power. But just as suddenly, he turned his mental back on them, preferring to remind himself how that night had ended. With shouts. With the sharp slap of betrayal. With slamming doors and banked tears.

His insides shifted and he folded his arms across his chest, lowered his chin and peered out at his world from beneath the wide brim of his D.I. cover. To look at him, no one would guess anything in his life had changed. And that's just how he wanted it. He wasn't the kind to wear his heart on his sleeve. He didn't want to moan to his friends or whine to his family. And he damn sure didn't want to be the hot topic of conversation on base again. Been there, done that.

What he wanted to do was forget that night had ever happened.

But his body wasn't about to let him get away with that. And neither was his heart.

"Dammit," he muttered, doing a quick about-face and striding toward the lot where his car was parked. He needed to get off base for a while. And since he was still officially on leave, he'd do just that. Clear his head. See his family. Maybe then he'd get a little peace.

Maybe then he could forget the sound of the musical bells Lilah wore on her wrist. But it wouldn't be that easy, he thought. Already, he missed hearing her voice, her laughter. He missed seeing the way her eyes lit up when she was excited about something. And damned if she didn't get excited over the dumbest things, he thought with a wry smile that faded as quickly as it was born.

He unlocked his car, slid onto the seat and buckled the belt. There was an emptiness inside him now that yawned wide with a blackness more terrible than anything he'd ever felt before. And Kevin knew that only Lilah could fill that void.

Steering his car toward the main gates, he shot a glance at the street leading to Colonel Forrest's house and had to fight his own instinct to turn onto it. Driving past, he tightened his grip on the wheel, clenched his jaw and told himself to get over it.

"You can't get over this that easy," Kelly said, once he'd taken a seat in her small, toy-strewn living room.

"Watch me," he said and congratulated himself on keeping his voice more firm than he felt.

"Just like that?"

He shot his sister a look that clearly told her to knock it off. Naturally she didn't pay the slightest bit of attention to it. Before she could get going again though, he said tightly, "Back off, Kel."

"Sure," she said, handing him a baby bottle filled with juice. As he offered it to Emily, she went on. "I'll stay out of it, just like you did when Jeff and I were having problems."

"That was different," he grumbled, keeping his gaze locked on his niece's beautiful face.

"Yeah," his sister said, "different because it was me, not you."

"Damn right."

"You sure talk a tough game."

"I'm not the one playing games," he said, flicking her a quick look, "that would be Lilah."

Kelly leaned back in her chair, crossed her arms over her chest and gave him the glare that told him he was in for either a fight or a lecture. Turns out it was the lecture.

"You're an idiot, Kevin."

"Hey…"

"Ever since Alanna, you've been shut down inside. You locked yourself away because that woman sucker punched you."

"Let it go, Kelly."

"Why?" she asked. "You haven't."

Yes, he had. Once Lilah had captured his mind and heart, Alanna had become nothing more than a bad memory. He was a different man, now. And a lot of that was due to Lilah. Dammit. He'd trusted her. "This is about Lilah. She lied to me."

"She lied to her father," Kelly pointed out. "You got sucked in."

"God, you sound just like her."

"She called today."

His heartbeat thudded. "You?"

"No, the mailman. He told me about it."

He gave her a tight smile. "What did she want?"

"To say goodbye." Kelly watched him as she

said, "She's going home tomorrow. Back to San Francisco."

He wouldn't have thought it possible, but that emptiness inside him blossomed until it felt as though he was being swallowed by darkness. She was leaving.

"And let me tell you something, big brother," Kelly was saying and he heard her voice as if from a distance. "If you lose the best thing that ever happened to you, because of the worst thing…then you'll deserve exactly what you get."

Next morning, Lilah sat outside Kevin's apartment, staring at the emerald-green door, trying to imagine what he was doing inside. Cursing her? Missing her?

She'd waited three days, giving him every opportunity to come to her. To tell her that he understood.

But he hadn't come.

She clutched the amethyst hanging around her neck and told herself she should just go on to the airport. Get on the plane and go back to her life. Obviously, he wasn't interested. What they'd shared these last couple of weeks—and the other night—didn't mean anything to him. At least not what it had meant to her.

But she didn't believe that. Not really.

"Lady?" the cab driver half turned in his seat and looked at her. "We staying or going?"

"He should have come," she said. "The least he could have done was come over to shout at me."

"Right."

She met the cabbie's disinterested gaze. "I mean, if a person cares about another person and that person lies to the person then shouldn't the person at least care enough to tell the person how they feel?"

His brow furrowed. "Huh?"

"Never mind." She grabbed the door handle and yanked it. "Wait for me, okay?"

She climbed out of the cab, stalked up the driveway, her long skirt flapping about her legs, the bells at her wrist keeping time. When she reached his door, she stepped up onto the porch and, loud enough to wake the dead, rapped her knuckles against the door.

When it was wrenched open, she almost stumbled backward. Kevin looked fierce. Barefoot, he wore faded jeans that were ripped at the knee. Whisker stubble shadowed his cheeks, his eyes looked wild and the red Marine T-shirt he wore looked as if he'd slept in it. But a closer look at his bloodshot eyes told her he hadn't been sleeping at all.

That was something, she supposed.

She stared at him for a long minute, and felt her heartbeat stagger. Her first instinct was to go to him, put her arms around him, hold him. But an instant later, she shoved her hormonal reaction to one side and pushed past him, marching into the apartment. Breath quickening, mouth dry, she kept walking until she was in the middle of the living room. Then she turned to face him as he followed after her.

It was so hard to be here again. To be with him and still be alone. Why couldn't he just see that she'd never meant to lie to him?

"I'm leaving," she blurted, hoping to see some reaction in his eyes.

"I know."

Pain slammed home and weakened her knees. He'd known she was leaving and still he hadn't come to her? "And you were just going to let me go?"

He opened his mouth, but she spoke up quickly, not entirely sure she wanted to hear his answer.

"Fine. You know I'm leaving. But there's something you don't know. And I came here to tell you. I love you," she said and relished the taste of the words on her tongue. She'd given up hope of ever being able to say those three simple little words. And now that she had, the feeling was bittersweet.

"Lilah…"

"No," she said, lifting one hand and only half listening to the chime of the bells around her wrist. "You had a chance to say what you wanted to."

"When was that?"

"The last three days," she snapped, giving in to

the temper rising within. "I waited for you. Thought you'd come. But you didn't."

He shoved one hand along the side of his head, then let it drop to his side again. He looked miserable. Well, good.

Tipping her chin up, she straightened to her full, less than impressive height and said, "I'm sorry I lied. I should have told you the truth. But the lie really didn't have anything to do with you—at first." She started pacing, needing to move, needing to do *something*. "And by the time it *did* concern you, well, it was too late to tell you without proving myself a liar."

"You did lie."

"And you never have?" she snapped a furious look at him. "Saint Kevin, is that it? You've never made a mistake?"

"Yeah, I made a big one a couple years ago," he reminded her.

"Oh, right," she said, nodding. "You trusted the wrong woman and now you don't want to trust the right one. Clever."

"Look, Lilah,"

"I'm not finished," she said hotly.

Kevin could only watch her, fascinated. She was so full of fire. Full of the life she'd brought into his world. Just marching up and down in his tiny living room, Lilah Forrest made the whole place seem bigger, warmer.

Seeing her again, here, in his house, made him want to grab her, hold on to her and never let her go. Her blue eyes flashed with indignation, words kept spilling from her mouth in a tumbling stream. Dammit, she was magnificent, he thought and knew without a doubt that he couldn't let her leave him. He had to be with her. Had to be a part of her life. But she was still on a tear and wouldn't give him the chance to say so.

"I talked to my father," she was saying. "Really talked. You were right about that. So thanks. Things are...*good* between us for the first time in a long time."

"I'm glad." And he was. He didn't want her hurting. Ever.

She stopped suddenly and stared at him through narrowed eyes. Hands at her hips, the toe of one suede boot tapping against his floor, she said, "You're glad now, but soon, you're going to be sorry."

"About what?"

"You'll regret letting me go, Kevin," she said, meeting his gaze and holding it. "And you know why? Because you love me, that's why."

He opened his mouth to agree, but there was no stopping her. Frustration simmered inside, but a part of him was really enjoying hearing her argue for their love.

"If I leave, you'll miss me forever." Folding her arms across her chest, she continued. "And once

I do leave, it'll be too late for you to change your mind. So you have to decide now, Kevin. Right this minute. Are you going to let me walk out of your life because of something stupid? Or do you want to admit you love me—because I know darn well you do—and take a chance on what we could find together?" Pulling in a long, deep breath, she said simply, "Decide."

That decision had probably been made from the first moment he'd seen her, Kevin thought. He hadn't stood a chance. Not from the beginning. And to prove it to both of them, he stepped forward, yanked her into his arms and lifted her clean off the floor before kissing her long and hard and deep.

When he was fairly sure that she was dazed enough to keep quiet for a minute or two, he lifted his head and stared directly into her eyes. "I *do* love you."

"Hah! I knew it!" She wrapped her arms around his neck and grinned at him.

"My turn to talk," he told her and tightened his grip around her waist. "I didn't plan on loving you. Didn't want to."

"Gee, thanks."

"Is kissing you the only way to keep you quiet?" he muttered, then kept talking before she could answer that. "I don't *just* love you though," he said. "I need you. I've been up all night thinking about this, Lilah. And dammit, I *need* you. Need you to light incense and hang crystals. Need to help you with all of the charities you've got running. Need you to be the chaos in my *way* too boring life." He planted a quick, light kiss on her mouth and added, "You've given me laughter. You've given me a new life. And I can't stand the thought of losing it or you."

She smiled at him and a single tear escaped the corner of her eye to roll along her cheek. "Oh, Kevin…"

"*But,*" he said, knowing that this was important, too. "I'm a Marine, Lilah and I can't change that. Won't change that. It's who I am. It's as much a part of me as you are."

"I know that," she said.

"Are you sure you're willing to reenter a world that didn't make you happy before?"

Another tear joined the first, but she nodded fiercely and gave him that blinding smile that he would never tire of seeing.

"It wasn't the military that made me unhappy, Kevin," she said and stroked his cheek, sending tendrils of warmth into a heart that had been like ice for three long days and nights. "It was trying to be something I wasn't. And as long as you love me for who I am, I'll always be happy."

"Who you are," he said, "is exactly *why* I love you. Never change, Lilah. I'm actually getting to be pretty fond of chaos."

"Then kiss me, Gunnery Sergeant," she said,

holding him tightly enough that he knew he'd never be lonely again, "and let's start talking weddings."

"My suggestion?" he whispered, bending his head to taste her neck, her jaw, the corner of her mouth, "small and fast."

"Good idea," she murmured, tipping her head to one side, to allow him access. Then, just to tease him a little and prepare him for their life together, she said, "You know, I've been thinking about starting a petition."

"For what?" his voice came muffled against her throat.

"I think maybe it's time the Marines stopped using such a dreary green for their uniforms." She paused for effect. "I'm thinking maybe a bright, cheerful red."

He pulled his head back and stared at her, appalled. Then when he saw her smile, he laughed aloud and said, "If anyone can bring it off honey, it's you."

Her heart filled until it felt as though it might burst from her chest. And as she pulled his head closer, she said, "Forget it. The only Marine I'm interested in is the one who'd better start kissing me, quick."

"Ma'am, yes, ma'am," he said and lowered his mouth onto hers.

A moment later, a car horn honked and Lilah pulled away. "The cabbie."

Guiding her mouth back to his, Kevin muttered, "Let him get his own girl."

Epilogue

Two months later...

The scent of sandalwood hung in the still air and Kevin smiled to himself. Candlelight flickered from nearly every corner of the room. And outside the bedroom window, delicate music lifted from the wind chimes dancing in the breeze.

Everything in his world has changed since meeting Lilah. And every night, he thanked God for it. He couldn't even remember anymore what it had been like to live here alone. He didn't *want* to remember.

The bathroom door opened suddenly and a pie wedge slice of light fell across the bed. Going up on one elbow, he stared at Lilah silhouetted in the doorway and wished he could read her expression. But with the light dazzling all around her, that was just impossible.

"Well?" he asked when she didn't speak. "What's the verdict?"

Instead of answering, she flipped the light off, bolted across the room and jumped onto the bed. She straddled his hips and Kevin's body leapt into action, just as it always did when she was anywhere close. But there was something he had to know.

"Come on, Lilah," he said, voice tight, "out with it."

She laughed and the sound of it lifted up and settled down on him again like a gift. What had he ever done in his life to deserve such a woman?

Laying her palms against his chest, she leaned down, letting her hair fall like a dark blond curtain on either side of his face. She kissed him then. Tiny kisses scattered in between her words. Kiss. "The—" kiss "—verdict—" kiss "—is—" kiss "—*yes*." Big kiss.

"Yes?" he repeated, when she lifted her head to grin down at him. "You're sure?"

"Way sure," Lilah said. "Very sure. Totally sure."

His heart kicked into high gear and his hands at her waist tightened before easing up again just as quickly. "Sorry," he said, wincing and held her more carefully.

Lilah shook her head and felt her love for him rise up inside her like a tide. "I'm pregnant, Kevin," she said softly, "not made of glass."

"Yeah, I know," he said, "it's just—"

"New?" she asked, still relishing the results of her pregnancy test.

"Yeah, I guess so."

"You're happy though?" She had to know he was as happy as she.

"Definitely."

She squirmed on his lap and felt his body tighten beneath her. A slow smile curved her lips as a deep, delicious tingle began to build and grow within her. "Well," she said, wriggling again, harder this time, pressing her warmth against his strength, "you *feel* happy."

"Baby," he said on a groan, "you ain't seen nothing yet."

Going up on her knees, Lilah slowly, seductively, pulled her night shirt up and over her head, then tossed it aside. In the flicker of candlelight, she watched his eyes darken as he reached to cup her breasts in his palms. His thumbs and fingers tweaked at her nipples and she threw her head back even as she arched into him. Every night it was the same and yet always different. Each time he touched her, it was like the first time. Fires quickened within. Her body raced—hot and wet and eager for him.

And she hoped it was always this magical between them.

"I've got to have you," he murmured.

"You *do* have me, Marine," she whispered and slowly lowered herself down onto his body. Inch by glorious inch, she took him inside her. Tantalizing them both with her restraint, she watched his features tighten as he fought for control.

He dropped one hand to her center and while she eased down onto his arousal, he rubbed her damp, wet heat until she was swiveling her hips back and forth into his touch and moaning his name like a chant.

And then he was fully craddled within her. His body locked with hers. His soul entwined with hers. He touched her again, rubbing that one tight, sensitive spot, and Lilah exploded. Shivers wracked her body, and she called out his name and swayed with the convulsions ripping through her.

Kevin gripped her hips, arched up, pushing himself deeper into her warmth, then gave her everything he was.

As the last of the tremors eased away, Lilah slumped down across his chest and his arms came around her, holding her to him. Her breath dusted across his flesh and he counted it as yet another blessing.

"You know," she said softly, her voice muffled

with exhaustion, "I think I should warn you, I always wanted a big family."

He smiled to himself and planted a kiss on top of her head. "How big?"

"Oh," she said around a yawn as she snuggled even closer to him, "seven's a nice number, don't you think?"

Seven kids?

With Lilah?

His heart filled to bursting, he reached down for the blanket and drew it up to cover them both. "Seven would be perfect," he murmured and held her while she slept.

* * * * *

MARINE UNDER THE MISTLETOE

Chapter One

She recognized his attitude.

Marie Santini stared out through the front windows of her auto repair shop at the man standing in her driveway. It wasn't easy to get a good look at him, what with the holly and snowmen painted on the window glass, but she gave it a try. Tall, she thought, dark hair, cut short, aviator-style sunglasses even though the day was too cloudy to make them necessary, and a hard, strong jaw with a stubborn chin.

Perfect.

Just what she needed. Another male with a protective streak toward his car. Honestly. A woman's car broke down, she brought it into the shop and picked it up when it was ready. A *man* hovered over the blasted thing like it was a woman in labor, questioning everything Marie did to his baby and winced with sympathy pains.

Now, Marie Santini liked cars as much as anybody else, but she knew for a fact that they didn't bleed when operated on. Still, she told herself, business had been slow in the last week. Maybe she'd better just step outside and coax Mr. Nervous into the shop. She grabbed her navy blue sweatshirt, tugged it on and left it unzipped to display the slogan on her red T-shirt that read Marie Santini, Car Surgeon. Then she headed for the door.

"*This* is a *garage?*"

Davis Garvey stared at the small but tidy auto repair shop. Wide plank walls were painted a brilliant white, the window trim and the cozy-looking shutters were an electric blue and some kind of purple and white flowers blossomed enthusiastically in terra-cotta planters on either side of the front door. Off to the side, a garage bay stood, its double doors open to reveal what looked like a mile of Peg-Board on which hundreds of obviously well-cared-for tools hung from hooks and glittered in the overhead lights.

Except for the garage bay, the place looked more like a trendy little tea shop than anything else.

He'd expected something bigger. Showier, somehow. The way the marines at Camp Pendleton talked about this shop, he had thought the place would reek of money and experience. Yet the proof that he was in the right place was emblazoned across the front of the little building. A boldly painted sign in red, white and blue proclaimed Santini's.

He frowned, remembering the guys who had told him about this place. Their voices hushed almost reverently, they'd told him, "If Marie Santini can't fix your car, nobody can."

Still, Davis thought, the idea of a woman working on his car was a hard one to swallow. But with things at Camp Pendleton as busy as they were, he had no time to do the job himself.

A cold winter wind whistled off the nearby ocean, and he jammed his hands into the pockets of his faded, worn Levi's. Tipping his head back, he watched gray clouds bunching and gathering above and wondered what had happened to the sunny California he'd always heard about. Heck, he'd been at Pendleton a week and it had either rained or threatened to rain some more.

Then a door opened and Davis snapped his attention to the front of the shop and the woman just stepping outside. He watched her as she walked toward him. She had black, shoulder-length hair, tucked behind her ears to show off small silver hoops in her lobes, and she wore a red T-shirt tucked into worn jeans, tennis shoes and a dark blue zippered sweatshirt that flapped like wings in the wind. Taller than she looked at a distance, the top of her head hit him about at chin level when she stopped directly in front of him.

"Hi," she said, and gave him a warm smile that took away some of the afternoon chill.

"Hi," he said, and looked down into the greenest eyes he'd ever seen. Okay, he didn't know if Marie Santini knew anything about cars. But hiring this woman to welcome customers was definitely a good business move. Not pretty exactly, but she had the kind of face that made a person look twice. It was more than appearance. It was something shining in her eyes, something...*alive*.

A second or two passed before she asked, "Can I help you?"

Davis blinked and reminded himself why he was there. To find out if the "Miracle Worker" the guys had told him about was worthy to work on his car. And he couldn't do that until he actually met Marie Santini. He could always get to know the welcoming committee later.

"I don't think so," he said. "I'd like to see Marie Santini."

She blew out a breath that ruffled a few stray wisps of black hair, then said, "You're looking at her."

No way. "You?" he asked, letting his gaze rake her up and down, noting her slender build. "You're a mechanic?"

She shook her hair back from her face when the wind tossed it across her eyes. "Around here," she told him, "I'm *the* mechanic."

"You're Marie Santini?" When the guys had told him about a female mechanic, somehow he'd imagined a woman more along the lines of a German opera singer. Brunhilde.

She glanced down, unzipped her sweatshirt a bit wider, then looked up at him again. "That's what my shirt says."

"You don't look the part," he said, and wondered just how good she could be if she didn't even have grease under her fingernails. What did she do? Wear elbow-length white gloves for oil changes?

"You were expecting maybe Two-Ton Tessie covered in axle grease?" She folded her arms across her chest, and Davis told himself not to notice the curve of her breasts. For Pete's sake, he was interviewing a mechanic. Breasts shouldn't come into this at all!

"Sorry to shatter your expectations," she said, "but I'm a darn good mechanic."

"You sound pretty sure of yourself."

"I ought to be," she muttered. "I spend half my time proving myself to men just like you."

"What do you mean, men like me?"

"Men who assume a woman can't know more about cars than a man."

"Hey, wait a minute," he said, folding his arms over his chest and glaring down at her. Nobody called him a chauvinist and got away with it. Hell, he worked with women every day on base. Darn good marines, too, all of them. He didn't necessarily have a problem with a woman mechanic. He had a problem with *any* mechanic working on his cars. Hell, if he wasn't so busy at the base right now, he'd have fixed the car himself and never have met Marie.

"No," she interrupted, "*you* wait a minute." She shook her head and threw her hands high. "You came to me. I didn't hunt you down and demand to work on your car."

"Yeah," he said.

"So have you changed your mind?"

"I don't know yet."

"Well," she said, "why don't we find out?" She started past him toward the Mustang he'd left parked at the curb.

He was only a step or two behind her. "Are you this charming to all of your customers?"

"Only the stubborn ones," she told him over her shoulder.

"I'm surprised you're still in business," he muttered, deliberately keeping his gaze from locking on to the sway of her behind.

"You won't be once I've fixed your car."

If he didn't know better, he'd swear she was a marine.

Marie didn't even want to think about how many times she'd been through this conversation. Since taking over her father's auto shop two years ago, every new customer who'd entered the place had given her the same look of disbelief.

It had stopped being amusing a long time ago.

So why, she wondered, was she enjoying herself now?

She stopped alongside his Mustang and glanced up into his big blue eyes. An utterly feminine reaction swelled in the pit of her stomach and she tamped it down fast. Honestly, she'd seen broad shoulders and strong jaws before. Silently she reminded herself that he was here to see her as a mechanic—not a woman. Hardly a rarity. "Let me guess. You've never seen a woman mechanic before."

"Not lately," he admitted.

She had to give him credit. He was recovering from his surprise a lot more quickly than most of her customers. But then, she thought, *he* was a lot more...*everything* than most men. Broader shoulders, more muscular build, longer legs, a square, firm jaw, and those sharp blue eyes of his looked as though he could see right through her.

Which, she told herself with an inward sigh, most men did.

She'd learned years ago that men didn't see their mechanic as possible date material. Poker buddy, sure. A Dear Abby to the lovelorn, great. But a *real* woman? Prospective wife and mother-type female? No way.

"A first time for everything, Sergeant," she said.

His eyebrows shot up and Marie just managed to swallow a smile at his surprise.

"How'd you know I'm a sergeant?" he asked.

Not a difficult call for someone who'd grown up in Bayside. With Camp Pendleton less than a mile or so up the road, the little town was usually crawling with marines. They were easy enough to spot, even in civilian clothes.

"It's not hard," she said, enjoying his surprise. "Regulation haircut—" she paused and indicated his stance pointedly "plus you're standing like someone just shouted, 'At ease.'"

He frowned to himself, noting his feet braced wide apart and his hands locked behind his back. Deliberately he shifted position.

"Then," she went on, smiling, "as to your rank… You're too old to be a private, too ambitious or proud looking to still be a corporal and you don't appear nearly arrogant enough to be an officer. Therefore," she finished with a half bow, "sergeant."

Impressed and amused in spite of himself, Davis nodded. "First sergeant, actually."

"I stand corrected." Marie looked into those blue eyes of his and saw what she briefly thought might be interest. No. Probably just instinctive, she told herself. A man like him was no doubt accustomed to flirting with women. *All* women. "So," she said, getting a mental grip of her hormones, "what's the problem?"

"You're the mechanic," he challenged. "You tell me."

A spurt of irritation rushed through her. She should be used to this. He wasn't the first, nor would he be the last man to test her knowledge of cars before entrusting his "baby" to her care. Although, she admitted with pride, once she'd fixed a car, it stayed fixed. And her customer base was a loyal one.

"Why is it, do you think," she asked him, "that men can design dresses for a living and be respected while a woman mechanic has to do tricks to prove herself?" He opened his mouth to speak, but she went on instead. "Do you think anybody makes Calvin Klein thread a needle himself before hiring him?"

He shook his head. "No. But then if ol' Calvin sews a crooked hem, the dress doesn't blow up, does it?"

Okay, maybe he had a point.

"All right," she said, surrendering to the inevitable, "let's take it for a test drive, shall we? Keys?" She held out her hand and Davis looked at it for a long moment before lifting his gaze to hers.

"How about I drive?" he asked.

"Not a chance." She shook her head and gave him a sympathetic glance, but didn't budge otherwise. "I have to drive it to get the feel of it," she said. Then she pointed out, "besides, you'll have to trust me with it eventually."

That smile on her face was confident and entirely too attractive. To stifle that thought and any that might follow. Davis dropped his keys into her outstretched palm. Sliding into the passenger seat, he watched her buckle up, then turn the key in the ignition. The Mustang rumbled into life.

He glanced over his shoulder at the still-open auto shop. "Aren't you going to—?"

"Shh," she told him with a frown.

He was so surprised, he did. It had been a long time since anyone had told him to shut up.

Cocking her head toward the engine, she closed her eyes and listened with all of the concentrated effort of a doctor holding a stethoscope over her patient's chest.

A moment later, she opened her eyes, sat back and shoved the car into gear. "What were you saying?"

"Don't you want to lock your shop?"

"Won't be gone that long," she told him with a grin. Then she glanced over her left shoulder, stepped on the gas and pulled away from the curb with enough speed to launch them into space.

Davis fell back in his seat as Marie drove like she was in the lead car at the Indianapolis 500.

The beach town's narrow streets were crowded with shoppers and bedecked with holiday garlands and plastic candy canes. He winced as she threaded her way expertly in and out of traffic. She squeezed past a city bus with less than a single coat of paint to spare, then turned down an even narrower, one-way street.

A couple of people waved to her as she passed and she smiled a greeting, never really taking her eyes off the road. She worked the clutch, brake and gas pedals like a concert pianist, and Davis found himself staring at her long legs as her feet moved and danced across the car's floor.

With the convertible top down, ocean air whipped around them, sending Marie's hair into a wild, shining black tangle. It was the first time he'd ridden in a convertible with a woman who wasn't moaning about the state of her hairdo and pleading with him to raise the top.

She took the next corner practically on two wheels and darted between a surfboard-laden station wagon and an ancient Lincoln. Ahead, the signal turned from green to red without benefit of yellow and she slammed on the brakes. He jerked forward in his seat, thanked the Fates for seat belts and ground his teeth together.

Glancing at him, she said, "It's got a flat spot."

"What?" he asked, trying to unlock his jaw.

"The engine," she told him. "A flat spot when you step on the gas. It pauses, then catches."

"You're right," he acknowledged, and rubbed the whiplash feeling out of the back of his neck. "But how you even noticed a pause while driving at light speed is beyond me."

She laughed, and damned if he didn't enjoy the sound of it.

Before he could say so, though, the light turned green and she was off again.

People, cars and scenery became a colorful blur. Davis's grip on the armrest tightened until he thought he'd snap the vinyl-covered shelf clean off.

A few seconds later, she was parking the car in her driveway, shutting off the engine and giving the dashboard a loving pat. "Nice car," she said.

He inhaled slowly, deeply, grateful to have survived. Hell, he'd been in combat zones and felt more optimistic about living through the day.

Now that their mad rush through traffic was over, he turned his head and gaped at her. "You drive like a maniac."

She grinned, clearly unoffended. "That's what my dad used to say."

"Smart man," Davis managed to grind out. "How about I deal with him, instead?"

She sobered quickly. "I wish you could. But he passed away two years ago."

"Oh. Sorry." He heard the echo of pain in her voice and knew that she still missed him.

"You couldn't have known," Marie told him. "So," she added, "do you want me to fix this baby for you or not?"

Spotting a problem and knowing how to fix it were two different things. Besides, if her car-repair skills were as reckless as her driving, he could be asking for trouble here. "How do I know you *can* fix it?"

She leaned one forearm across the top of the steering wheel and shifted in her seat, turning to face him. "I guess you don't, Sergeant. You'll just have to take a chance."

"I just took enough chances for a lifetime."

Her grin widened. "I thought you marines liked a little risk now and then."

"Lady, I'm just glad you don't drive a tank."

"Me, too," she said, then added, "though I'd like to give it a try someday."

Davis laughed shortly. "I bet you would."

If he wasn't careful, he could get to like this woman. She was damned unusual, though. No open flirting. No coy smiles. Just confidence and a take-no-prisoners attitude. She had a great laugh, amazing eyes and a figure that would be able to thaw the polar ice caps. Damn, if he wasn't responding to her in a big way.

"So? Are you going to trust me with your baby?"

A challenge gleamed in her eyes and he automatically responded to it. But what marine wouldn't?

"Okay, Car Surgeon," he said, "you're on."

She nodded. "Come on into the shop, I'll write it up."

He watched her as she climbed out of the Mustang, cheeks flushed, eyes bright, her long, lean limbs carrying her in an easy stride toward the office. And Davis knew he'd never think of mechanics in the same way again.

Chapter Two

Marie felt his gaze on her as surely as she would have his touch. At *that* thought, a small shiver of anticipation rattled along her spine even as the still-rational corner of her mind told her to forget it.

Guys like him were never interested in women like her.

Behind her, she heard his car door open, then close. The soft crunch of his footsteps on the gravel drive heralded his approach. Her mouth went dry. Ridiculous. She was way too old to get butterflies just because some man gave her a second look. Some *gorgeous* man, she silently corrected. She stepped behind the counter, picked up a pen and started filling out the work order.

He walked into the office and stopped directly opposite her.

"So," she asked, with what she hoped was a professionally casual tone, "I need your name and address and a phone number where you can be reached."

He nodded and took the pen from her, his fingers brushing hers lightly in the process. Her skin tingled and she shrugged it off as static electricity. The fact that no one else had ever given her a spark like that in the office was beside the point. As he filled in the form, he asked, "How long is this going to take? I need my car."

Ah, she thought, there was definitely safety in sticking to business.

"Everybody does," she pointed out. "But I'm pretty open right now. Shouldn't take more than a couple of days."

He glanced at her. "You do all the work yourself?"

Was he still hoping there'd be a man overseeing her work? A bit defensive, she said, "Yes, it's just me. Well, except for Tommy Doyle who comes in three afternoons a week. Does that worry you?"

"That depends. Who's Tommy Doyle, and is he going to be working on my car?"

"Tommy's sixteen, and no, he's not." She waved one hand at the open doorway leading into the service bay. "He cleans up and gives me a hand sometimes."

His expression clearly said, "Keep that kid away from my car."

"Look, Sergeant—"

"Call me Davis."

Oh, she didn't think so. No point in getting on a first-name basis with the man. Better she keep this professional. As she knew it would stay. He might give her behind and her legs the once-over, but when it came right down to it, men just weren't interested in dating their mechanic.

"*Sergeant,* I can fix your car. If you want to leave it here, I can give you a loaner for a couple of days."

His eyebrows lifted. "A loaner?"

"Yeah," she said, knowing he was thinking that a business as small as hers wouldn't have anything so civilized as loaner cars. But she had a few. Of course, they didn't look like much, since she tended to buy old junkers and get them into running condition for just such situations. "You can take the Bug out there."

He glanced over his shoulder at the battered gray-and-red Volkswagen. Dents dotted its surface and splotches of primer paint made it look as though it had a skin condition.

She noted his expression and fought down a smile. "It's not a beauty," she admitted, "but it will get you back and forth to the base."

"Will it get me to a restaurant, too?" he asked, sliding his gaze back to her.

"Wherever you aim it, it will go," she assured him. "Though the valets at the Five Crowns might not want to park it for you."

Just the thought of her poor little Bug cruising up the elegant drive of the best restaurant on the coast brought a smile to her face. That smile faded when he spoke again.

"I was thinking more along the lines of that coffee shop I passed on my way here—if I could buy you some lunch."

Her stomach skittered nervously and she didn't like it. She much preferred being in control. And as long as she was being Marie the mechanic, she was. But heck, nobody ever asked her out. Men didn't usually look past her skills with tools to search for the woman within.

And now that it had happened, she wasn't real sure how to respond. So she settled for what felt natural—making a joke.

"At three o'clock in the afternoon?" She forced a laugh she didn't feel to let him know she wasn't taking him seriously and so he shouldn't worry about a thing. "A little late for lunch."

"And early for dinner," he agreed. "But they'd probably serve us anyway."

"Uh…thanks," she said, shaking her head and

taking the completed form from him. "But I've got work to do and besides, I don't date—"

"Marines?" he finished for her.

"Customers," she corrected, though if she wanted to, she could have told him her sentence had been pretty much complete the first time. She didn't date. Period. In fact, Marie couldn't remember the last time she'd had a real date.

No. Wait a minute. That was wrong. She could remember. She'd just made a conscious effort to forget the experience. As any sane woman would.

Two years ago it was, just before Papa died. And the night had ended early as soon as her date blew a tire. He didn't know how to fix the flat and had wanted to call the auto club. But since they were already late for the movie, Marie had fixed it herself.

Judging from her date's expression as he rolled past her house fifteen minutes later and practically shoved her out the door, she'd committed a sin the equivalent of a girl beating up the bully picking on her boyfriend.

"Well, then," he said with another of those slow smiles, "we'll just have to wait until my car is officially off your lot and I'm no longer a customer."

Where was all this coming from? she wondered. On the test drive, he'd looked like he wanted to strangle her. Now he's all smiles and invites? Why?

And why did that gleam in his eyes make her as

nervous as she'd been the first time she'd done a brake job on her own? Man. Spending your growing-up years in a garage with your dad really didn't prepare you much for the whole man-woman game.

"Is it a deal?" he asked.

She was saved from having to answer him by the sound of a car pulling into her driveway. Marie looked past Davis's shoulder and almost sighed with relief. The cavalry was here. Her little sister, Gina, could always be counted on to monopolize a conversation when a man was around.

Gina jumped out of her compact, slammed the door and ran across the gravel drive to the garage. Dressed in white jeans, a deep green T-shirt and girly sandals that were no more than tiny straps attached to paper-thin soles and completely inappropriate for the weather, she looked like an ad for summer in the middle of the Christmas season. Her short, dark brown hair curled around her head in careless waves that Marie knew took her sister at least an hour to create. Gina's brown eyes lit with undisguised interest as she spotted the sergeant.

"Hi, Marie," she said, never glancing at her sister. "I came to tell you we're going to miss all the good sales if you don't close up now."

Saved! She'd forgotten all about promising to take their nephew Christmas shopping. Grateful for an excuse to get Davis Garvey moving along, she said, "Right. I'll be ready in a second."

"Aren't you going to introduce me?" Gina practically purred, apparently forgetting about the big rush to leave. She didn't bother waiting for an introduction as she walked up to Davis, held her hand out like a Southern belle at a debutante ball and said, "Gina Santini. And you are…?"

"Davis Garvey." He took her hand briefly and gave her a distracted smile.

"You're a marine, aren't you?" Gina asked, smiling.

"That's right." He didn't even look surprised that she'd known his identity as easily as Marie had.

A part of Marie watched in envy as Gina turned on her charm. Honestly, she didn't know how her younger-by-two-years sister did it. Flirting came as easily as breathing to Gina. Her eyes narrowed thoughtfully as she noted the practiced moves. A light touch on Davis's arm. Flipping her hair back with a subtle movement. A ripple of laughter that floated out around them musically.

Marie had been witness to Gina's flirting hundreds of times over the years, and she'd always enjoyed watching the hapless target of her intentions stumble over his tongue. But for some reason, she didn't particularly want to see Davis Garvey reduced to a puddle of drooling male. In fact, for the first time ever, Marie felt a surprising spurt of resentment at her little sister's quick moves.

Honestly, you'd think the girl could have a little

self-control. Did she really have to make a conquest wherever she went?

At least though, Marie told herself, the sergeant wouldn't be pretending interest in *her*. Who would, when faced with Gina's more obvious charms?

But, he managed to surprise her again. Far from succumbing to Gina, Davis was actually looking *past* the tiny bundle of dynamite to stare at Marie instead.

A small curl of pure, feminine pleasure floated through her. And when she met Davis's steady gaze, that pleasant feeling thickened and warmed inside her. Good heavens, the man had amazing eyes. And the rest of him wasn't bad, either.

When Gina paused for breath, he said, "If you'll give me the keys to the loaner, I'll leave you my car and you can take off for your shopping."

"Okay." She should have been ashamed of herself. There was a small part of her that was really enjoying Gina's stunned surprise at being overlooked. Smiling, Marie opened a drawer and grabbed up a set of keys.

As he took the keys from her, his fingertips scraped the palm of her hand, sending new bolts of electricity along her nerve endings. Marie curled her fingers into a tight fist and fought to ignore the sensation.

It wasn't easy.

Smiling as if he knew just what she was feeling,

he dropped his own keys onto the workbench. "You'll take good care of my car?"

Did his voice really have to take on such an intimate note? Or was she reading more into it than he'd intended? Opting for the latter, and struggling to get her imagination under control, she quipped, "I'll sing it to sleep every night and tuck it in personally."

His eyebrows lifted and one corner of his mouth twitched. "Lucky car."

Her stomach flipped again. Oh, for heaven's sake.

"Two days?" he asked.

"Uh…yes. Two days."

"I'll see you then." Turning, he walked past Gina with a nod. Then he stopped, looked at Marie and said, "Think about lunch."

As he walked slowly to the Volkswagen, Gina stepped up beside her sister. Both women watched him as he fired up the little car and pulled out of the drive onto the street that would take him back to the base.

"Lunch?" Gina asked.

"Yeah."

"He asked you to lunch?"

Why did she say that in the same tone someone would ask, "You were abducted by aliens?"

"Yes, he asked me to lunch." She turned to glare at Gina. "Is that really so hard to believe?"

"'Course not," Gina said, giving her a pat on the shoulder. "You're going, aren't you?"

"No."

"Why not? He's gorgeous."

"He's a customer."

"That is so medieval." Gina crossed to the far corner of the counter, opened a drawer and pulled out one of the candy bars Marie kept stocked there. As she unwrapped the chocolate, she muttered, "You really need to get a life."

"I have a life, thanks." Marie told her and locked the connecting door to the service bay. Then she led her sister outside and walked to Davis's car. She had to pull it into the garage and lock it up. Wouldn't do to take chances with the sergeant's car. After she'd parked the Mustang alongside an ancient Fiat in for a brake job, she got out of the car to discover Gina still talking.

"Okay, then, at the very least, you need glasses. Did you see the way he looked at you?"

"He had to look at me to talk," Marie said briskly. "It's polite."

"Polite had nothing to do with it."

"Cut it out, Gina."

"Me?" She took a bite of candy and waved one hand in the air. "Heck, I gave him my best smile and even fluttered my big baby browns at him and it was like I wasn't there."

Marie smiled and shook her head. "Just because

you're slipping doesn't mean he was interested in me."

"Honey," Gina said, "any man who looks at you like that, despite the fact that you're a *mechanic* of all things, is *not* just being polite."

Pleasure whirled through Marie briefly at the thought. But a moment later, she firmly stomped it into oblivion. She wasn't going to play that game again. Convince herself that a man was interested in her. Indulge in daydreams and wicked fantasies and then have to pick her heart up off the garage floor when reality kicked in.

No, thanks. Been there, done that. Way too many times. Not lately, of course. But her memories of splintered crushes and hurt feelings were vivid.

"Honestly, Marie, don't you *like* men?"

"What's not to like?" she asked, again retreating into humor that was comfortable. Safe.

"Then for pity's sake, make an effort."

"What do you want me to do, little sister? Hit some guy over the head with a socket wrench and drag him into the garage?"

"A woman's gotta do what a woman's gotta do."

"Gina," she said as she keyed in the code in the electric alarm system, pushed her sister out the garage doors, closed them and firmly set the padlock in place, "give it a rest, okay? I'm perfectly happy. Believe it or not, you do not *need* a man to make your life complete."

"Doesn't hurt," Gina mumbled as she finished the candy and stuffed the wrapper into her jeans pocket.

Sure it did, Marie thought. It hurt plenty. Every time she took a chance, only to be flattened by the fist of love, it hurt.

"There's nothing—" she paused for effect "—repeat *nothing* going on here. The sergeant just wants his engine worked on."

Gina's eyebrows wiggled and she grinned at her sister. "I bet it's a real nice engine, too."

A heartbeat passed before Marie laughed. "Good God, girl," she said with a shake of her head, "take a pill. Your hormones are in overdrive again."

"Better overdrive than stalled."

This is what she had to put up with because she'd loaned her car to Mama. Putting up with Gina should be enough to curb future bouts of generosity.

"My hormones are just fine. Thanks for your concern."

"Sometimes, Marie," Gina said thoughtfully as they walked to her car, "I wonder if you even *have* hormones."

Oh, she thought as they pulled out of the driveway and headed toward home, she had them all right. At the moment, in fact, they were all standing straight up and screaming at her.

But she'd had a lot of practice at taming them, and she had no doubt she could do it again. Although, she admitted silently as the scenery whizzed past, Davis Garvey was more of a challenge than she'd ever had to face before.

"Cheer up, sis," Gina said on a laugh, "maybe Santa will leave you a marine in your stocking!"

Oh, now, *there* was a mental image.

Davis drove through the guard gate, nodded at the sentries and ignored their barely muffled snorts of laughter. Okay, so the Volkswagen looked like hell. Its engine purred like a kitten.

Amazing woman.

Not only did she kick-start his body into high gear, she knew cars, too. He could really get to like Marie Santini.

But even as he thought it, alarm bells went off in his head. Having a nice, mutually satisfying affair was one thing. Actually getting emotionally involved was something else again. He didn't want to *like* her. It was enough that he simply *wanted* her. Just touching her hand had given him as big a rush as surviving that test drive.

Marie Santini definitely had his attention. And what was wrong with a hot, satisfying, temporary relationship?

Camp Pendleton would be his home for the next three years or so. After that, he'd be reassigned. He made a point of never getting so involved, he couldn't walk away easily. Because Davis *always* walked away.

One of the things he liked best about being in the corps was the fact that rootless types like him fit right in. There was no room for roots in the marines. You went in, did your job, then moved on. All in all, a good way to live your life. See the world and never have to stay in one spot long enough to notice you don't fit in.

He dismissed that train of thought, turned the steering wheel and drove along the nearly empty road, headed for the NCO barracks. He passed a fast-food place, a small, tidy-looking church and a basketball court where a dozen or so kids raced back and forth across the asphalt. In the winter twilight, multi-colored Christmas lights twinkled on rooftops, around windows and in the bare branches of trees.

Christmas again. The one time of year he almost envied his married buddies. But the season would pass soon, as would those brief longings for something more in his life.

Pulling into a parking slot, he got out, locked the car and headed for his apartment. One that looked much like every other place he'd lived in for the last fifteen years.

Before he could open the front door though, his neighbor, Sergeant Mike Coffey, stepped out of his place and said with a pointed look at the VW, "I see you found Santini's."

"Recognize the loaner, do you?"

"Hell, yes." Mike grinned. "Drove it myself last month."

Pocketing his keys, Davis cocked his head and looked at the other man. "So how come you didn't tell me your Miracle Worker was a good-looking woman?"

"Good-looking?" Mike asked with a shrug. "To tell you the truth, I never really noticed."

How could he not have noticed those green eyes and the suggestion of a dimple in her cheek? Was Coffey blind or was Davis nuts?

"Doesn't really matter what she looks like," Mike was saying, "she's a whiz with cars."

Hmm. Maybe it didn't matter to Mike, but Davis could still see her in his mind's eye. Still, he didn't admit to it. "She'd better be," he said.

Mike laughed. "Don't worry. Your Mustang's perfectly safe."

Don't worry? Hell, Davis was extremely picky about who worked on the Mustang. Or any of the other cars he had tucked away in storage garages all across the country. Then he remembered Marie's confident smile and the concentration on her face when she listened to the rumbling of his car's engine. He had a feeling Mike was right. He didn't have anything to worry about. As far as his car was concerned, anyway.

"Trust me," Mike said. "Once Marie works on your

car, you'll never want anyone else's hands touching it."

The other man gave him a wave and ducked back into his own apartment. Davis stood there in the lowering darkness for a long minute and thought about Marie Santini's hands. Strong, slender, delicate, capable.

And he had to admit, it wasn't just his cars he was thinking about her hands being on.

Chapter Three

Could she really kill her sister at the dinner table? Sure she could, Marie told herself silently. But someone was sure to notice.

"I'm talkin' *hunk* here," Gina said emphatically, and plopped down into her chair at the dinner table. "I swear, if he wasn't a marine, he could be a model or something."

Marie gritted her teeth, set the salad bowl down on the dining room table and walked to her seat. She shouldn't have agreed to eat with the family tonight. Should have known that Gina would still be talking about Davis Garvey. Heck, she'd been talking about him all afternoon. Even shopping in the crowded mall hadn't shut her up.

With a mental sigh, she thought longingly of the peace and quiet of her garage apartment.

"We understand, dear," Maryann Santini said, and smiled at her youngest daughter. "He's handsome."

"Beyond handsome," Gina corrected, and slanted a look at Marie. "Wouldn't you say so?"

If given the chance, which she hadn't been, Marie might have said a lot of things. Like, he wasn't really handsome in the traditional sense, but he had a sort of inner strength that appealed to her—and apparently Gina. But all she said was, "I think you've already said plenty on the subject."

Far from looking abashed, Gina just grinned. "All I'm saying is that he's one hot property and he was looking at Marie like she was the last steak at a barbecue."

"Thank you so much for the lovely analogy." But she couldn't help thinking that Gina had seen one too many movies. Although a part of her wanted to believe that the first sergeant had been interested, another, more rational part reminded her that she wasn't the girl guys asked out. She was the girl guys talked to about *other* girls.

"So is he a nice young man?" Mama asked, eyebrows lifted into high arches, her gaze locked on her middle daughter.

Marie stifled a sigh. If he looked like a gargoyle, Mama wouldn't care as long as he was "nice." Being Italian wouldn't hurt, either.

Better to head her mother off at the pass. Maryann Santini loved a good romance better than anything. And the only thing worse than having to live with her own disappointing love life was knowing that her mother had given up all hope of Marie finding a boyfriend.

According to Mama, feminism was all well and good—but it would never take the place of a big wedding and lots of kids.

"For heaven's sake," Marie sputtered. "How do I know if he's nice? I just met the man. And he's not up for grabs, either," she said with a pointed look at her little sister. "I'm just fixing his car. That's all. End of story."

Gina snorted.

"He seems taken with you," Mama argued.

"According to Gina." She slid her gaze toward the tiny brunette across the table from her. Justifiable homicide. No jury of big sisters would ever convict her.

"Gina's very wise about these things," Mama said, giving her youngest daughter a quick smile of approval.

Meaning, of course, that Gina knew how to catch a man's eye. Something Mama had given up on teaching Marie years ago. Apparently though, old hopes die hard.

"No one's asked me," Angela, the oldest of the

Santini girls said quietly, "but who cares if he's interested? It's obvious that Marie is *not*."

"Thank you," Marie said heartily, surprised, but pleased at the support. "At last a voice of reason."

"Besides," Angela went on as she poured her son, Jeremy, a glass of milk, "Gina was probably wrong. After all, when she's at work, Marie's hardly the stuff men's fantasies are made of. All that grease and grime... What man is going to take the trouble to look past the surface?"

Well, thanks again, she thought, but didn't say.

"I can solve that," Marie said lightly. "I'll just wear one of your old prom queen dresses the next time I rebuild a carburetor. Oh, and maybe a small, but tasteful tiara. Just think how the diamonds will twinkle in the fluorescent lights."

"Funny," Angela muttered.

"I like Aunt Marie just how she is," Jeremy piped up.

She sent him a grin and a wink. "Have I told you lately that you are my absolute favorite eight-year-old person?"

"Yep," he said. "But I think you should tell Santa, just to be sure *he* knows, too."

"Count on it, buddy," she said. If it struck her as just a little sad that her most ardent male admirer was her nephew, Marie buried the jab quickly.

Her mother and sisters continued to talk around her, but she stopped paying attention. It didn't matter what they thought, she told herself as she concentrated on getting through dinner as quickly as possible. But, of course, it did matter. Always had.

And that was both the blessing and the curse of being a member of a close family.

She glanced at the familiar faces seated around the dining table that had been in the Santini family since God was a boy. The solid mahogany table shone from years of polish and bore the scratches of innumerable generations of Santinis like badges of honor.

There was Gina, always perky enough for three cheerleaders. Angela, pretty but quieter, sadder since being widowed three years before. Jeremy, bustling through life with all the grace of the proverbial bull in a china shop. And Mama—patient, loving, *there*.

She missed her dad. A pang of old sorrow twisted around her heart briefly. Two years he'd been gone now. Papa had been the one male in Marie's life to really appreciate her.

A tomboy from the time she could walk, Marie had grown up in Santini's garage. She'd been the son Papa'd never had. And though she'd loved her special relationship with her father, she'd always been sorry that she and her mom weren't closer. Angela, Gina and Mama had shared girly things, and though Marie had sometimes wistfully watched them all from the sidelines, she had never really felt comfortable enough to try and join in.

Still, she thought, letting go of old regrets, they

were family. And family—love—was all-important and always there.

As much as they drove her nuts, Gina knew she'd be lost without them. A sudden, unexpected sting of tears tickled the backs of her eyes. Family. Tradition. Roots. The Santinis were big on all of them, and that was a good thing, wasn't it? To know that there were people who loved you, supported you, no matter what?

She nodded to herself, feeling much more magnanimous toward them all.

"So!" Gina spoke up loudly to get her attention. "If Marie's not interested, like she claims, I say she brings the hunk home to dinner so we can have a shot at him."

So much for magnanimity.

"The man's not a prize turkey, you know," Marie snapped.

"Methinks she doth protest too much," Gina said.

"Oh, for heaven's sake," Marie told her in irritation, "he's not the last living man on the planet. Why are you so intent on him?"

"Why are you so defensive?"

"I'm not." Was she? An uncomfortable thought. After all, what did it matter to her if Gina made a move on him?

She shifted uneasily in her chair.

"Good," Gina said with a brisk nod. "Then it's

settled. You'll bring him to dinner. What's good for you, Mom?" she asked. "Saturday?"

"Saturday's fine, if Marie's sure."

"Marie didn't agree to any of this," Marie pointed out.

"You will, though," Angela said, "if only to prove to Gina that you don't care."

She shot her sister a nasty look, mainly because she was right. "Fine. Saturday. I'll invite him." And feel like a fool for asking a perfect stranger home for a family dinner. "Happy, now?"

Gina smiled. Angela nodded. Mama was already planning the menu.

Marie sat back in her chair and glared at all of them.

You know, maybe family was overrated.

Davis held down the channel button on the remote and idly stared at the TV as images flipped on and off the screen. He really wasn't in the mood to watch; it was simply something to do. In the darkness, the rapidly changing pictures and sounds dispelled the quiet emptiness of his apartment.

Not that he was lonely, he assured himself. Far from it. He set the remote down on the table and picked up the carton of cold chow mein that was his dinner. Propping his feet up on the coffee table, he stared blankly at the screen, not really interested in the life cycle of the honeybee.

He liked his life. He liked being able to eat in the living room right out of the carton. If the place was a mess, there was no one around to complain. He liked not having to unpack his moving boxes until he was good and ready—which usually meant two or three months. Liked moving to new bases every few years. Seeing new faces, new places.

New faces. Instantly one particular face rose up in his mind—as it had all evening. Marie Santini.

He'd never spent so much time thinking about a woman he hardly knew. Whether it was her big green eyes or the adrenaline rush her driving gave him, something about her had hit him hard. Hard enough to make him rethink that casual invitation to lunch. If spending less than a half hour with her was enough to get him thinking about her, did he really want to pursue this?

He much preferred a simple, no-ties-involved relationship. And Marie Santini was practically encircled by a white picket fence. Everything about her screamed out hearth and home. Altogether a dangerous female.

But then, marines were supposed to thrive on danger, right?

A knock on the door exploded his thoughts and he was grateful for the distraction. Setting the carton of chow mein down with relief, he walked across the room and opened the door.

"Hey," Mike Coffey said, "a couple of us are going into town for dinner. Want to come?"

Davis glanced over his shoulder at the darkened room, the flickering TV and the half-eaten chow mein container. There was such a thing as too much time to yourself, he thought, and suddenly he wanted out of that too-quiet, too-lonely apartment. "Yeah. Just let me turn off the TV."

She had plenty of work to do.

And she would do it, she promised herself, just as soon as Davis Garvey had picked up his car and was gone again. Until then, she kept busy at her desk.

Marie hated paperwork. She'd much rather be under a car than hunched over a computer. Unfortunately she didn't have a car to work on at the moment. Jim Bester had picked up his Fiat that morning and Davis Garvey would soon be by to pick up the Mustang. Apparently, every other automobile in Bayside had decided to stay healthy throughout the Christmas season.

Davis.

As soon as he got there, she'd have to ask him to dinner.

Grumbling to herself, she tossed her pen down onto the desk and stood up. She never should have given in to Gina's goading. Why in heaven would Davis even *want* to come to dinner at her house? For

Pete's sake, the man wasn't going to want to sit down with a bunch of strangers.

Although, she thought as she marched into the service bay and flicked on the overhead lights, the idea wasn't as strange as some might think. Every year around the holidays, an informal Adopt A Marine program started up. Families in town would invite young marines away from home to holiday dinners, so they wouldn't be stuck on base eating in the commissary. Her own family had participated a few times over the years and it had always worked out well. The marines were grateful for a respite from the base and the families enjoyed the company of some lonely young men. She supposed she could think of Davis in that context.

Sure. Why not? Just imagine him a lonely marine away from his own family at a special time of year. The fact that he didn't look like the image of a lonely young soldier didn't really have to come into this. Did it?

"Besides, it's Christmas," she said aloud, her voice echoing slightly in the empty service bay.

"According to my watch," a familiar, deep voice said from the open doorway behind her, "we still have about three weeks until Christmas."

Surprised, Marie jumped and turned around to face him. "Do the marines teach you to sneak up on unsuspecting civilians?"

"Oh, yeah," he said, walking toward her until he

was stopped just inches from her. "Sneaking 101. A very popular course."

Too close, she thought. He was standing way too close for comfort. She could smell the sharp, citrusy scent of his aftershave and see a small nick beneath his chin where he'd cut himself shaving.

And what was going on with her stomach, pitching and rolling like she was on a roller coaster? "Well," she said, trying to get a grip. "I hope your teacher gave you an A."

"An A plus, actually." He moved closer still and Marie took a short half step backward. "They like us to be able to walk quiet in our line of work."

"Yeah," she said. "It probably comes in handy. In a jungle."

He laughed and Marie didn't even want to admit to herself what a nice sound it was.

"So," he asked, "my car ready?"

"Yes," she said. "It is." And the sooner he took it, the better. She'd spent way too much time already thinking about him. The last two days, his face had cropped up in her mind far too often for comfort.

"Good." He reached out and laid one hand on her forearm. Even through her sweater's bulky material, a series of small electrical charges pulsed through her. Marie's breath caught and she pulled away, stepping around him to lead him into the office. Mentally she did the multiplication tables in a futile effort to reclaim her mind.

As she walked behind the counter, he took up position directly opposite her. Laying his palms flat atop the laminate surface, he waited for her to look at him, then asked, "So how about lunch?"

"No thanks," she said and stopped silently counting at four times twelve. If she went out to lunch with him, that would mean she was interested in him. Which she wasn't. Besides, with her stomach twisting and untwisting, who could eat?

"I remember," he said. "You don't date your customers."

"No, that's not it," she said quickly before she could lose her nerve. Just ask him, she told herself. Ask him to come to dinner and prove to her sisters *and* to Mama that she wasn't attracted to him. Heck. Maybe she could prove it to herself, too. "I just thought maybe you'd like to have dinner tonight instead. At my house."

Davis just looked at her for a long moment. He'd told himself all the way over here that he wasn't going to repeat the invitation to lunch. Any woman who interested him this much this quickly was one to stay clear of.

But then he'd seen her again. Stood close enough to catch a whiff of the flowery scent she wore. Looked down into those green eyes and had known that he had to spend more time with her. Risky or not.

Still, he couldn't help wondering what had changed her mind. A couple of days ago, she wouldn't go out to lunch with him. Now she's inviting him to a cozy dinner at her place?

Marie Santini was one confusing woman, he thought. But as his gaze swept over her again, he told himself it would be interesting trying to figure her out.

"Well?" she prompted.

"Sure," he said. "I'd like that."

She inhaled deeply and blew the air out in a rush again. "Good."

"What time?" he asked, smiling at her obvious signs of nervousness.

"Oh. Six, I guess." She picked up a pad of paper and scribbled down the address.

When he took it from her, his fingertips brushed across hers and instantly, tendrils of heat exploded between them.

She yanked her hand back as if she'd been burned by that same blast of energy, and Davis wondered if he was doing the right thing. If they set sparks off each other that easily, could a fire be far behind?

Chapter Four

So much for a cozy dinner for two.

He should have known better. Should have guessed that she was up to something. Marie had gone from refusing his lunch invitation to inviting him to dinner at her home. And he'd already noticed that she didn't seem the type to move fast and loose.

But who would have figured on this? His gaze flicked across the faces gathered around the oblong dining table. Gina, the flirty brunette he'd met earlier at the garage. Angela, the eldest, a stunning widow and the mother of Jeremy, an eight-year-old who would one day make a great interrogator. The kid never ran out of questions. At the end of the table sat Maryann Santini—Mama. Her green eyes were the image of Marie's and had hardly left him in the last hour.

He shot a glance at Marie on his right and wondered why she hadn't told him she'd be throwing him into a family dinner.

Of course, if she had, he wouldn't have come. He'd never been comfortable around families. He'd always felt like a kid standing outside a candy store. He could see good stuff inside—he just couldn't get to it. After a while he'd stopped looking.

"So," Jeremy piped up from the other end of the table, "how come you're not wearing a uniform, and where's your gun?"

Clearly Davis's khaki slacks and pale blue sportshirt were a big disappointment to the kid. "I don't usually wear the uniform off base and we don't bring guns to dinner."

"Man, what a rip-off," the boy muttered.

He knew exactly how the kid felt. He'd expected candlelight, a bottle of wine and some quiet conversation. Just him and Marie. What a rip-off.

"That's enough," the boy's mother said, and turned a smile on Davis. "So how long have you been at Camp Pendleton, Davis?"

"Just about a week, ma'am," he said, concentrating on finishing dinner. He had to get out of there.

"And where are you from?"

He took another bite of lasagna, and when he'd

swallowed, answered, "My last posting was in North Carolina."

"No," Gina said, giving him one of those practiced, flirty looks she'd been sending him all evening. Damn, the girl was good. Too bad he wasn't interested. For some reason, Gina's obvious sexuality didn't have near the appeal for Davis as Marie's inherent sensuality.

She continued talking, though, and Davis couldn't think of a way to stop her. "My sister meant, where are you from originally?"

His fingers tightened around his fork. Everywhere, he thought. Nowhere.

"Where's your family?" Marie's mom asked.

"I don't have a family, ma'am," he said, and hoped they'd leave it at that.

He should have known better. For the last hour, the Santini women had been pumping him for information about the base, the corps in general and himself specifically. All of them but Marie, that is. The woman he'd come to see had hardly spoken to him. He shot another look at her. Her green eyes met his briefly and once again he felt that indefinable something that coursed between them.

He shouldn't have given in to the impulse to come here tonight. Hell, he'd known from the get-go that he shouldn't be seeing her. Just pulling up in front of her house had told him that.

It was an old Craftsman-style with a wide front

porch and a big bay window, through which lamplight poured out into the darkness. A rainbow of Christmas lights were strung across every surface. Every bush sparkled, and the porch pillar posts were wrapped with strings of flickering lights that seemed to move like those on an old movie marquee. On the roof, Santa's sleigh had slipped to a precarious angle and a couple of his reindeer looked ready to fall. Hell, it had been like looking at a Christmas card. An advertisement for cozy warmth and home fires burning. He wasn't used to dealing with women so grounded. So rooted. He preferred impersonal apartments and women who recognized the beauty of a brief, but mutually satisfying affair.

So what was he doing here? Mistake, he thought. Big mistake.

Marie Santini and he came from two different worlds and it would be easier for both of them if they stayed that way.

"No family?" Mama Santini repeated with a shake of her head. "I'm so sorry. You must miss them terribly. Especially at this time of year."

He didn't say anything and wondered what she would think if he told her you couldn't miss something you'd never had. But she wouldn't understand that. None of them would. How could they?

"You won't spend Christmas alone, will you?" Gina asked.

"Oh, no," Mama put in before he could answer. "You'll come here."

He choked on a bite of lasagna and had to force it down with a gulp of wine. Spend Christmas with the Santini women? He didn't think so. Three eager faces watched him as he tried desperately to come up with an excuse that would get him out of this without offending them.

Marie had been quiet all evening, as if to prove to her too-inquisitive family that she wasn't the slightest bit interested in Davis Garvey. She'd sat by while Mama and Angela grilled him. While Gina batted her eyelashes and coyly smiled. While even Jeremy quizzed the poor man about everything marine.

But the look on Davis's face told her that the family had gone too far. She didn't know what it was about the mention of family that had shuttered his features, but she figured it wasn't any of hers—or her family's business.

"You know what?" Marie spoke up, changing the subject, and the other three women looked at her. "It's getting late. I've gotta get Jeremy to the batting cages."

"Cool!" her nephew shouted, and jumped out of his chair.

"Yes," his mother called out after him, "you can be excused."

"Batting cages?" Davis asked, clearly grateful for the shift in conversation. "In December?"

"Sign-ups for Little League are in February," she told him and stood up. "Gotta get in shape."

As she'd expected, Davis took the opportunity she'd handed him.

He pushed himself up from the table and stood beside her. "I think I'll be going, too, but thank you for dinner, Mrs. Santini."

"Call me Mama," she said. "Everyone does."

He actually paled.

Apparently the combined forces of the Santini women could bring even a marine to his knees.

They escaped the dining room together and headed for the front door. Behind them, three female voices broke into a whispered conversation. From upstairs came the sound of Jeremy's running feet and Marie knew she only had a minute or two to get rid of Davis.

And she did want to get rid of him, she reminded herself.

She walked him to the door and opened it. "Thanks for coming," she said.

But he didn't leave. He only stood there, looking down at her. "Why didn't you tell me?" he asked.

"Tell you?"

He shook his head. "About your whole family being here?"

"Oh," she said with what she hoped was a convincingly innocent tone, "didn't I?"

"No."

"Okay," Marie said, and tightly gripped the doorknob with her right hand. Watching him at the table had stirred up a bit of guilt inside her. He'd looked so ill at ease, she'd almost felt sorry for him when the questioning had gotten fast and furious. "I should have told you. But Gina wanted to see you again and I thought…"

His eyes widened and he chuckled under his breath. The sound had a strange effect on her. Almost as if it had danced along her spine, sending goose bumps trailing across her flesh. She took a slow, deep breath and told herself—*again*—to get a grip.

"So you were trying to set me up with your sister?"

"What's wrong with my sister?" she demanded, instinctively defensive, despite the fact that only a few minutes ago, she'd wanted to kill Gina for pouncing on the man.

"Nothing that a couple dozen Valium wouldn't cure," he muttered. Then he asked, "Is she *always* so perky?"

Marie ducked her head to hide a smile. Gina's perpetual cheerleader attitude could get a little wearing. "She has a positive personality."

"You could say that," he said, and moved in a little closer. "But," he reminded her quietly, "I didn't ask her to lunch. I asked you."

"And I asked you to dinner. So we're even."

"Not yet," he said.

Did he practice giving women that long, soulful look? Or was it a gift he was born with? Marie's breath hitched in her chest. He seemed to loom over her—and she wasn't exactly on the petite side. But Sergeant Garvey was not only tall, he was broad, and from what she could see, in fantastic shape.

She was way out of her depth.

"Look," she said, drawing in a deep breath, but keeping her voice low enough so that her family wouldn't overhear her, "why are you doing this?"

"Doing what?" He actually sounded confused.

"This. Acting like you're interested in me."

"Who's acting?" he asked, and lifted one hand to smooth her hair back from her face. The slightest touch of his fingertips sent short bursts of excitement fluttering through her, and Marie took one hasty step back.

All night she'd watched him, listened to him and tried to remember that she wasn't attracted to him. Wasn't interested in him. So why did he have to touch her and shoot all of her fine notions clear to the moon?

"You ready, Marie?" Jeremy called, and thundered down the stairs and past them out the door.

"Yes," she yelled after him gratefully. And then to her family she called, "We'll be back in an hour or so."

Davis followed her onto the porch, and in the glow

of the Christmas lights, he asked, "So where are the batting cages?"

"Why?" she responded warily.

He shrugged. "It's been a long time since I've done any hitting. Thought it might be fun."

Oh, for heaven's sake.

With her hair pulled back into a ponytail, she looked about seventeen. And entirely too good.

Davis stood outside the cage, curling his fingers into the wire mesh as he watched Marie teach her nephew the proper batting stance. His gaze followed every wiggle of her hips, and the curve of her behind in those tight black jeans was enough to stop his heart.

She'd paid no attention to him at all since they'd arrived at the cages. Every bit of her concentration was on the nephew who clearly adored her. She was patient, firm and surprisingly knowledgeable about the intricacies of batting.

Along the line of cages, baseballs thumped into the netting and slammed against wooden backboards. Piped in from overhead speakers came a stream of Christmas carols, and the cold ocean air whipping over the crowds gave the whole place a seasonal feel.

Dozens of kids ran loose, their harried-looking parents handing out quarters for the cages and the video machines. It had been years since Davis had been to one of these places and he found himself enjoying it. He took a last gulp of really bad coffee, crushed the now-empty hot cup, tossed it into the trash and turned his attention back to Marie.

He couldn't help himself. She captivated him, and that was a bad sign, he knew. He should have gone home and forgotten all about the sexy mechanic. But even knowing that, he hadn't been able to leave her yet. Damn. It was like going into combat. You knew it was dangerous and your gut told you to run like hell. But a stronger instinct—something primal and undeniable—took over, making you stand your ground.

And a purely male instinct was telling him to grab Marie and kiss her so long and hard and deep that neither of them would worry about the consequences.

She fitted the batting helmet on Jeremy's head, patted the top and then slipped out of the cage, closing the door behind her.

"Okay, kiddo," she called out. "Get ready. The first one's coming in hard and fast."

"I know, I know," the boy answered in that patient tone that all kids adopt when talking to adults.

"You're good with him," Davis said, sliding a look at her.

"He's a great kid." She shrugged, keeping her eyes on Jeremy. The first pitch went past him. "Keep your swing even."

"So how'd you learn so much about baseball?" Davis asked, more for something to talk about than anything else.

"My dad taught me," she said. Then she called out, "You have to keep both hands on the bat."

"I didn't think little girls played baseball."

She shot him a glance, and smiled and said, "Welcome to the twentieth century."

"Baseball and auto repair, huh?"

"What can I say? I'm a Renaissance woman."

She was that.

"Did your sisters play, too?" He didn't care about her sisters. He just wanted to hear that smoky-sounding voice of hers again.

Marie laughed and shook her head, still watching Jeremy. She clucked her tongue when the kid missed another pitch. "Angela and Gina? Play baseball? No way."

"So you were the tomboy in the bunch?"

"Were?" She shook her head. "Still am." She winced when Jeremy took a pitch on his arm. "Rub it out, kiddo, and get ready for the next one."

She intrigued him completely. He'd never known anyone quite like her. The women he dated wouldn't be caught dead playing ball with a bunch of kids. Marie seemed to thrive on it. She was just so damned *alive.*

"You're patient, too," Davis commented.

She turned a quizzical look on him. "You expected me to slap Jeremy around?"

"No," he said with a smile. "But usually adults get a little testy—start yelling—when a kid's not learning."

"Speaking from experience, are we?" she asked.

When he didn't answer, Marie looked up at him, and he felt as though she was looking deep inside him. To where he kept his secrets. And he didn't like it.

He shifted, tearing his gaze from hers and effectively cutting off any question she might have asked. He didn't want to talk—or think—about his past. He wanted to talk about the now. With her.

"Hey, Santini!" A deep voice called out from just behind them.

Davis glanced over his shoulder in time to see a tall, hulking guy step up next to Marie and give her behind a swat. She yelped and Davis took a step closer, to put himself between her and the guy who'd actually hit her. Instinct had his right hand curling into a fist even as Marie turned, rubbing her bottom with one hand and grinned at the guy.

"Nicky, hi! I didn't know you were back in town."

His fisted hand relaxed but that didn't mean his guts weren't still churning. Just who the hell was this guy, and how did he have the right to be slapping Marie's butt?

"Davis, this is Nick Cassaccio. An old friend."

"Hi," Nick said, and offered a hand to Davis. He took it, but kept a wary eye on the guy anyway. Just how old and how good a friend was he?

"So how'd it go with Patty?" she asked.

"Just like you said," Nick told her on a big smile.

"Good, I'm glad."

"Yeah, me, too." He reached out tugged her ponytail and said, "I gotta be going, brat. Just wanted to say hi."

"See you, Nick," she called after him as he drifted off into the crowd.

"Brat?"

Marie shrugged. "He's always called me that."

Davis frowned. How long was *always?* "Who's Patty?"

"Nick's girlfriend. Well," she corrected herself, "fiancée, now, I guess."

"Oh." That's good. But if the guy was after some other woman, what's he doing slapping Marie's behind? And most important, he demanded silently, why the hell did *he* care?

He didn't. No. It had been purely instinct to want to hit a man who'd hit a woman. It had nothing to do with the woman in question being Marie. Right. Even he didn't believe that.

"So what was he thanking you for?"

Marie gave him a quick look, then turned her

attention back to Jeremy. "Nothing, really. Patty broke up with him and he came over to the garage whining about it, and I told him that she was probably tired of waiting for him to pop the question."

"So he popped?"

She grinned. "Apparently."

Davis's eyebrows arched. "Batting instructor, mechanic and giver of advice to the lovelorn?"

"I am a woman of many talents," she said lightly.

"I do believe I agree with you," Davis told her and watched as her small smile faded into a look that was part nerves, part excitement. He reached out and ran one finger across the nape of her neck. She shivered and that tremor rocked him, too. "So," he asked, his voice low and suddenly thick, "what advice would Dear Marie have for me?"

She shrugged his hand off and looked up at him from beneath lowered lashes. "I guess I'd have to tell you to stop working so hard to convince me you're interested. And to move on to greener pastures."

"Maybe I don't see any pastures greener."

"Then you should have your eyes checked."

Does she really not know how attractive she is? he wondered. "My eyes work just fine," he said. Then he asked, "And what makes you think I'm not interested?"

She gave a short, strained laugh. "I've never exactly been the belle of the ball, sergeant. Men don't usually chase me down the street shouting their undying love."

Why the hell not? he wondered, but didn't ask. Instead he said, "Maybe you just haven't been listening."

"Yeah?" she said pointedly. "Same to you."

He grinned. Whether he should or shouldn't, Davis knew that he wouldn't be staying away from her. Trouble or not, he had to see this through, wherever it led.

"Aunt Marie," Jeremy called from the cage, "I'm not getting it."

"Just keep your swing even, sweetie."

Davis looked at the kid and mentally flashed back to his own childhood. When he'd wanted to be in Little League more than anything. When the thought of belonging to a team and being good at something was the most important thing in the world.

But his childhood had been different from Jeremy's. Growing up in a series of foster homes where he was never sure from one week to the next where he'd be living, Davis hadn't been much of a joiner.

Until the corps. Now he *did* belong somewhere and the past couldn't touch him anymore.

He shook off old thoughts and stepped past Marie into the cage. "Try this," he said, and positioned the boy's hands on the bat. Then drawing Jeremy's arms back, he showed him exactly how to hit high and away.

When he rejoined Marie outside the cage, he fed another quarter into the slot. He really didn't want to think about how good it felt to be here. With her and the boy.

He just wanted to enjoy it.

The next pitch came and Jeremy connected solidly, sending the baseball high into the overhead nets. Excited, he turned around, beaming at them. "Did you see it? Did you see how far I hit that?"

"You bet I did," Marie said.

"Do it again, kid," Davis told him.

"Just watch me," Jeremy yelled and turned around to face the pitching machine.

"Thanks," Marie whispered.

"No problem," Davis answered, and enjoyed the first real smile she'd given him.

Chapter Five

"Thanks, Davis," Jeremy said, "that was great!"

The kid was bouncing with excess energy. Davis knew marines who didn't have as much get-up-and-go as this small boy. And the kid didn't quit, either. Even when he wasn't doing well at the cages, he hadn't stomped off. He'd just set his feet and tried harder. There were a few privates on base who could learn a lesson from this boy.

A cold ocean wind rattled the naked branches of the tree standing sentry in the front yard and set the strings of Christmas lights swaying. The motion left a rainbow pattern of sliding lights trailing across the front of the house.

"You did good, kid," Davis said with a smile.

"You wanna hit some more balls tomorrow?" the boy asked, hopping from one foot to the other in his eagerness to recapture the glow of slamming a homer in the batting cages.

Davis paused before answering, mainly because he didn't know what to say. And in that pause, Marie jumped in to fill the silence.

"Sergeant Garvey doesn't have time to take you to the cages, Jeremy." She reached out to ruffle the boy's hair. "You and I will go again soon, okay?"

Jeremy ducked his head, then squinted up at Davis. "If you're not too busy, you could always just come anyways, though, right?"

"We'll see how it goes, okay?" A stall. Perfect. Why didn't he just tell the kid flat-out that he wasn't interested in an unofficial Big Brother program? He was only here to see Marie. He'd never had any intention of getting to know her family.

As if she knew what he was thinking, Marie gave him a cool look before turning to her nephew. "Go on in now, Jeremy. Your mom's probably wondering where you are."

The boy nodded and headed across the lawn toward the house. Before he climbed the front steps though, he turned back and yelled, "Remember, tomorrow…just in case."

Davis lifted one hand in acknowledgment, but it was so dark, he doubted the kid saw him. Once the boy was inside, Davis slid a glance at Marie, standing beside him. It was the first time he'd actually been *alone* with her all night. This *date* hadn't exactly gone as planned, he thought, but standing here with her in the cold winter night, he didn't really mind.

Her scent drifted to him on the breeze and everything inside him felt as though he was going on full alert. Every sense was heightened, every breath seemed measured. She stared at him and he wished he could see every emotion flickering in the depths of her green eyes. But the light wasn't strong enough. There was only the darkness and the soft wind blowing around them.

Then she spoke and the spell was shattered.

"So," she said in a too-hearty voice, "thanks for everything and maybe I'll see you around."

In other words, *Shove off, Sergeant.*

"Around where?" he asked, just to hear her voice again.

"Just…around." She shrugged. "It's a small town."

Not good enough. He suddenly wanted to know when he was going to see her again. "What if I asked you to dinner? Just the two of us this time."

"Why would you do that?"

Why indeed? He should be climbing into his car and heading for the base. But he wasn't ready to leave just yet. He'd come here tonight to see her. And he hadn't had more than a minute or two of her time all night. Davis wasn't used to sharing.

He took a step closer to her, and even in the darkness, he saw wariness flicker in her eyes. That bothered him more than he wanted to admit. Damn it, what was there to be wary of? "Let's just say I'd like to spend time with you. Alone."

She laughed, and it was a second or two before he heard the nervous note in that chuckle. "You don't have to do this," she said. "Your car's fixed. No reason to smooth-talk the mechanic."

Davis frowned slightly. "Who said anything about my car?"

"Look," Marie said, and backed up a step or two. "I appreciate your being so nice to Jeremy…." her words picked up steam until she was nearly babbling. "I mean, your showing him how to hit a fly ball was really great. I've been concentrating on showing him an even swing, so he could lock into solid base hits. But I guess every kid wants to blast a grand slam…."

"I guess," he agreed, and moved with her as she started to cross the lawn. "But I really don't want to talk about Jeremy at the moment."

"Apparently not," she muttered, and sighed heavily. "You're just not going to leave, are you?"

He smiled at her. "Not until I walk you to your door," he said, then glanced at the front of the house off to his left. "Which, by the way, is over there."

"Yeah," she told him and pointed down the

driveway toward the frame, two-storied garage. "But I live there. In an apartment upstairs."

"Good," he said, glad to know he and Marie could have a little quiet time without her family hanging in doorways. Now all he had to do was convince her that she wanted a little quiet time with him.

They walked along the side of the house, the only illumination the overhead Christmas lights and a moon that peeked in and out from behind rain clouds.

At the foot of the stairs, she stopped, turned around and held out one hand toward him. "Okay, Sergeant. Mission accomplished. I'm at my door. Good night."

He took her hand and instantly felt a swell of heat dance from her fingertips to his. That heat rushed along his arm and settled in his chest, filling him with a sort of warmth he'd never felt before. She felt it, too; he knew it. Even in the shadows, he saw her reaction written plainly on her face.

His thumb stroked the back of her hand when she tried to pull free. He didn't want to break that connection just yet. Didn't want to lose the warmth still pulsing inside him.

"Technically," he whispered, "you're not at your door yet."

"Who pays attention to technicalities?" she asked, and he heard the slight tremor in her voice.

"Marines," he answered. "And mechanics."

She licked her lips and took a backward step up onto the stairs. He followed her.

"What is it you're after?" she asked quietly, still halfheartedly trying to tug her hand free of his grasp. "Bucking for a discount oil change?"

Did she really think a man would be interested in her solely for her mechanical abilities?

"What do you think?" he asked.

Another step up, toward the door on the landing.

"I think you've got the wrong Santini," she said. "Gina's in the house. I could go get her for you."

He shook his head. "I didn't come here tonight to see Gina." Her younger sister might be a nice woman, but she never shut up long enough for him to be sure. "Hell," he added, "I thought dinner was going to be just you and me. But you knew that, didn't you?"

Another step backward and Marie almost stumbled. Just what she needed—to go pitching headfirst down the flight of stairs. She'd probably kill him in her fall and have the entire Marine Corps down on her for knocking off one of their sergeants. On the other hand, if she didn't kill him, they'd end up at the bottom of the steps, all wrapped up together. Arms and legs touching, bodies pressed tight. Oh, my...

If he'd only let go of her hand, maybe she could think straight. But his grip didn't lessen and the ridiculous spurts of heat she'd felt at that first contact with his skin showed no signs of tapering off. Another step up. Careful, Marie, careful.

Oh, jeez, she thought as she drew in a long, steadying breath. He smelled like Old Spice, marine and—she took another whiff—*trouble*. Now she knew what it felt like to be an opposing army in those old war movies. Marines never retreated. Always advancing. Always closer. And closer. The poor bad guys never stood a chance.

"So tell me," he said, still climbing the stairs with her, "why'd you really pull the whole family dinner thing tonight?"

"Family dinners are more fun, don't you think?"

"I think you haven't had dinner with the right guy if that's what you think."

She was definitely not used to this. Marie had practically offered Gina to him on a silver platter and he didn't seem the least bit interested. But that couldn't be right. *All* men were interested in Gina. She was bright and perky and pretty and dainty and everything else men liked.

Marie was a *mechanic,* for Pete's sake.

Female mechanics weren't exactly the stuff of men's fantasies. She climbed up another step.

How many stairs are there here, anyway? Shouldn't she be near the top? She didn't want to take her eyes off Davis long enough to check. She had the distinct feeling that he'd been militarily trained to take advantage of an opponent's momentary lapses.

Just as that thought whipped through her mind, she reached the second-story landing. Her own little porch, where two pots of dead geraniums decorated her doorway. The last frost had killed them off and she hadn't had time to replace them yet. Stupid, she told herself. This is no time to be thinking about flowers.

With her free hand, she dug into her purse to find her keys. Naturally they hid from her. She had nowhere else to go. She couldn't back up another step, unless she decided to jump over the railing to the driveway below, and that seemed just a tad excessive.

Talk, she told herself. Say something. *Anything*.

"We're here," she announced as if he hadn't figured that out for himself. "So... thanks again."

He still didn't let go of her hand. Instead he pulled her closer to him. Close enough that she felt as though *she* was wearing the aftershave whose scent was doing such odd things to her knees.

He lifted his free hand to cup her face, and she felt the distinct imprint of each of his fingers on her skin. Not a good sign. Breathe, Marie. Breathe. He tipped her face up until she was staring directly into his eyes. In the muted light, she saw determination glinting in their depths and she knew without a doubt that he was about to kiss her.

"I, uh...don't think this is such a good idea," she whispered, forcing the words past a throat so tight, she could scarcely draw a breath. "I hardly know you."

He smiled and Marie's heartbeat skittered wildly for an instant. "Lady," he said, "I'm a marine. You can trust me."

"Yeah?" she asked on a squeak of sound. "To do what?"

He lowered his head. "Whatever's necessary," he told her just before he slanted his mouth across hers.

Marie gasped, shocked silly by the flood of sensations rippling through her. She'd been kissed before. Not often, but enough to know how to do it without bumping noses or biting lips. But none of the kisses she'd experienced before tonight had prepared her for this.

The earth actually did stand still.

Davis's arms came around her, and as he pressed her tightly to him, she wound her own arms around his neck. She sighed into his parted lips as her body began a slow meltdown. Then his tongue slipped into her mouth and circled her own in a long, lazy, caress that left her struggling for air and clamoring for more.

Heart pounding, knees wobbling, Marie leaned into him, giving herself up to the sensations rushing through her. And when he finally pulled his head back, breaking that incredible kiss, she was grateful for the strength of his arms still holding her upright.

"So?" he whispered, "how about lunch to-morrow?"

"Sure," she said and knew that if he'd just said *Why don't we fly to the moon tomorrow morning?* she'd have said, "Sure." But how could she be expected to think rationally when she'd just had what could only be described as a monumentally life-shattering moment?

"I'll see you, then," he said, and left her.

She listened to the sound of his footsteps as he went down the stairs. Then alone, she gripped the banister tightly and prayed she'd be able to move before it started raining again.

Things are starting to get interesting, Davis told himself as he parked outside Santini's auto repair shop. Heck, even the sun had decided to shine for a change.

He got out of the car and stood in the street, staring at the little shop that Marie's talent with cars kept going. But he wasn't seeing the garage. Instead he was reliving that kiss on her landing. As he had all last night, he remembered every instant of the time he'd held her close. The pounding of her heart, the taste of her, her soft breath brushing his cheek and the crisp December wind that seemed to envelop them both.

At the first touch of her lips, he'd known this woman was different. Different from every other female he'd ever known before. There was a chemical reaction between them that seemed to linger on in his bloodstream throughout the night.

In that one kiss with Marie, he'd found more than he had expected…and enough to worry him. But not nearly enough to make him back off. He needed to explore what he'd found with her, but he could still keep it simple, he told himself. Keep what they had intimate. He didn't have to get involved with her family.

And on that thought, he started for the open service-bay doors. Even on a Sunday she was busy. A testament to her abilities.

As he entered the garage, he heard a muttered "Damn it."

He smiled to himself. Even miracle workers get frustrated, he supposed. "Marie?"

The loud clatter of a metal tool hitting the concrete floor sounded out and a second later, she stepped out from behind the upraised hood of a small Honda. She wore a pair of bib overalls that shouldn't have looked cute, but did, and a tiny white T-shirt. Her hair was pulled back into a ponytail from which one or two strands had escaped to hang on either side of her face. As he watched, she lifted one hand to push the hair out of her way and left a streak of oil behind on her cheek.

"Davis, hi," she said and pulled a shop towel out of her hip pocket. Wiping her hands on the once-white fabric, she walked toward him. "Is it lunchtime already?"

Not exactly the eagerness he'd been hoping for, but at least she hadn't forgotten all about their date.

"Yeah," he said. "You ready?"

"Actually," she told him, with a glance at the Honda, "no."

"No?"

She lifted both hands and shrugged. "Well, a friend of mine dropped her car off this morning and it's an emergency, so I told her I'd fix it right away."

"She could drive it here and it was an emergency?" he asked, sure she was just trying to slip out of their lunch date.

"More like it lurched its way here," Marie told him. "The points and plugs are bad and Laura really needs this car for tomorrow morning."

Disappointment rose up inside him, but he pushed it away. It was just lunch, right? "What about one of your loaners?" he asked, and turned to where the three junkers were usually parked.

They weren't there.

"Well, see," Marie said, "that's the problem. I've already loaned them out."

Okay, now he was confused. Loaners were supposed to be for her customers' use. But the Honda was the only car at the shop. Curious, he asked, "Who'd you loan them to?"

She shoved the rag back into her pocket, then tucked both of her hands behind the bib front of her overalls. Rocking back and forth on her heels, she said, "Well, Tommy needed a car to get to band practice…."

"The kid who works for you."

"Yes." She gave him a smile, as if proud he'd remembered. "And Margaret Sanders, a friend of my mom's, needed a car to get to her daughter's house, because her daughter just had twins and Margaret had to be there."

"Well, sure." Why Margaret couldn't have gotten there on her own was beyond him, though.

Marie just looked at him. "And the third one is halfway to San Diego by now. Angela needed to go pick up Jeremy's Christmas present."

"In San Diego?"

"All the stores around here were sold out." She cocked her head to one side. "Do you have any idea how fast video games sell out in stores? It's amazing."

He'd take her word for it. Since he'd never had to do Christmas shopping for anyone, he had no idea what sold and what didn't. Looking at the Honda, he asked, "So how long before you have it up and running?"

Marie followed his gaze and sighed. "At least another hour."

"I'll wait."

She whipped around to look at him, then let her gaze slide to the closed door between the garage and the office. "There's something else, too," she said. "Last night, when you asked me, I forgot about—"

The closed door opened and Jeremy came through, his eyes widening when he caught sight of Davis.

"Hi! Are you coming with us?" the boy asked.

"Us?" Davis repeated, looking from the kid to Marie.

She shrugged again and smiled.

"To see Santa," Jeremy said. "Well, not the real Santa, but the one at the mall. His helper."

"Santa?" Davis repeated before he could stop himself.

Jeremy grinned. "Some of my friends say there's no Santa, but I figure what if there is and he gets really mad 'cause nobody believes in him? Then maybe he won't bring me the presents I want, so I don't want to make him mad just in case, you know?"

"Yeah." Davis looked away from the boy, idly wondering if all kids talked that much and that fast, or if it was something in the Santini blood. Meeting Marie's eyes, he said, "So after Laura's car, it's Santa?"

"Sorry," she said, "but I promised."

"And a promise is a promise, huh, Marie?" Jeremy sounded like he was gloating.

Davis started thinking. Damn it, he wasn't going to lose out to a tune-up and a visit to Santa. He'd been wanting to get Marie all to himself for several days now and he figured with a bit of finagling, he could still manage it.

"How about," he offered, walking to Marie's side, "if I do the tune-up on this heap while you take Jeremy to see Santa? I'll be finished by the time you get back and then we can drop him off at home and go to lunch." Not bad at all, he told himself. A solution worthy of Solomon.

"Nope."

He was getting very little appreciation for his brilliance.

"What do you mean, no?" he asked. "I know as much about cars as you do."

"Maybe," she said, "but this is my shop. I work on the cars here. It's my reputation, my responsibility."

"Okay, I can understand that," he said. He didn't want to, but he did. "But there's got to be a way to work this out."

From the corner of his eye, he saw Jeremy watching them and he half wondered if she'd planned this, too. Like last night's family dinner. Was she deliberately trying to avoid being alone with him?

After a long minute, she offered, "There is one way…if you're up to it."

He responded to the implied dare like any true Devil Dog. "Lady, I keep telling you. I'm a marine. We're up to anything."

"All right, then," she said, "you take Jeremy to the mall to see Santa. And as soon as I'm finished here, I'll meet you in Santa's Village."

"Now, wait a minute," he said loud enough to be heard over Jeremy's shouts. "There's got to be another way. I'll go to your house. Pick up Gina. She could—"

"Gina's at a ballroom dance class."

"Your mother…"

"Is getting her hair done."

"Angela…"

"San Diego," she reminded him.

Why, Davis wondered, did he suddenly feel like he was being surrounded by heavily armored tanks?

"This is the only way, Davis," Marie said.

He glanced at the boy waiting for his decision. Well, hell. He had two choices here. Charge or retreat. Like any good marine, he made his decisions quickly.

"All right."

Jeremy shouted again and raced out of the garage toward Davis's car.

A mall. On a weekend. At Christmastime.

Davis had gone into battle feeling more confident of his chances for survival.

"One hour," Marie said, breaking into his thoughts. "Outside Santa's Workshop."

Santa's Workshop.

Ooh-rah.

Chapter Six

The parking lot was like a battlefield.

The only difference was there were no sides here. It was every man—and woman—for himself. Davis gripped the steering wheel tight enough to snap it in two and tried to keep his eyes on everything at once. Heck, his military training actually helped here. Watch for your chance to advance and protect your flanks.

"We're gonna be late," Jeremy whined from the passenger seat beside him.

"Don't worry, kid," Davis said, "I'm never late."

A woman in a red BMW convertible with a holly wreath attached to her front grille, cut him off, then flipped him a hand gesture substantially lacking in holiday spirit. Gritting his teeth, Davis decided to quit trying to get close to the actual mall and settled instead for a parking space that looked to be miles from the shopping center.

At least they were out of the fray.

He shut the engine off and looked at the boy. Jeremy practically vibrated with excitement. No matter if he denied it or not, the kid obviously placed high faith in Santa Claus. He looked down into those shining eyes and knew without a doubt that *this* kid's Christmas dreams would come true. The Santini women would see to it. This child wouldn't know the disappointment of a Christmas morning with nothing to show for it.

Memories swelled inside him, and Davis fought them back valiantly. The past had no more power over him, he reminded himself. He'd come a long way from the boy he'd been. From the boy who'd learned early that to believe in people was to set yourself up for a letdown.

"Can we go now?" Jeremy asked, unhooking his seat belt and reaching for the door handle.

"Yeah," Davis said, suddenly wanting to hurry up and get this whole Santa thing behind him. "Let's go."

He got out, locked up the car and came around the back end where Jeremy stood waiting for him. As they started for the mall, the boy slid his hand into Davis's and started tugging, trying to make him hurry.

Glancing down at the kid, Davis felt warmed by the small hand in his. He'd never been around children much and when he had, he'd deliberately kept his distance. But lately it seemed distance was the one thing he couldn't seem to maintain.

"Christmas is almost here, y'know," Jeremy said, and anticipation colored his voice.

Doing a quick mental count, Davis told him, "There's still nearly three weeks to go."

"But it's *almost* here."

Apparently everyone agreed with the boy. Even on base, the holiday season was in full swing. Most of his friends had already scheduled leaves to be with their families, and those that were remaining on base were planning celebrations. Davis, though, couldn't even remember a time when Christmas wasn't just a hard time to get through.

Not that he had anything against Christmas. Or Easter. Or Hanukkah. Or the Fourth of July. But all of those things meant family. The one thing Davis had never known. The succession of foster homes he'd moved through as a child hadn't been more than places to sleep—and to escape from. Maybe there were *good* foster homes out there, but he'd never been in one.

As soon as he was old enough, he'd joined the corps and found his place in the world. It had been more than enough for too many years to count. And that place was still his, right?

"What do you want for Christmas, Davis?"

"Huh?" His mind had wandered and he came back now with a jolt as a VW sailed past them. He'd better pay attention or they'd both get run down by holiday maniacs.

"For Christmas," Jeremy repeated. "What do you want?"

"Oh," he said, then shrugged. Instantly, visions of Marie, wrapped up in a red ribbon and not much else rose up in his mind. But since he could hardly say so to her nephew, he said only, "Nothing."

The boy laughed and shook his head. "Everybody wants something."

Wanting and getting are two very different things. And a part of Davis hoped the boy never found that out. Changing the subject slightly, he asked, "What does your aunt Marie want? Do you know?"

Jeremy grinned and tugged a little harder on Davis's hand. It still looked as though the mall was miles in the distance.

"I'm getting her a new wrench," the boy said proudly.

Davis smiled. "She'll like that."

"I know," Jeremy said, obviously sure of himself. "Gina says Santa should bring Marie a man."

Davis's eyebrows lifted.

"But my mom says Marie wouldn't know what to do with one anyway."

Remembering that kiss in the dark, Davis thought he'd have to argue Angela's point. Still, it did him good to know that there weren't other men in Marie's life. That thought sobered him for a minute. He wasn't *in* her life. Was he?

"Marie doesn't have boyfriends?" he asked, allowing himself to be pulled along in the boy's wake.

Jeremy laughed and shook his head. "No way," he said. "She's not like Gina."

True, Davis thought. And for himself, he was grateful for the differences. But he wanted to hear what the kid had to say, so he prodded him a little. "What do you mean?"

"Marie does neat stuff," Jeremy said. "Like fishing and baseball. She doesn't have time to go on dates."

That was certainly true. Davis had never had to work so hard to try and get a woman alone.

"Are *you* gonna be her boyfriend?" Jeremy asked suddenly.

Davis looked down at the kid. The boy watched him warily, waiting for his answer. When it came, it was another question. "Do you think I should be?"

Jeremy stopped dead, tilted his head to one side and thought about it for a long moment. Finally he said, "Yeah. 'Cause you could teach me how to hit really good, and I think Marie kinda likes you."

"You do, huh?" he asked, surprised at the jolt of warmth that rushed through him at the idea. "Why?"

"'Cause she acts kinda funny when you're around. Like she's breathin' weird or something."

Last night stormed into the front of his mind again and he remembered her rapid heartbeat and the brush of her breath against his cheek. They'd both been breathing weird then.

"So I think you should, okay?"

Davis looked at the kid and smiled. "I'll do my best," he said, and had every intention of keeping that promise. He wouldn't mind being Marie's boyfriend at all. At least, temporarily.

Kids.

Millions of them screamed and laughed and cried and jumped up and down in excitement. The line leading around Santa's Workshop, through the Village and up to the throne where the big man sat, crawled forward at a snail's pace. Davis shifted from foot to foot, held Jeremy back from climbing the decorative fence that separated them from the artificial snow and wondered wildly how he'd let himself get talked into this.

The whole place was nuts. The kids around him were worked up to a fever pitch and the Christmas carols coming in over the loudspeaker had repeated themselves three times. And yet, despite everything, a part of him had enjoyed it all.

Finally an elf escorted Jeremy to the throne and the boy took his seat on Santa's lap. While the two of them talked, another elf snapped a picture and turned to Davis with a smile.

"Would you like a picture of your son with Santa?" she asked, giving him a slow look up and down. "Only four dollars."

"He's not—" Davis broke off before he could deny fatherhood. This elf didn't know or care who he and Jeremy were. And for some odd reason, as he stood there, surrounded by children and their parents, he actually *wanted* to belong. To be a part of this madness.

For the first time in his life, he felt close to the joy that other people took for granted. He turned his gaze to Jeremy and watched as the child told all his secrets to a man in a Santa suit, and he found himself hoping that the kid would never be disappointed. He wanted to think that the boy would always feel the magic that he felt now. That he would never lose the happiness that wreathed his face.

"Sir?" the elf said. "The picture?"

Davis shifted his gaze from the pretty young elf to the boy still whispering secretively to Santa. His heart swelled suddenly. He didn't stop to question the unusual emotions taking hold of him. He didn't want to examine them too closely.

"Yeah," Davis told her, his gaze still fixed on Jeremy. "I'll take it." He reached for his wallet to buy a little piece of Christmas.

Marie hurried through the mall, dodging harried shoppers laden down with overflowing bags. The tune-up had taken longer than she'd thought and then she'd had to go home and change clothes. Even she refused to go to the shopping center covered in motor oil and grease.

Hurrying her steps toward the center of the mall, she ran the flat of one hand down the front of her beige sweater and stopped atop her nervous stomach. Most people got butterflies when they were nervous. She felt as though bats were flying around inside her.

The crowd of kids was still thick around Santa's Village and her gaze scanned the mob, looking for two familiar faces. They weren't there, though, so she turned to look at the surrounding stores and finally spotted them sitting at a café opposite the Workshop.

Her heartbeat staggered and her mouth went dry. Even across a crowded mall, he had the ability to destroy her equilibrium. Mind spinning, she wondered how it had happened that in less than a week she'd become so...involved with this man? It had been years since she'd indulged in the kind of dreams that had haunted her sleep last night, and that fact worried her as much as it excited her.

Mainly because Marie still didn't know why he appeared to be so interested in her. But she was beginning to enjoy it. And a part of her was already dreading the day he'd move on in search of a more female female.

Surely soon, the novelty of chasing after a woman mechanic would wear off. Then he'd quit coming around—or worse yet, start treating her like a pal. Something cold and tight squeezed around her heart and Marie almost winced at the sensation. She didn't need or want another "buddy."

But darned if she didn't want him.

Gathering what was left of her unraveling self-control, she hurried through the crowd separating them.

"Hi," she said as she slid into a seat beside Jeremy.

Davis's gaze locked onto hers and she felt a slow heat climbing inside her. So much for self-control.

"I already talked to Santa, Marie," Jeremy said, "and Davis bought a picture of me so you could see it." He handed her the photo and added in a whisper, "But don't show it to anybody except Mom and Grandma, okay?"

"Okay," she told him, and hardly glanced at the

picture before looking at Davis again. "Thanks. Thanks for bringing him and for this."

"No problem," he told her. "Get the tune-up finished?"

Good, she thought. Safe ground. "Yeah. But the car's nearly done for. I don't know if I can keep it running much longer."

"How come Laura doesn't buy a new car?" Jeremy piped up.

"She can't afford to, honey," Marie said.

"Maybe Santa will bring her one."

"Maybe." But Santa didn't usually take adults' dreams and wishes to heart. Maybe he figured adults were capable of making their own dreams come true. And speaking of dreams...

Marie couldn't seem to tear her gaze from Davis's. Ever since last night, she'd been thinking about him, reliving that kiss and warning herself not to pump up her balloon to the bursting point. A kiss that had curled her toes didn't necessarily mean the same thing to him. Maybe he hadn't felt the same connection she had.

But now, staring into his blue eyes, she had the decided impression that he, too, was remembering those few minutes in the darkness.

"How about we take Jeremy home and go for an early dinner?" he asked suddenly, and she wondered if his voice had really dropped a couple of notches or if she was just imagining it.

Dinner. She thought about it for a long second or two, then decided yes, she'd go to dinner with him. Once they had a little time alone, he'd see she wasn't his type and go away. Hopefully before she got hurt too badly. Besides, she wanted to be with him again, if only for the last time. She wanted to be kissed again. She wanted to feel the heat rising within her. To feel his arms wrapped around her. For once in her life, she wanted to know what it felt like to be *wanted* by a man. By this man. And she had to do it quickly, before he came to his senses.

"Okay," she said simply and hoped he hadn't heard the slight tremor in her voice.

"Hey," Jeremy complained, "I'm hungry, too."

One of Davis's eyebrows lifted in a silent question.

She answered him by speaking to her nephew. "Not tonight, kiddo." Her gaze slid back to Davis's as she added, "Tonight is for grown-ups."

"Lord, girl," Gina exclaimed, "don't you *ever* condition your hair?"

"Of course I do," Marie said, then yelped, "Ow!" when her little sister dragged a brush through the tangled curls.

She glared into the mirror at Gina's reflection and when her sister was unmoved, shifted that glare to the other two women encamped in her bedroom.

Since finding out about Marie's dinner date,

the three of them had pulled out all the stops. Apparently they were bound and determined to push Marie through the doors of femininity, kicking and screaming if need be.

Her bedroom, her sanctuary, looked like a bomb had gone off in it. A mound of dresses that had been tried on and discarded covered the mattress. Shoes, stockings and more makeup than Marie had ever seen before lay strewn across every other possible surface.

Jeremy had been left in the main house to play video games on the TV while the Santini women transformed Marie into—she looked at her own reflection and sighed inwardly—a gorgeous stranger.

Gina yanked the brush through the still-warm curls again and Marie made a grab at her hair. "You don't mind leaving a few strands on my head, do you?"

"Only if they're curled and shining," Gina snapped.

"You have to suffer for beauty," Mama said from her perch on the edge of Marie's bed.

"And who made up that rule?" she demanded hotly. "A man?"

"Probably," Angela conceded as she slapped Marie's hand away from the dangerously low-scooped neckline of her borrowed red dress. "And stop tugging on the fabric. It's not going to come up any higher and you'll wrinkle it."

"My boobs will fall out," Marie told her, and laid the flat of her hand atop the swell of her breasts. She'd never worn a dress cut so low and knew that she'd have pneumonia before the end of the night. Figures that Gina's dress would be cut low enough to display all of her charms.

How had she let herself be talked into wearing the slinky red number? But even as she thought it, she knew the answer. Because just for tonight she wanted to be more than she usually was. Just for tonight she wanted to be the homecoming queen, the prom princess and Miss America all rolled into one.

"Your boobs will *not* fall out," Gina told her with a grin. "But if you're lucky, they may be helped to escape."

"Gina…" Mama's voice sounded stern, but they all knew the woman had long since given up trying to rein in her youngest daughter.

"If they don't freeze and break off before then," Marie whispered.

Angela picked up a tube of lipstick and a tiny brush, then turned Marie's face toward her. "God knows, I hate to agree with Gina on anything, but honestly, Marie, it's high time you did something like this."

"Amen," Gina muttered, and jabbed Marie's skull with a rhinestone barrette.

Marie winced and tried to pull away. Angela's fingers tightened on her chin.

"You're a pretty girl," Mama said. "You should make the most of it."

"By wearing enough paint to hide my identity?" Marie asked, giving a sideways glance into the mirror. Hmm. The rhinestones looked kind of nice the way they held back a wave of curls and twinkled against her dark hair.

"To accentuate your inner beauty," Gina said, making her voice high and pompous.

Inner beauty. Right. What all men were interested in.

Angela finished painting on lipstick and released her chin. Then she studied Marie's face as though it was a just finished work of art. "Good," she said to herself before reaching for the tiny bottle of expensive perfume she'd brought with her.

Leaning forward, she dabbed some of the luxurious scent behind each of Marie's ears, then handed her the crystal stopper. "Touch the scent between your breasts," she ordered.

Marie gripped the crystal tightly enough to snap it. This was getting out of hand, she thought for what had to be the hundredth time since submitting herself to her sisters' care. "Isn't it enough they're exposed to the entire world? Do they have to smell, too?"

"Oh, brother," Gina muttered as she jabbed another rhinestone barrette into place on the other side of Marie's head. "All of this is wasted on you, you know that?"

"That's enough, Gina," Mama told her.

"Well, really," the youngest Santini sister went on, curling some of Marie's hair around her finger and smoothing it into place. "She's Italian, for heaven's sake! Hot-blooded, just like the rest of us."

Oh, Marie thought, her blood was plenty hot and getting hotter every minute.

"Italian doesn't mean sex crazed," Angela chimed in.

"Then it's been so long, you don't remember," Gina snapped.

"All right!" Mama clapped her hands and said, "That's enough now. Marie will be who she is and—" she looked into the mirror to meet her middle daughter's gaze "—that's more than enough for any man."

Marie gave her a soft smile and, touched, whispered, "Thanks, Mama."

The older woman smiled back and lifted one hand to emphasize her next point. "Though that's not to say that a little advertising doesn't hurt. Now put that perfume where your sister told you to. And Gina, I really don't want to know about your hot blood, all right?"

"None of us do," Angela added.

"Jealous," Gina told them. "You're all jealous."

Marie dutifully touched the stopper to the valley between her breasts and shivered at the feel of the cold glass against her heated skin. When she handed the perfume back to her sister, she took a last look at herself in the mirror.

It was her reflection and yet so different.

"Nice, huh?" Gina said, admiring her handiwork.

"Nice nothing," Angela said. "She's gorgeous."

"She always has been," Mama put in.

Marie stared at herself for a long moment, then took a deep breath that swelled her breasts high enough to convince her not to do *that* real often, and stood up. "Okay, I guess I'm as ready as I'll ever be."

"Wait'll Davis gets a load of you," Gina said with a grin.

Angela smiled and reached out to smooth the skirt of Marie's dress. "His eyes'll pop out, honey."

Marie's eyes suddenly stung with the threat of tears. She'd never done this before. Shared a feminine bonding session over makeup and clothes with her sisters and her mother. It felt strange, and…good.

"Don't you *dare* get all weepy and ruin your makeup," Gina warned sternly.

Marie laughed, as she was meant to, and thought maybe they were right. Maybe it was high time for her to come out from under her overalls and take a look at the world through female eyes.

A knock at the door sounded.

And maybe, she thought with a sharp pang of

insecurity, it wasn't too late to cancel this whole thing.

"He's here," Gina said unnecessarily.

"Oh, God," Marie whispered through a suddenly tight throat.

"You look wonderful, Marie," Mama said as she crossed the room to hug her. "Now don't worry about a thing. Just be yourself."

Marie knew it was good advice, but how could she be herself when she didn't even look like herself? Nope. That wouldn't work. Tonight she would be someone else. Someone as hot-blooded as Gina. Someone as beautiful as Angela. Someone as confident as Mama.

Tonight she was the best of all the Santini women—and the Marie she'd always secretly yearned to be.

Chapter Seven

Davis knocked on the door again and couldn't help wondering if she'd changed her mind again. Maybe she wouldn't go out with him at all. And maybe, he told himself, they'd be accompanied by one of her sisters. Or her mother. Or Jeremy.

He'd never before been involved with a woman so devoted to family. And he still wasn't sure he liked it.

Overhead, a clear winter sky gleamed with millions of stars, and the ever-present ocean wind pushed at him with its cold breath. He stuffed his hands into his trouser pockets and wished his suit coat was warmer.

Then the door opened and every thought in his head, but one…dissolved.

Beautiful. Marie Santini was absolutely the most breathtaking woman he'd ever seen. Backlit by a solitary lamp, her dark hair shone around the glittering clips holding the thick mass back from her face. For the first time since he'd known her, she was wearing makeup, but only enough to emphasize the beauty of her eyes and the lush fullness of her lips. A soft floral scent reached out to him, and he inhaled it greedily as his gaze drifted down and over her. His heart lurched a bit and his breathing quickened as he admired the swell of her breasts above the low neckline of her dress. Long red sleeves encased her slender arms and the short hem of the dress swirled around a pair of amazing legs.

Slowly he lifted his gaze again until he was looking into her green eyes. Then he smiled, shook his head and said, "Lady, you're incredible."

She smiled and lifted her chin a bit higher, giving her hair a shake. "Thank you. Tonight I *feel* incredible."

And he felt lucky. So damned lucky, he was sure something would go wrong.

"Are you ready?" he asked, and held out one hand toward her.

"As I'll ever be," she said, and picked up her coat from a nearby chair. Then she stepped out onto the porch and closed the door behind her.

That scent of hers enveloped him, and Davis had all he could do to keep from grabbing her and pulling her close. He wanted to taste her mouth again. But they had a dinner reservation to keep. Which was too bad, since the only thing he was hungry for was her.

Small bouquets of holly and poinsettias decorated every table, and in the far corner of the restaurant a fire blazed on the brick-faced hearth. The soft clink of crystal and the hush of muted conversations drifted through the room, but Davis paid no attention to any of it. He only had eyes for Marie.

Unfortunately so did their waiter.

At the thought of him, the man appeared with their dessert, and keeping his fascinated gaze locked on Marie, damn near dumped a slice of apple pie into Davis's lap.

"Hey!" he said, and caught the china plate just in time.

The waiter spared him a fast glance and a less-than-apologetic shrug. "Sorry." Then shifting his gaze back to the object of his affections, he asked, "Would you like more coffee, miss?"

Davis gritted his teeth. He was used to other men admiring his dates. What he wasn't used to was this smattering of anger that churned in his guts every time the waiter drooled on Marie. Jealousy? he wondered, surprised at himself. Hell, he'd never been jealous before and had even laughed at his friends when they described the ugly emotions he was now experiencing. But damn it, there was nothing funny about watching a stranger ogling Marie.

"Coffee?" the waiter asked again, and Davis prepared to scoot out of range.

She gave him a small smile and shook her head, "No, thanks."

As the man walked away, Davis said, "I appreciate your turning down the coffee. Otherwise, I might get third-degree burns in an area I'd rather keep unharmed."

Marie chuckled. "I think he's sweet."

"You would," he said, giving the man's back a hard look. "He didn't dump a salad in your lap."

"At least it was served with dressing on the side," she said on a laugh.

True, he thought. Instead of picking dry lettuce off his slacks, he could have been doused with blue cheese dressing.

"And have you recovered from the waiter's slip?" she asked, laying her forearms on the linen-covered tabletop and leaning forward. Her movement gave him an excellent view of the breasts he'd been trying all evening not to stare at.

Recovered? he thought. Hell, no. He was sinking fast.

"I'll live as long as he doesn't come back with some flaming dessert."

She laughed again and he found himself enjoying the sound.

"This was really nice, Davis," she said, dragging his attention back to her face and the eyes that haunted him. "Thank you for bringing me."

"I've been trying to get you to go out with me since I met you," he reminded her.

"Was it worth the wait?" she asked, a teasing note in her voice.

"Oh," he said with a slight nod, "definitely."

"Good." She picked up a spoon and took a small bite of sherbet. Her lips closed over the icy sweet, and he watched her sigh as the flavors dissolved on her tongue.

He shifted uncomfortably in his seat and was privately grateful that the room was so dimly lit. Otherwise he'd have to keep his suit coat buttoned when they left, to avoid embarrassing himself.

"How long have you been a marine?"

"Hmm?" He shook his head to clear it. "What?"

She grinned at him. "I asked how long you've been a marine."

"Oh." Keep your mind on the conversation, he thought. "Forever."

"That long?" Marie smiled and took another bite of sherbet. "You look pretty good for your advanced age."

And he was aging by the minute, thinking about her and him and what he'd rather they be doing instead of sitting here making polite conversation. "Thanks, I think."

She licked her spoon, and the slow swipe of her tongue did incredible things to his pulse rate.

"So how long really?" she asked.

"Close to fifteen years," he managed to say.

"Are you a lifer?" she asked, dipping that spoon back into the sherbet he was beginning to envy.

"Yeah," he said, tearing his gaze from her mouth and the sensuous way she ate the damned dessert. "Always figured to be in for the long haul."

"Really? There's nothing else you'd want to do?"

For one brief minute, Davis thought about his old dream of opening a car-restoration place. Heck, he had several different cars tucked away in various storage garages across the country. Wherever he was stationed, he'd buy an old junker and slowly restore it himself. He'd always told himself it was a hobby, but the truth was it gave him something to do when he wasn't on duty. A man with no family and ties had too much free time.

He'd never told anyone else about that old dream, and even though somehow he knew that Marie would be encouraging, he just couldn't form the words to tell her.

"No." Davis shook his head and pushed the slice of apple pie to one side. "I like moving around. I don't know if I could stand staying in one place too long."

"Funny," she mused, and pushed her unfinished sherbet aside. "I don't know that I could relocate as much as you do." She shook her head slowly. "A new home every few years? No place to call your own?"

"Root-bound, huh?" he teased.

"And you're rootless," she said softly.

"I guess there's no middle ground between the two, huh?" he asked.

"I don't think so," she said softly.

He reached across the table and covered her hand with his. The quick flash of heat that erupted when they touched warmed him through as he asked, "Haven't you ever wanted to just…take off? Move somewhere new?"

"Take off?" she repeated.

"Yeah. Go somewhere where no one knows you."

Marie shook her head. "No. Why would I?"

Davis frowned and linked their fingers together. "To be on your own. Alone to do whatever you want."

She smiled at him, but her eyes looked confused. "I already have that."

"Do you?" he asked. "I've known you several days and I almost never see you without Jeremy or Gina or your mom…."

"They're my family," she protested.

She didn't understand, and he knew he shouldn't have expected her to. She hadn't grown up being shuttled from place to place. She hadn't learned early that "he travels fastest who travels alone." There was no way she could possibly know the benefits of having no one to lay claim to your time. Your life.

"Quicksand," he muttered.

"What?"

He inhaled deeply and linked his fingers with hers. Her thumb stroked the back of his hand and a part of his mind concentrated solely on the sensations she was stirring within him.

"Families," he said thickly. "I've always thought of them as quicksand." Explaining, he went on. "Stay too close and they suck you in and then under. You're trapped. Never free to be whoever you might want to be."

Marie watched him and tried to read his expression, but it seemed Davis Garvey had had too many years to learn to hide what he was thinking. She couldn't understand his feelings about family and thought his way seemed a lonely way to live.

Instantly images of her family rose up in her mind and she knew that without them, her life would be an empty thing.

"I've always thought of my family as a lifeboat," she said quietly, trying to ease the shadow of old pain from his eyes.

"What do you mean?"

"You know," she said, continuing to stroke the back of his hand with her thumb, "a safety net, sort of. Where each of us is there to help the other. To back each other up in times of trouble and to cheer for each other when things are great. Mama says that home is a place that, when you go there, they have to let you in."

He didn't say anything and Marie asked quietly, "Where's your safety net, Davis?"

He gave her hand a squeeze, then released her and reached for the leather folder that held their bill. Giving her a smile that didn't quite hide the shadows still lurking in his eyes, he said, "I guess right now it's Camp Pendleton."

As he glanced at the bill and counted out the appropriate amount of money, she asked, "I know you said you don't have a family. But surely there's someone?"

"Just the corps," he said, then must have noticed the sympathy in her eyes. "Don't bother feeling sorry for me," he said with a half smile. "Quicksand, remember?"

"Yes," she said, "I remember." But she couldn't help wondering if he'd still feel that way if there was a family standing beside him.

She'd seen his patience and kindness with Jeremy and his friendliness toward her sisters and her mother. Marie had a feeling that Davis Garvey didn't even realize how starved for family he really was. This was a man who'd obviously spent so much of his life alone, he'd come to believe that it was the only way to live.

Her heart ached just a little for the man who had so much to give and no one to give it to.

While Davis settled their bill, Marie waited on the wooden deck that stretched along behind the row of restaurants lining the harbor. The cold, sea-kissed breeze whipped around her, sending her skirt hem into a wild dance around her thighs.

She tipped her face into the wind and felt the sting of salt air caress her cheeks and chest with dampness. With her earlier worries about pneumonia banished along with the rest of her rational mind, she let her coat hang open so that the wind could wrap itself around her.

"You must be freezing," Davis said as he came up behind her.

Startled, she turned to look at him, and in the soft glow of the deck lights, she saw his eyes darken as he stared at her. Maybe a part of her should be offended that he was so obviously attracted to the "new and improved" Marie—the stranger she was tonight. But watching his eyes as he watched her sent spirals of heat unwinding throughout her body. A slow, deep ache settled low in her belly, and it felt as though an iron band was wrapped tightly around her chest, making it difficult to breathe.

He draped one arm around her shoulders and pulled her close to him. Her back to his front, she felt the hard, solid strength of him, and a skittering of heat dazzled her bloodstream. This was something elemental. A powerful connection lay between them and this was the night Marie had decided to explore it. To discover what she'd always dreamed of discovering. To find in Davis's arms the magic she knew other women had found.

His arms came around her and they stood, staring out at the harbor. The luxury homes across the water sparkled with thousands of twinkling Christmas lights. Reflections of those lights shone on the black water, looking as though handfuls of multicolored stars had fallen from the sky.

From somewhere far off, the muted strains of "Silent Night" drifted toward them. Marie's breath caught in her throat. It was all so beautiful. So perfect.

He held her tighter and she shivered.

"You *are* cold," he whispered close to her ear, and the brush of his warm breath on her flesh made her tremble.

Cold? She didn't think she'd ever be cold again. Not with the fires blazing inside her.

"No," she whispered with a shake of her head, "I'm not cold. I'm…"

"What?" He turned her in his arms and held her tightly, pressing her body into his.

Looking down into her eyes, he captured her gaze and held it until Marie thought she might drown in the crystal-blue depths that held so many secrets and so much warmth.

How could it be possible she'd known him only a few days? At that moment, she felt as though she'd always known him. That a part of her had always been waiting for him. And it didn't matter anymore that he would leave her one day. All that mattered now was that tonight, for now, he was hers. And she suddenly wanted to be his.

"Marie?" he asked, and lifted one hand to smooth his fingertips along her cheek.

She swallowed heavily and closed her eyes briefly at the sensation of warmth trickling from his fingers into her soul. Looking at him again, she said only, "Kiss me, Davis."

"My pleasure," he whispered, and bent his head to claim her mouth.

Gently at first, his lips met hers. Softly, tenderly, he kissed her as the wind raced around them, binding them together in an icy embrace. Then he cupped her cheek with his palm and deepened that kiss, entering her mouth when she sighed, his tongue caressing her warmth, stealing her breath.

Marie's heartbeat raced, her stomach flip-flopped and her knees wobbled. She leaned into him, trusting him to hold her upright as her world spun. It was everything their last kiss had been and more. So much more that Marie didn't want it to stop. She didn't want these sensations to end. And when he lifted his head to look at her, she looked deeply into his eyes and said, "Let's go home, Davis."

She knew he heard the need quivering in her voice and saw the desire shining in her eyes. "Are you sure?" he asked.

Marie inhaled deeply, drawing the scent of him deep inside her. She would never be able to catch a whiff of Old Spice again without remembering this moment in the Christmas-lit darkness with him. Every nerve tingled with anticipation. Every sense strained to the breaking point. Her breath hitched, her stomach rolled and that ache low in her body seemed to throb in time with her pulse beat.

Sure? Dear heaven, if he didn't get her home quickly, the new and improved Marie was going to toss him to the wooden deck and have her way with him. And the mental images inspired by *that* notion nearly pushed her over the precarious precipice on which she felt balanced.

Mouth dry, heart pounding, she lifted her hands to the lapels of his coat and hung on. Then tipping her head back to look at him squarely, she whispered harshly, "Davis, trust me on this. I'm *very* sure."

He groaned tightly, pulled in a long, deep breath, then winked at her. "Me, too."

Chapter Eight

Okay, she *had* been sure.

On the deck, on their hurried walk to the parking lot, for most of the drive home. But, as the silence in the car thickened, her nerve had started slipping.

What was she doing?

She wasn't a one-night-stand kind of girl.

For pity's sake, was she out of her mind?

Davis parked the car in the driveway and Marie tossed a quick glance at the main house. Why did she suddenly feel like a hormone-enraged teenager sneaking around with her boyfriend? She was a grown woman. Twenty-six years old and about to finally lose the humiliating fact of her virginity.

She choked back an hysterical laugh.

Sure. Nothing to be nervous about.

"Marie?" Davis asked, and she lifted her gaze to his. In the dim light, she saw his concern warring with the desire still thumping through her despite a sudden rush of doubts. "Are you okay?"

"Yeah," she muttered, and groped blindly for the door handle. "Dandy." She got out of the car and started walking toward the stairs leading to her apartment. Every click of her heels against the cement seemed to be echoing a message. Unfortunately it was a very confusing message. At first she heard, *Do it, do it.* And in the next instant, she imagined a voice shouting, *Stop this, stop this.*

Oh, great. Even her conscience was muddled.

Just when she needed to be able to think straight, her brain was a jumble of wants and desires and warnings and guilt pangs. But what did she have to be guilty about?

She lifted one hand to her forehead as she started up the stairs. Hearing Davis only a step or two behind her did nothing to calm the frenzy roaring through her.

At the landing, she dug out her house key, slid it into the lock and turned it. Before she could step inside, though, Davis's hand on her arm stopped her.

"Hey," he said quietly, and his breath misted before him in the cold. "I don't know what's going on in that mind of yours, but—"

"It's nothing," she said quickly, fighting down her nerves. She'd come this far. She didn't want to quit now, did she?

A single lamp had been left burning in the apartment and a fragile slice of light framed the two of them as they stood there, staring at each other.

"It's something," Davis said, and laid both hands on her shoulders. "Marie, we don't have to do this. If you've changed your mind—" he forced a strained laugh "—I'll just crawl back to my car and limp back to the base."

A groan squeezed from her throat and Marie rested her forehead on his chest. She felt the pounding of his heart and knew the frantic beat matched her own. If he left now, he wouldn't be the only one crawling to safety. She wanted him so badly, her whole body seemed to be crying out for the feel of him. So why was she hesitating now when before it had felt so right?

Lifting her head, she looked at him and whispered, "Davis, I don't know *what* I want…."

One corner of his mouth tilted into a half smile and he shrugged. "Then we wait."

"But I don't—"

"Shh…" He laid one finger across her mouth and a splinter of warmth touched her. "It's okay."

"No, it's not." Disgusted with herself, Marie stepped back from him, halfway through the doorway and tossed her purse into the apartment. When she looked back at him, he was smiling. "What?"

"That." He pointed over her head to the tiny green plant nailed to the door frame. A red ribbon dangled from its leaves and Marie knew darn well the plant hadn't been there when she left.

Gina.

She didn't know if she wanted to throttle her sister or thank her.

"It's mistletoe," he said unnecessarily, and took a step closer.

"So it is," she whispered, and felt her body light up again in anticipation.

"Then before I leave, I think we'd better kiss," he said, stepping into the doorway to join her. "Don't want to buck a tradition as old as mistletoe. Who knows what might happen?"

She nodded jerkily. "No point in taking chances."

"Exactly," he whispered, and pulled her into the circle of his arms.

When their lips met, Marie felt it again. That flash of heat and sense of rightness. This is what she'd been missing. On the deck, when he was kissing her, she'd known instinctively that tonight was the night. It was only on the drive home, when she'd had too much time to think, that she'd started doubting her own decision.

She should have known better. This wasn't a

time for thinking. This was a time for feeling.
Experiencing. For letting go of everything else and
grabbing hold of what was being offered. A chance
to find a little Christmas magic all her own.

Parting her lips for his tongue, she welcomed him
inside and gasped at the intimate caress. Her nerve
endings felt frazzled. The pounding of her own heart
was deafening. Swirls of want and need and pure,
unadulterated lust swam in the pit of her stomach.
This time, when he broke their kiss, Marie didn't let
go of him.

Instead she curled her arms around his neck,
met his gaze with her own and whispered brokenly,
"Make love to me, Davis. Now."

"Marie…" He looked haggard, pushed to
the breaking point, and yet there was a gleam of
uncertainty in his eyes. As if he was waiting for her
to change her mind again.

"I mean it," she said, moving one hand to cup his
cheek.

He turned his face into her touch and kissed the
center of her palm, tracing the tip of his tongue along
her skin until she was shuddering in his grasp.

"I want you," he whispered, and his breath came
warm against her flesh.

"I want you right back," she said in a hush. "Now,
Davis. For heaven's sake, please, now."

Apparently he saw the truth in her eyes, because
he picked her up, stepped into the apartment and

kicked the door closed behind him. Nestled in his strong arms, Marie tugged at his knotted tie and when it was free, unbuttoned the top two buttons of his shirt as he walked blindly across the small living room to the couch.

He set her down on her feet and she slipped out of her coat as he did the same. Gazes locked, the only illumination the one small lamp in the far corner, they faced each other and hurriedly yanked at their clothes.

Marie reached behind her to undo the zipper on her borrowed dress and groaned aloud when the blasted thing stuck. Davis came to her side, turned her around and worked it loose, skimming the backs of his knuckles along her spine as he slid the zipper down the length of her back.

"Ohhh…" Marie sighed heavily at the contact, and when he turned her back around to face him, leaned into him, loving the feel of his bare chest and back. She ran her hands up and down his muscular back and pressed herself close to him. And even through the material of his slacks, she felt the hard, rigid proof of his desire straining against her abdomen.

"Davis," she whispered, leaning back in his arms to look up at him, "I need…" How was she supposed to ask for what she needed when she wasn't completely sure herself?

"I need you, too, babe," he said, and began to drag his mouth along the line of her throat and down to her chest and the swell of her bosom. And then he stopped one last time. "No more doubts?" he asked quietly.

"None," she told him, more sure of this than anything before in her life.

He nodded and continued on his exploration. "I've been thinking about your breasts all night," he whispered, brushing his breath against her already-heated flesh.

"You have?" she said on a sigh, and felt his talented fingers flick her bra strap open in a single move.

The delicate lace came away in an instant and Davis tossed it to the floor. Before she could even think about embarrassment or anything else for that matter, he lowered her to the couch, cupped her breasts in his palms and bent his head to taste one erect nipple and then the other.

What was left of her brain dissolved into a puddle.

"Oh, my," she said. Mouth dry, eyes wide, she stared up at the ceiling as Davis's lips and teeth did incredible things to her body. Her back arched when he pulled one nipple into his mouth and suckled her. A drawing sensation started in the pit of her stomach and radiated outward until she felt as though he was pulling her soul into his. And just when she thought she would die from the pleasure, he abandoned that breast for the other. Again she felt his lips tug at her as the edges of his teeth nipped and teased her so sensitive skin.

"Davis," she said softly, her hands groping for him. She held the back of his head, pressing him to her so that she could keep him there and continue feeling the amazing sensations rocking her world.

He groaned tightly, and as he suckled her, his fingers toyed with her other nipple until she felt as though she was being pulled in four directions at once. As taut as a wire, her body ached and burned like nothing she'd ever experienced before.

And then it was over and he was sliding down along her body, trailing damp, warm kisses across her rib cage, her abdomen and...lower.

"Davis, do you think...?" She half sat up on the couch and watched through wide eyes as he pulled her black bikini panties down her legs then tossed them to the floor as he had her bra.

Excitement warred with awkward discomfort as she looked at herself to find she was stretched out on her sofa wearing nothing but a pair of black thigh-high stockings. Then her gaze locked with Davis's heated stare and as he watched her, she felt moisture pool at her center. Her flesh seemed to be simmering, her blood boiling, and as he leaned back and scooped her bottom off the couch, even her hair caught fire.

His strong fingers kneaded her tender flesh as he looked at her and Marie couldn't look away from his eyes. The blue depths looked silver in the half-light and they seemed to gleam with an inner blaze that burned as brightly as the flames consuming her.

He lifted her higher off the couch and inched closer to her. She licked her lips and tried to steady her breathing enough to allow air into lungs that felt starved for nourishment.

"Davis, what are you—" She broke off as he bent his head close to the juncture of her thighs. Her leg muscles contracted and she tried to pull free. She hadn't counted on *this*. She'd expected—no *wanted* sex. But this, this was something else again, and she wasn't at all sure that she could let him—

His mouth came down on her and she groaned aloud. Her hips bucked in his hands and she only half felt him ease her legs across his shoulders. She was flying. No longer tethered to the earth, the only hold on reality existed in the touch of Davis's hands on her bottom and the feel of his mouth on her—oh, good heavens!

Her head twisted from side to side on the sofa cushion. She arched into him and tried to concentrate on every sensation he offered her. His tongue swirled delicately over the tender folds of skin and teased an especially sensitive button of flesh. Marie jerked in his grasp as a lightning-like flash of pure, undiluted pleasure rocketed through her. He did it again, and another jagged bolt, stronger than the first, grabbed at her.

She gave herself up to him, leaving modesty,

awkwardness and shyness behind. She tried to part her legs wider, inviting him closer, deeper. Marie sighed when his tongue swept into her depths and groaned when his mouth closed over that one small area that seemed to hold every sensation in the universe.

She rocked against him, her hands reaching for him, her eyes still locked on the ceiling as she felt something hot and dark coil within her. The feeling built and built, feeding on itself, feeding on the pleasure only Davis could bring her. Every cell in her body tightened. Something was there. Just beyond her reach. Hovering, waiting for her to discover its treasures. Her mind blanked to everything but this silent, hungry quest.

She turned her head to look at him and her heart somersaulted in her chest. So intimate. So close. He touched her as no other man ever had and as she wanted no other man to do. Marie felt the strength in his hands and knew that he would keep her safe. Hold her, guide her to the end of this road he was propelling her along.

His tongue swept over that one certain spot again and she caught a scream and swallowed it as she hurtled toward oblivion. And when the first, glorious shake of completion rattled through her, she rode its wave, secure in his grasp, and let the tiny explosions shatter what was left of her composure.

Moments…maybe hours later, she heard his voice whispering in her ear.

"Come with me, Marie."

Her body still trembling, she opened her eyes to look at him, and when he helped her to her feet, she went with him, leaning against him as he headed for her bedroom.

Outside the window, she could see the strand of Christmas lights twinkling in the darkness. Moonlight slanted through the panes, falling across her double bed as if to point the way toward heaven.

Davis stopped beside the bed, grabbed the comforter and tossed it to the foot of the mattress. Then he eased himself down onto the clean sheets and drew her with him, laying alongside her, holding her tight.

His own heart pounding, he levered himself up on one elbow and looked down into her incredible face. Her hair tumbled about her cheeks. One rhinestone clip was missing and the other clung tenaciously to a single strand of hair.

Gently he disentangled it and set it down on the bedside table. Then he indulged himself. Running his hand across her body, he luxuriated in the soft, smooth feel of her. She sighed and turned toward him. Opening her eyes, she looked up at him and said, "That was amazing, Davis. Absolutely amazing."

Oh, he knew that. He'd felt her climax as surely as if it had been his own. Just the memory of her wild, untamed response to him was enough to make him hard and ready. The taste of her, the feel of her in his hands, was more than he'd ever expected to find. Never before had he felt this kind of... connection to a woman. And that thought both terrified and intrigued him.

But there would be time enough later to think. Now all he wanted was to become a part of her. To claim her body fully with his own. Slipping off the bed, he quickly got rid of the rest of his clothes. And when he lay back down, she opened her arms to him and Davis had the strangest sensation of *coming home*. Looking down into the liquid darkness of her eyes, he felt himself falling—into what, he wasn't sure.

He banished that thought and all others though, a moment later. Her hands moved on his body with a featherlight touch. Tender, gentle, yet demanding. Apparently, she, too, felt the same driving force to join. To couple their bodies and to feel the world drop away.

He bent to her breasts and kissed their soft brown tips again. She arched into him and he smiled against her skin. This they shared. The hunger, the joy.

His left hand dropped lower, crossing her abdomen to the small triangle of curls at the juncture of her thighs. She took a breath, held it and released it in a heavy sigh when his fingertips explored her depths.

A groan built inside him and Davis fought it back.

He touched her, stroking her silky body, finding everything he'd ever searched for within her. He dipped one finger, then two inside her. She lifted her hips into his touch and Davis shifted, giving in to the urge to hurry. To enter her. He couldn't wait another minute. Pulse pounding, heart racing, he moved to position himself between her legs.

Then he looked down into her eyes and kept her gaze locked with his as he eased himself in.

Her big green eyes widened farther at his intrusion and he paused, aching to hurry but suddenly needing to go slow. So tight, so warm. He inched farther into her heat and felt her body welcome him, closing around him in a soft grasp.

"Marie," he said on a choked-off groan, and leaned over her, bracing his weight on his hands at either side of her head.

"Come inside me, Davis," she whispered, and licked her lips just to torture him further. "I need to feel you inside me."

He needed that, too. More than his next breath.

Bending his head to hers, he took her mouth in a hard kiss and pushed himself the rest of the way in. She gasped aloud and held perfectly still for a moment. And in that instant, Davis knew what he should have suspected all along.

Her nervousness. Her heated response. Her tight warmth.

Marie Santini was a virgin.

At least she *had* been.

Marie's head tipped back into the pillow and she smiled at the glorious feeling of Davis *inside* her. It was like nothing she'd ever known before. Everything she'd heard, everything she'd read, couldn't have prepared her for the simple *rightness* of it all.

Bodies joined, hearts beating in unison, the power, the magic of it swamped her, leaving her breathless. She looked up into Davis's surprised gaze and knew in that heart-stopping moment that she loved him. As ridiculous as it might sound, she loved a man she'd known less than a week.

And even as logic cried out that it was impossible, her heart knew the truth. It didn't matter if a week or a year had passed. When you found the one person meant for you, the feelings were real. Undeniable. She opened her mouth to say the words she'd always wanted to utter, but Davis spoke before she had the chance.

"Why didn't you tell me?" he ground out.

"It didn't seem important at the time," she told him, and brushed aside his concerns for her virginity. *She* hadn't been worried. She'd thought only to silence the ache inside her and she had. Closing her eyes, Marie started, cautiously, to rock her hips against his. "Mmmm," she said quietly, relishing the delicious sensations that movement caused, and moved again, deliberately taking him deeper.

"Oh, damn it," Davis said tightly, and dropped

his head to her shoulder. Anger dissolved under the onslaught of need and pleasure.

"Could we argue about this later?" she asked, and somehow swiveled her hips in a circular motion that nearly undid him.

She was right. No talking. Not now. Not when all he could think of was burying himself so deeply inside her, they would never be free of each other.

"Yes…" He gasped and withdrew from her only to plunge inside again. Her legs locked around his waist, she pulled him deeper with every thrust. Demanding everything he had to give and offering him all that she was.

Blind to everything but her and the overwhelmingly powerful urge to become one with her, Davis turned his back on rational thought and raced toward oblivion.

Together they hurtled along the path leading them toward a release so shattering that neither of them could have been prepared.

When they reached that pinnacle, Davis called her name and felt her arms go around him to cushion his fall.

Chapter Nine

Slowly, carefully, Davis pulled away from her and shifted to one side of Marie where he collapsed like a dead man.

Body still humming with lingering flickers of delight, Marie summoned the last of her strength and turned her head on the pillow to look at him. Love, she thought dazedly. Who would have thought it? She'd long since given up on finding love, and now that she had, she must remember that just because she loved him…it didn't mean that he loved her.

She'd gone into this with her eyes wide-open, knowing that one day Davis Garvey would get over his fascination with her and move on. That realization hadn't changed.

Still, there was nothing saying she couldn't enjoy things while they lasted.

"You okay?" he asked.

Oh, more than okay, though she didn't think she'd be confessing her undying love anytime soon.

Instead, she met his steady blue gaze and said softly, "If there's a fire or an earthquake in the next few minutes, I'm going to have to simply lie here and take it."

A half smile touched one corner of his mouth. "Me, too."

"So," she said, easing one hand off the mattress to reach out and pat his arm, "just in case, I wanted to say, *thanks*."

He blinked. "Thanks?"

Inhaling deeply, Marie realized she felt completely and utterly relaxed—from tip to toe. It was glorious. "Oh, yes. Thanks. Mmm…Davis, you were…that was…" She paused, thought for a moment, then shrugged and chuckled. "I'm at a loss for words."

He slowly pushed himself up onto one elbow and looked down at her. Strangely enough, he didn't look nearly as happy as she felt at the moment.

"Well," he said quietly, "I'm not."

Puzzled, Marie didn't have a clue why he was so grumpy. She knew darn well he'd enjoyed himself every bit as much as she had. But then, she didn't have much experience with this sort of thing. She smiled to herself at that thought. She had more experience now than she'd had an hour or two ago.

"I don't know what you've got to smile about."

Marie stared at him and grinned. "If that's true, then you underestimate yourself."

"That's not what I meant."

"What did you mean?"

"Damn it, Marie," he said tightly, "why didn't you tell me?"

"Tell you what?"

"That you were a virgin."

She snorted a laugh. "Why would I do that?"

"Because…" He shoved one hand across the top of his head in frustration. "Because you're supposed to, that's why."

"There are rules about that sort of thing?" she asked, surprised.

"Hell, yes," he snapped and sat up, clearly frustrated.

"Gee, I'm sorry," she told him, completely unapologetic. Rolling to one side, she tugged the edge of the quilt out from under her so she could yank it across her naked body. Starting to feel cold from the inside out, she suddenly wanted to cover her nudity. "I guess I forgot to study my copy of *The Beginner's Guide to Sexual Situations.*"

"Oh," he told her solemnly, "that's very funny."

"Thank you," she said, fumbling with the quilt. "We aim to please."

"Do you really?"

"You have a complaint you'd like to register?" For heaven's sake, why couldn't she get the stupid quilt off the blasted bed?

"Oh," he said, leveling her with a glance, "several."

"Perhaps it'd be better if you wrote a letter," she snapped and wondered where that gloriously indolent sensation had gone. Marie glared at him when she noticed that it was his body holding down the quilt. "Move," she said.

"Move?"

"You're on my quilt and I want it."

"Oh, pardon the hell out of me," he said, and levered himself off the mattress long enough for her to snatch the quilt up and cover herself.

"You're forgiven," she said. Then she added, "See how easy that was?"

"Damn it, Marie," he said, "this isn't a joke. You should have told me."

"Uh-huh," she said, holding the quilt up over the swell of her breasts. Raking one hand through her hair, she gave him a look that should have curled his. "And when was I supposed to do that?"

"What?" He shook his head and stared at her.

"When?" she demanded, and sat up straighter against the headboard. "Oh! I know," she went on, giving in to the rising tide of anger inside her. "When you brought your car in that first day."

"Huh?"

"Sure." Marie nodded abruptly. "When we went for that test drive, I should have said, 'Give me your keys, and by the way, did you know I'm a virgin?'"

"Marie…"

"Oh, and then later, at dinner with my family," she went on in a rush. "I could have said, 'Davis, would you please pass the lasagna to the only virgin at the table?' Of course that might have been a little embarrassing for Gina, but at least *you* would have been forewarned."

"You're being ridiculous," he said, his voice a tight, hard thread.

"Not at all," Marie went on, meeting those blue eyes of his in a staring match she was determined to win. "I'm agreeing with you. You're right, I missed several key opportunities to admit to my humble station. Just think, at the batting cages, I could have said, 'I'm a virgin, so would you mind helping Jeremy hit a home run?'"

He jumped off the bed and started pacing the room. But it was angrier than pacing really. More of a stalking. Her gaze followed him, and even though her temper was beginning to boil, she felt a different kind of burning inside as she watched him move through the darkened room.

"You should have told me tonight, damn it."

"At dinner?" She went up onto her knees, still clutching that quilt to her front like a shield. "Maybe after the waiter dumped your salad in your lap. Something along the lines of, 'Let me help you pick up that lettuce, Davis, I'm a virgin.'"

He stopped dead, swiveled his head to glare at her and Marie's breath hitched in her throat. In a shaft of moonlight, his muscular body was outlined, defined. He could have posed for a marble statue. Something titled Infuriated Lover.

Oh, wow, she had a lover.

Marie swallowed the smile that thought brought. At the moment he didn't look particularly loving, and the way this conversation was headed, their one night of lovemaking could very well be their first *and* last.

He just looked at her. "I mean you could have told me here, tonight."

"Precisely when, Davis?" she asked, crawling off the mattress to stand on her own two feet. "On the couch a while ago?" Memories rushed back at her and her knees wobbled in response. "Or here, in bed? What was the point? You found out eventually."

"Yeah, when it was too late to stop."

"Good. I didn't want you to stop."

He scraped both hands across his face, growled deep in his throat, then walked toward her. Grabbing her shoulders, he gave her a little shake and said, "Don't you get it? You deserved better your first time."

Is that what this was all about? For pity's sake.

Was he grading his performance? Well, she could reassure him on that score anyway.

Lifting one hand, she cupped his cheek and looked deeply into his eyes. "I don't see how it could have been any better."

He shook his head, pulled her to him and wrapped his arms around her. Resting his chin on top of her head, he said, "That's just it. You don't see how. But I can. And if I'd known…"

If he'd known, Marie thought, he might not have gone through with it and then she would have missed out on one incredible experience. No, whatever he might think, things had worked out better this way.

She snuggled in close, letting the quilt drop between them, so that she could feel the warm brush of his flesh against hers. His heart beat steadily beneath her ear as she said, "I wouldn't change a thing, Davis. Really."

He squeezed her tight enough to snap her ribs, then eased up the pressure, still keeping her in the circle of his arms. "Why am I the one making noises about this? Damn it, Marie, you should be the one upset here."

"Why?" She tipped her head back to look up at him. "It was wonderful. I'm glad it was you. I'm glad I'm not a virgin anymore. Don't make such a big deal out of it."

"You *deserve* a big deal," he said tightly.

Didn't he have a clue just how big a deal this had

been for her? Good heavens, she'd only just realized
that she loved him. How many women were fortunate
enough to always be able to remember their first time
with the knowledge that they'd been with a man they
loved?

Of course, it was very nice to have him so
concerned for her feelings. But what he couldn't know
was that, having realized she loved him, it made what
they had shared all the more beautiful. Heck, darn
near miraculous.

"I *deserve* to enjoy the lovely glow you gave me,"
she countered.

He laughed shortly, the sound coming harsh and
strained from his throat. "Glow, huh? There are other
kinds of glows, you know."

"Hmm?"

"There's something else we have to talk about,"
he said.

"Now what?" Really, if *she* was happy, why
couldn't he be?

"We didn't use any protection, Marie."

"Protection." The first drops of rain started to land
on her parade.

"I'm clean," he said quickly as if to reassure her.
"And if you're on birth control pills, then we have
nothing to worry about."

Birth control pills. Sure, what twenty-six-year-
old virgin wasn't taking the Pill in the hopes that

someday, someone *might* come along and *maybe* she'd finally have sex?

"Marie?"

"In a perfect world…" Okay, now she was upset. Protection. She hadn't given it a thought. Oh, brother, wouldn't it be just retribution for a virgin to get pregnant her first time out?

"No Pill?"

"No Pill."

"Oh, man." He inhaled deeply, and tightened his hold on her. "It'll be okay. It's my fault," he said. "I should have—"

"There were two of us there, Davis," she pointed out. And therein lay the problem. But she'd be darned if he'd take all the blame for this. "We're both grown-ups. We made a mistake."

"A big one."

"Well, if you're going to make a mistake," she muttered, "might as well go whole hog."

Davis stared blankly at the darkened ceiling for a long moment and mentally called himself all kinds of uncivilized names. He hadn't done anything this stupid since he was seventeen and got lucky with the girl next door.

A virgin, he thought. He'd never been with a virgin before, and the fact that Marie had allowed him to be her first both shocked and touched him. She'd trusted him to initiate her into lovemaking, and brother, had he let her down.

Not only had he taken her virginity, he might have made her pregnant. All because he hadn't been strong enough to withstand his hormones. But in his own defense, he admitted silently, it had been much more than hormones. It had felt like his very life had depended on having Marie. Being a part of her. And now, both their lives might very well change forever because of it.

Leading her to the foot of the bed, Davis sat down and dragged her onto his lap. The feel of her naked skin against his had him wanting her all over again, and that was a new sensation. Always before, once the rush of desire had been sated, he'd been content. But with Marie, being with her had only fed the hunger that continued to grow inside him. A warning bell went off in his head, but he ignored it.

"You're taking this pretty well," he said softly.

She scooted around to get comfortable, and Davis drew in a long, deep breath, hoping to keep his body from responding. It didn't help.

"Do hysterics act as an after-the-fact birth control method?" she asked with a shrug.

"Nope," he told her, and laid one hand across her thighs, trying to hold her still.

"Then what would be the point?"

Amazing woman. Over the last several days, he'd really grown to *like* Marie. Kind and patient, funny and smart, not to mention being a hell of a mechanic, Marie Santini was a frighteningly perfect woman.

Now he was finding out that she was great company in a crisis situation. No losing her head. No shouting or blaming. Just a woman way too good for him. If he were a different sort of man, he might right now be thinking about getting down on his knees and begging her to marry him.

Instead, he looked into her eyes, saw the softening gleam in those green depths and had to battle down the urge to run. Marie was the kind of woman who wanted family. Hell, she *needed* family. And Davis wouldn't know what to do with a family if he fell into the middle of one.

Still, a part of him wished that he and Marie belonged together. That he could call this woman *home*.

"You're really something, you know it?" he asked, and knew it for the understatement that it was.

"Yeah," Marie said with a smile, "Jeremy says I'm the bomb."

"The bomb?"

"Apparently a good thing."

Then she was definitely the bomb.

"I want you to know," he said, "if you're pregnant—"

"I'll deal with that problem if it presents itself."

"*We'll* deal," he said firmly. He wanted her to know that in this, at least, she could trust him. He'd be there. For her. For a baby. A baby. God help them all.

She looked into his eyes and nodded. *"We'll deal."*

At least that much was settled. "When will we know for sure?"

She thought about it for a moment, then said, "Before Christmas."

Less than three weeks, he told himself. He'd lived through boot camp and combat. He could last until Christmas.

"But for now…" she said, dragging his attention back to her as she wrapped her arms around his neck.

"Yeah…?" He pulled his head back to watch her warily.

She smiled at him and he felt the power of that smile like a punch to the midsection. His body stirred and a fresh wave of need swelled inside him. Oh, he was in serious trouble when even the threat of possible parenthood wasn't enough to make him head for the door.

"We're here together…." She tossed her hair back from her face and ran the tip of one finger along his jaw and then across his lips. "Do you have any of that protection you mentioned?"

Everything inside Davis tightened a notch or two. She'd never been with a man before tonight, a possible pregnancy was hanging in the balance and yet, here she was, rekindling the fires between them. And he was leaping into the warmth she offered.

"As a matter of fact, I do," he said, thinking of the foil packets he'd been carrying around for the last few days in the hope he and Marie would come together. And naturally, when they did make love, he'd been so intent on her, he'd forgotten all about the little packages that could have saved them a couple weeks of worry.

She smiled at him again and it was a different smile. The age-old feminine smile that had been bringing men to their knees for centuries.

"Man," he whispered, sliding his hand up the nape of her neck to thread his fingers through the black silk of her hair, "I thought virgins were supposed to be shy...."

"But as you pointed out a few minutes ago," Marie told him as she leaned in for his kiss, "I'm not a virgin anymore."

"I stand corrected."

"Oh," she said softly, "don't stand on my account."

Two days later, Marie lay half under her mother's kitchen sink and bonked her head hard when she sat up suddenly and asked, "Was that my phone?"

"No," Gina said from her seat at the kitchen table. She turned the page of her magazine, shot Marie a quick, amused look and added, "just like it wasn't your phone ten minutes ago, too."

"So sue me," Marie snapped, and eased her head

back down beneath the pipes. "I thought I heard something."

"I'm not surprised you're hearing bells the way you slammed your head into the bottom of the sink."

Marie ground her teeth together, gripped the wrench handle more tightly, ignored her sister and tried to turn the frozen-in-place bolt again. Damn it, she didn't have time for this. She should be at the shop working on Laura's car. She should be Christmas shopping. She should be…with Davis.

That was the real problem, here. Not her mother calling her to help out with a plugged sink. Since their night together, Marie hadn't heard a word from Davis Garvey. Nothing. No phone call, no visit to the garage, no drop-in at the apartment. It was as if in one magical night she'd found the love of her life and chased him off in the process.

"So who are we expecting to call?" Gina asked in a much-too-innocent-sounding tone. "Plumbers Unlimited?"

"Very amusing," Marie said through gritted teeth. "When is Mama going to be back from the store?"

"There's no telling. I get my love of shopping from Mom."

"Well," Marie said, "I'm never going to get this darn elbow joint off. We'll have to call a plumber."

"And tie up the phone line?" Gina countered, then *tsk-tsked*. "We wouldn't want that, would we?"

Marie squirmed out from under the sink, hefted the

wrench in one hand and looked at her sister. "Watch it, Gina. I'm armed and just a little cranky."

Gina flipped the magazine closed, got up from the table and walked to where Marie was sitting on the floor. Then, squatting, she looked her sister dead in the eye. "It's Davis, isn't it?" she asked.

Marie shifted her gaze away and made a big production out of precisely placing her wrench back into the toolbox. She didn't want to get into this with Gina. She didn't want to have to admit out loud that not only had Davis left her—like every other guy she'd ever known—but that he'd left her in record time, carrying her virginity like a trophy.

Besides, she was making too big a deal out of this. She'd known all along that Davis wouldn't be interested in her forever. And yet, only two nights ago, he'd seemed very interested indeed.

"This has nothing to do with Davis," she said, forcing conviction into her voice. "It's raining, I've got work backed up at the shop and I'm hip-deep in stubborn kitchen appliances only two weeks from Christmas. Isn't that enough to make a person crabby?"

"Uh-huh," Gina said, "but not enough to make a person imagine a telephone ringing."

"A simple mistake."

"Once maybe, but twice?"

"Maybe I should try the heat gun on that bolt," Marie said. "It could warm up enough to turn."

"Who cares?"

"Mama."

"This is about Davis, isn't it?" Gina demanded. "That's why you're not looking at me. That's why you've been avoiding me for the last couple of days."

Bingo, Marie thought, but didn't say. Gina was way too observant.

"You're nuts."

"Then look me dead in the eye and deny you're waiting to hear from Davis."

"Fine." Steeling herself to keep her emotions shuttered, Marie looked into Gina's dark brown gaze and hoped her sister wouldn't notice a thing.

"Ohmigod!" Gina sputtered.

Marie gasped and turned away, looking back at the floor, the ceiling, the windows, the darned sink that had brought her here in the first place.

But Gina wouldn't be ignored. Not now, anyway. "You did it, didn't you?" she asked, plopping onto the floor and grinning. "You and Davis did the deed!" She whooped, clapped her hands and actually chortled, "And the last Santini virgin bites the dust."

Boy, her little sister was good. What did she have—radar?

Chapter Ten

Rain drummed against the canvas, convertible roof of the Mustang and pinged off its hood and fenders. Davis parked at the curb in front of the Santini house and stared through the streaming passenger-side window at Marie's apartment. Was it only two days ago he'd been here? Had it really only been two days since he'd spent hours wrapped around Marie's willing, responsive body?

It felt longer.

He shoved one hand across the top of his head, then dropped that hand to the steering wheel. His fingers tapped out a rhythm to match the pounding rain as he reminded himself that he'd stayed away purposely. He'd wanted to give Marie some room.

Whether she admitted it or not, what had passed between them that night *was* a big deal. And he had to be sure she'd had time to think about what she wanted to do. He'd seen that softening gleam in her eyes that night and known it for exactly what it was. Reaction to the temporary closeness of lovemaking. But she'd been a virgin. She didn't know that you could feel the same sense of intimacy with anyone.

"Liar," he muttered to himself as the inside of the windows began to fog over. He'd been with enough women to know that what he'd found in Marie's arms was unlike anything he'd ever experienced before. Something had happened between them. Something strong and elemental. Davis had touched and been touched on levels he hadn't known existed.

And then he'd stayed away.

His right hand gripped the steering wheel tightly enough to snap it in two. Hell, by now Marie might be wishing she'd never heard of Davis Garvey. And though it'd probably be better for both of them if she told him to get lost, he hoped to hell she wouldn't.

Two days without her had taught Davis one thing. How much he liked being with her. He'd missed seeing her smile, hearing her sing along to the oldies radio station she listened to. Missed the sound of her voice and her smart-aleck remarks.

Bottom line…he missed Marie.

Still, they had to talk. If they were going to keep seeing each other, then she had to know that as much as he liked her, enjoyed being with her, there was no future in this.

"Oh, good idea, Marine," he muttered darkly. Just the thing you should tell the woman who might be pregnant with your child. A flicker of something he didn't want to call fear rippled through him. A child. He shook his head. No. Wouldn't happen. No way would God sentence an innocent kid to a life with a father like him.

And on that happy thought, Davis opened the car door and stepped into the mouth of the storm.

"Give me details," Gina demanded, leaning toward her sister, an eager expression on her face.

Outside, the wind whipped rain against the windows, rattling the panes, and the winter cold seemed to seep through the glass into Marie's bones. She suddenly felt like a bug on a slide under a microscope. And knowing her sister, Marie was sure Gina wasn't going to quit until she got the information she was after.

Of course, that didn't mean she'd make it easy on Marie.

"No way," Marie snapped, shaking her head. That night was special…secret. Sharing the memory of what had happened between her and Davis would make it less real, less *hers*. And she had a feeling that as the years passed away and she lived her life alone, she'd be wanting to pull up the memories of that night. Often.

"Oh, c'mon," her younger sister prodded. "The mighty Marie finally takes the plunge—this is news."

"This is private," Marie said flatly, even though she knew it wouldn't stop the smiling woman facing her.

The Santini family was world-renowned for their stubbornness. The two of them entered a staring contest, each of them looking for signs of weakness in the other.

A long moment passed in silence, the only sound the rain tapping wildly at the windows. Finally though, Gina's shoulders slumped in defeat. Folding her hands in her lap, she took a breath and said quietly, "At least, tell me what it was like."

An interesting development.

Marie stared at her little sister as a surprising notion presented itself. Was it possible? she wondered, tipping her head to one side to study the other woman she'd thought she'd known so well. Could it be that big-talking, always-dating Gina wasn't as experienced as she let everyone believe?

"What was it like?" Marie repeated at last. "Are you saying…?"

Gina shrugged, lifting both hands high in the air before letting them drop to her lap again. "What can

I say?" she said. "I lied. You weren't the last Santini virgin. I am."

Okay, Marie thought, stunned. This little piece of news ranked right up there with finding out the world really was flat, after all. Remembering all the times she'd taken Gina's teasing about her lack of experience, Marie scowled and demanded, "Why?"

"Why not?" Gina countered, a bit defensively, Marie thought. "It's nobody's business what I do… or don't do, right?"

Amazing.

"Oh, but my business was your business?"

"Sure," Gina said with a grin. "That's what sisters are for."

Completely unrepentant and totally Gina.

"But—"

"But me no buts," Gina interrupted her. "Just tell me if I have something good to look forward to."

Good? That didn't half cover it, Marie thought, remembering the liquid heat in Davis's touch. The fires that had burned all night. The incredible sensation of reaching for a pleasure so deep, it almost scared you to claim it, only to grab it and find that it made you more complete than you ever thought you could be.

How could she explain to Gina what you couldn't possibly understand until you'd discovered it for yourself? Like tuning a carburetor, you could learn the steps, know what's expected of you, but until you rebuilt one for yourself, you just couldn't know what it was all about. And she could just imagine trying to look her sister in the eye while comparing sex to a carburetor.

Besides, how could she tell Gina how glorious it was and then admit that Davis had been avoiding her for two days? Nope, she told herself, she'd keep her comments short and sweet.

"Yeah, it's good." And as Gina smiled, Marie's eyes closed on memories and she added, "With the right person, it's wonderful."

"You're in love with him, aren't you?" Gina asked.

Marie's eyes flew open again and she stared at her sister. The brightly lit kitchen offered her no shadows to hide in, and sitting this close to the very observant Gina would make it impossible to disguise the emotion she knew was shining in her eyes. So why bother denying it?

Because that's why.

"Of course not." As a lie, it wasn't much, but it was the best she could do.

"Yeah, I'm convinced," Gina said, placing both hands on the floor behind her and leaning back.

"Good. Now leave me alone to fix this bloody sink."

"Forget the stupid sink."

"Mom thanks you."

"Marie, I know you're in love with him."

"What makes you so sure?"

"Because—you wouldn't have gone to bed with him otherwise."

Simple, but true. "*Please* leave it alone, Gina."

"Not gonna happen," she said with a slow shake of her head.

One look at Gina's determined features convinced Marie that—to borrow a quote from a popular science fiction character—"resistance was futile."

Gina sensed her sister's surrender and was prepared to be generous in victory. "So what's the problem?" she asked softly.

"How much time do you have?"

Gina grinned. "As much as you need."

"Problems, huh?" Marie asked. "Okay, let's see. I've only known him for about a minute and a half…"

"Mama and Papa only knew each other a week before they got married. Worked for them."

"That was different." Marie turned and noisily searched through the toolbox for a smaller-headed wrench. "We have nothing in common except interest in cars. And I have the distinct feeling that if anyone mentioned the word *love,* Davis would take off so fast, and so far, a marine recon platoon wouldn't be able to find him."

"Why don't you try it and find out?"

"Huh?" Marie's head snapped up and she stared at her sister as if she was nuts.

"I said, try it." Gina shrugged and smiled. "You've got nothing to lose. If he bolts, good riddance. If he doesn't, we've got another romantic Santini story to hand down the generations."

"Easy for you to say," Marie said while her mind toyed with the idea of confessing her love. But how could she set herself up for rejection like that? What was she supposed to do when after hearing her out, Davis paled and said, "Thanks but no thanks"?

No. Better to just leave secrets unsaid and enjoy whatever time she had with him.

"And here's your chance," Gina crowed, looking past Marie to the window.

Marie followed her gaze. Through the rain she saw Davis knocking on her apartment door. Her heart did a quick spin in her chest and the fingers clutching the wrench suddenly weakened, dropping the tool into the box with a clatter of sound.

He'd come back.

Before Marie could do or say anything, Gina was on her feet, racing to the back door and throwing it open. Wind-thrust rain rushed into the kitchen as she shouted, "Hey, Davis. Marie's over here."

He turned, nodded and sprinted down the steps. Coming to a stop just inside the kitchen door, he raked his gaze around the warm, bright room until he found Marie. Then he just looked at her with enough feeling that she felt her toes curl inside her shoes.

"You're right on time," Gina said, half dragging him into the room and closing the door against the storm.

Marie gave her sister a quick look. She wouldn't put it past Gina to announce, "Marie's in love with you, and what are you going to do about it?"

Apparently sensing what she was thinking, Gina grinned.

"For what?" he asked, still watching Marie.

She paused long enough to give Marie a heart attack before saying. "Mom needs that sink fixed and our little mechanic can't seem to pull it off."

Temporarily relieved, Marie shot her a glare before looking back at Davis. "You don't have to help, really. I'll get it."

Gina, standing behind Davis, waved her arms and mouthed. "Don't be dumb."

Marie ignored her.

Davis did, too.

As far as he was concerned, there was no one else in the room besides him and Marie. The minute he locked eyes with her, his chest tightened and every breath became a battle. Damn, this was going to be harder than he'd thought.

"Well," Gina said loudly enough to get their attention. "I guess I'll leave you guys to the dirty work. Here, Davis." she added, reaching for the shiny wet windbreaker he wore, "I'll hang this up on the service porch."

"Thanks," he said as he slipped out of the lightweight coat and handed it over. Gina left, and neither of them noticed. Gaze still fixed on Marie, he reminded himself that he was here to have a serious talk. To let her know that he wasn't the root-bound kind of man she needed. Unfortunately, all he could think as he stared down at the ponytailed woman in blue overalls was how much he wanted her.

To combat the sexual urges raging inside him, he went down on both knees beside her and looked under the sink. It'd be best to keep his mind busy. "What's wrong with it?"

"Just backed up," she said, leaning down for another look herself.

Davis turned his head toward her and realized her face was just a kiss away from him. His gaze dropped to her mouth, and when her teeth tugged at her bottom lip, he felt the gnawing sensation deep in his guts. Oh, man, what the hell was happening here?

"It's good to see you," she said, and he felt the brush of her breath against his cheek.

"Good to see you, too," he admitted. Good, great, fantastic. Seeing her was all of those things and more. But he wouldn't—couldn't—say so.

Instead, breaking the spell between them, he

turned away, crawled beneath the sink and rolled over onto his back.

"I think the elbow joint's frozen," she said.

Amazing to think that anything could be frozen when he was on fire, but there you go. "Hand me the wrench," he said.

She did, and as he worked at the old pipes, he heard her say, "You're good with your hands. Do the marines have you doing mechanical stuff?"

"Nope," he said through gritted teeth as he forced the wrench down. "Just paperwork and riding herd on the rookies."

"A waste of talent," she said.

"Thanks," he mumbled as the joint moved beneath the pressure. The next few minutes went quickly as they worked together like a seasoned team. In no time at all, they had the pipe clear and a new elbow joint installed.

She checked out his handiwork, then smiled in approval. "Like I said, a waste of talent."

He scooted out from under the sink and took the towel Marie handed him. As he wiped the grease and dirt from his palms, he said, "I used to think about opening my own shop."

"A shop?"

"Something like Santini's, I guess," he went on, half wondering why he was telling her this. It was an old dream. One he hadn't really entertained in years. But over the last week or so, the time he'd spent at

Marie's garage had somehow rekindled that nebulous dream. He hadn't been able to tell her about it before, but now it seemed natural. It felt *right,* sitting here in this kitchen, beside her, with the storm raging outside.

"I wanted to restore classic cars," he mused, thinking about the cars he had tucked away all over the country. He started talking and didn't stop until he'd described his dream shop and the way he would run the business. When he finally finished, Davis couldn't remember a time when he'd talked so much. Yet Marie didn't look bored, she looked interested. In him. His dreams.

"Did you do the Mustang yourself?" she asked quietly.

"Yeah," he said with a proud smile.

"Nice work."

He nodded, accepting the compliment and relishing it all the more because he knew she was well aware of what went into such a job. Most people didn't have a clue about these things. Marie and he could speak the same language.

"I also did a '56 Corvette, a '64 Thunderbird and a '69 Roadrunner," he told her.

Marie laughed and Davis realized anew how much he'd missed that sound. "What's so funny?"

"Muscle cars, every one of them," she said, still smiling. "How very male of you."

He grinned. "The relationship between a man and

his car is a primal one, lady, and not to be taken lightly."

"'I stand corrected,'" she said, tossing one of his quotes back at him.

Instantly Davis did the same, saying, "'You don't have to stand on my account.'"

And in that moment, they were both thrown back into the memory of their night together. Tension rippled in the air around them. Marie held her breath, fighting down the swirling sensations fluttering to life in her stomach. The look in his eyes warmed her through, despite what she'd just heard him say. Or rather, what he *didn't* say.

In all his talk about opening a shop and restoring cars, there hadn't been a mention of family. A wife. *Her.* He clearly saw his future as a solitary one. Marie pushed the twinge of regret aside. She'd never expected him to stick around forever. In fact, she'd thought she'd seen the last of him two days ago.

She was in love with a man who, figuratively speaking, was keeping one foot outside the door, ready to run. Gazing into his eyes, she saw the desire in those blue depths and knew he found her attractive. Knew he wanted her. But she also knew it couldn't last.

On that thought, she shifted her gaze from his. "I, uh," she said, as she straightened out the toolbox, "used to think about expanding Santini's. But I don't know enough about restoration to make it work.

Besides," she added, "there never seems to be enough time or money."

The back door flew open, letting another rush of rain and wind sweep in. Mama Santini groaned, slammed the door, then dropped her packages onto the kitchen table.

"Hi, Mom."

Mama gasped, clutched the base of her throat and whirled around, all in one move. "Marie! Lord, girl, you scared ten years off me. Hello, Davis. Nice to see you again."

"Ma'am…" He pushed himself to his feet, then offered a hand to Marie. She took it, and when he pulled her up, too, he kept a firm hold on her hand.

Mama noticed, but thankfully didn't say a word about it.

"The sink's fixed?" she asked.

"Yes," Marie answered, reluctantly tugging her hand free. Her fingers felt suddenly cold without the warm clasp of Davis's hand. "Davis fixed it."

"Well, thank you," Mama said with a smile. Taking off her coat and draping it cross the back of one of the chairs, she said, "You'll stay to dinner, won't you? It's only fair to let me thank you for all your hard work."

Marie slanted a look at him and was surprised to find him staring at her. His eyes held a question and she knew he was waiting to see if *she* wanted him to stick around. She met his gaze squarely and echoed her mother's request, though she was hoping for much more than just dinner.

"Please stay."

He nodded, then glanced at her mother. "Thank you, ma'am, I believe I would like to stay for a while."

A while, he'd said, and Marie had a feeling he, too, was referring to more than just dinner. He wanted to stay…be with her, for *a while*. She wondered just how long he considered a while to be and knew that even if he'd meant years, it wouldn't be long enough for her.

The next few hours passed quickly. Though he and Marie were surrounded by family every minute, he'd discovered that he didn't feel nearly as out of place as he had before. And Davis wasn't sure if that was a good thing or a bad thing. Becoming used to the feeling of being sucked down by quicksand didn't prevent a person from sinking. It only served to blind you to the coming danger.

Davis helped Angela set up her new CD player, wiring in the speakers and laughing with the family when Jeremy insisted on playing his CD first. They all stoically sat through what seemed like years' worth of children's folk songs, though he managed to avoid joining in on the choruses. While the women went in to finish dinner and set the table, he and Jeremy played video games.

"This is cool that you're here," the boy said, and pushed a button that destroyed Davis's onscreen car.

He winced and pushed his own button, but nothing happened. What is it with kids? he wondered. Were they born knowing how to play these things?

"My dad died, y'know," Jeremy said suddenly, and Davis looked at him.

"Yeah, I know." A pang of sadness for the boy rose up inside him. Davis knew all too well what it was to lose a parent. But at least Jeremy still had his mother and grandmother and two aunts who loved him. The kid was luckier than a lot of others his age.

Luckier than Davis had been.

"I don't really remember him," Jeremy was saying.

Davis thought that was probably best. If he did remember, he'd only torture himself with memories and spend his free time constructing imagined "what if" scenarios. As he himself had done for too long.

"And except for me, it's always all girls around here," Jeremy said with a sneer, "so I like it when you come over."

"Thanks," Davis said, smiling. The boy was learning early to take comfort from his own kind. "I like it, too." In fact, it surprised him how much he was enjoying himself.

The house was cozy and filled with a warmth that seemed to beckon a person farther inside. Laughter and hushed conversation flowed from the kitchen, and Davis caught himself listening for the sound of Marie's voice.

"Why don't you marry Marie and then you can be here all the time?" Jeremy said.

Swiveling his head to look at the boy, Davis just stared at him for a long minute or two, wondering what to say.

"I mean," the kid continued, sparing Davis a reply, "I'd like it if my mom got married again even better. 'Cause having a father would be pretty awesome. But havin' an uncle would be pretty good, too."

Uncle. Uncle Davis.

Damn. He was fairly sure he liked the sound of that. Frowning to himself, Davis felt the unmistakable suction of quicksand pulling him under.

Jeremy set his game paddle down on the floor in front of him and turned to look at him. When he didn't get the man's attention, he patted his knee until Davis looked at him.

"Can you come back tomorrow evening?" he asked quietly, shooting a nervous look toward the kitchen, as if hoping the females would keep themselves scarce.

"Why tomorrow?" Davis asked.

Jeremy leaned into him and whispered in a voice that could have been heard in Chicago, "Because tomorrow we go to get our Christmas tree, and if you don't come then we can't go to the chop-it-down place."

"Why not?"

"'Cause a girl can't chop down a tree." Disgusted, Jeremy shook his head.

"Is that right?" Davis asked, smiling at the boy's scowl.

"Everybody knows that. That's how come we always go to the grocery store to buy one."

"Ah…"

"So will ya?"

Christmas tree shopping. "Uncle Davis." He was getting in too deep here, and for the life of him, couldn't find a way out. Looking into the boy's eager expression, he knew that way out didn't lead across Jeremy's wounded feelings. So, he thought, Christmas tree shopping it was. After all, there was a first time for everything. And it was a good excuse to see Marie again. "Sure."

"Promise?' the boy asked, studying his face.

He thought about it for a moment, knowing that once he'd given his word, he wouldn't break it. Did he really want to do this? And a voice inside him whispered, *"Yes."*

"Promise."

Chapter Eleven

The evening with the Santini family was over, and Marie led Davis up the steps to her apartment. For the last few hours, she'd watched him with her family. Had seen how easily he fit in and how much her mother, sisters and nephew liked him. And yet she hadn't been blind to the fact that even while enjoying himself, Davis had held a part of himself back.

Only a couple of weeks ago, she hadn't known Davis Garvey existed. She'd lived her life and thought it complete. She'd been *happy,* if a little lonely. But now that he'd entered her life, she knew that once he left it, happiness would never be harder to find.

The rain had slackened off to a drizzle that dampened her clothes and seemed to soak right down to her bones. A chill crept over her, but Marie had the strangest sense that it had nothing to do with the weather. In her heart she was already preparing for him to leave.

As she sensed he was.

The door swung wide and the single lamp she'd left burning cast a soft, golden light over the small living room. Her gaze went directly to the overstuffed sofa where Davis had first made love to her and she knew she'd never be able to enter this room without remembering every tiny detail of that night.

Even thinking about it made her body burn and hum with a kind of frenzied energy. And knowing that whatever she had with Davis wasn't permanent did nothing to smother the flames she felt inside.

She closed the door behind him, and when she turned around, he was there. Just inches from her. She tipped her head back to look up at him, and her breath caught at the expression on his face. Desire, tenderness, regret, all pooled together and simmered in his eyes. A deeply throbbing ache settled around her heart.

"Marie…" He reached for her, and she caught his hand in hers, curling her fingers around his. "We have to talk. About the other night. About what's between us."

Was it just her, or was the word *goodbye* hidden in that statement? Marie didn't want to hear it. Not tonight. Not now. She wanted one more night with him. Well, actually, she wanted a lifetime's worth of nights with Davis. But she would settle for one more… before he turned and stepped out of her life. She held on to his hand and brought it up to her face. Then, nuzzling her cheek against his palm, she said, "Don't talk, Davis. Not now."

He pulled in a long, shuddering breath and she watched different emotions chase each other across his features. But finally, regret was eased aside to be replaced by desire, and Marie knew that this one time, at least, she'd won.

"This is a mistake," he said quietly, even as he moved in closer to her. "We're too different. We want different things."

"Tonight," she said just as softly, "we want the same thing. Each other."

"Yeah," he muttered, "you're right about that," and cupped her face in his palms, tipping her mouth up to meet his. The kiss began as a gentle brush of lips against lips, but the instant their mouths met, an urgency burst into life between them.

He devoured her, his tongue opening her lips for his invasion, and when he swept inside her warmth, Marie leaned into him, groaning her surrender. Again and again he stroked her tongue with his, electrifying her bloodstream and sending shivers of expectation from the roots of her hair to the tips of her toes.

Marie wrapped her arms around his neck and held on, feeling as though she was sitting in the lead car on a roller coaster. Highs and lows seemed more frantic, more pulse pounding. Her stomach pitched, her mouth went dry and even the palms of her hands itched for him.

Hunger, raw and powerful roared through her, leaving her shaken but determined. She pulled at his windbreaker and he let her go long enough to tear it and his shirt off, baring his chest for her exploring hands. Then he turned his nimble fingers to the brass catches of her overalls. He flicked them open, and the overalls dropped to below her waist. Then he grabbed the hem of her tiny tank top and yanked it up and over her head.

The rush of cool air against her bare breasts puckered her nipples and Marie groaned again, more loudly this time, when Davis dipped his head to take first one, then the other into his mouth. Sensations rose up and shattered inside her. Incredible, the swell of emotions churning within. She clutched at his shoulders and his arms came around her, lifting her, bracing her back against the closed front door. The shock of the cold wood along her spine made her gasp and that gasp only built as she felt him ease her overalls and then her panties down and off her legs.

Free of her clothes, Marie gave herself up to the wildness rattling around within and wrapped both legs around his waist. He dipped his head, kissing her nipples one after the other. Tasting, sucking, nipping at their sensitive tips, he pushed her higher, higher, closer to the edge of the precipice she knew was waiting for her. She leaned her head back against the door and stared unseeing at the ceiling while Davis did unimaginable things to her body...to her soul.

One strong arm supported her while Davis's other hand dropped. She heard the unmistakable sound of a zipper being yanked down and everything within her tightened. Soon, she told herself. Soon, she'd feel him inside her again. Know that sense of completion again.

"Damn it," he muttered thickly, and Marie forced herself out of the sexual fog settling over her brain.

Breathless, she asked, "What? What is it?"

"I can't do this one-handed," he said, and every word sounded as though it had been squeezed from his throat.

She opened her eyes, looked at the small foil packet he held and understood. "Let me," she said, and reached for it.

He gave it to her and kept his gaze locked with hers as she ripped the foil and pulled the condom from its wrappings. Letting her slide down against the door, Davis held her steadily as she reached for him. Slowly, tenderly, she smoothed the satin-thin material down over the length of him and he winced with the effort to hold himself in check.

"Marie…" He said her name on a moan, and the sound of his need fed her own.

She couldn't wait. Couldn't stand the tension coiling inside her. She needed him with a desperation she never would have thought possible. Marie closed her eyes and bit down hard on her bottom lip before saying softly, "Now, Davis. Please, now."

"Now," he echoed, and still bracing her against the door, slid himself home.

She gasped and arched into him, instinctively drawing him deeper inside. He buried his face in the curve of her neck and groaned like a dying man granted a last-minute pardon.

After savoring their joining for a brief moment, Davis withdrew from her only to plunge back inside deeper, harder. Her legs held him to her, her hands clawed at his back as she felt the tightness inside her grow and build. Higher, faster than ever before, they raced together toward the edge of oblivion, and when they found it, they tumbled into the abyss together, safe in each other's arms.

Before the last tremor shuddered through her body, Marie whispered, "I love you." And in the very next instant she knew she'd said the wrong thing.

Davis went utterly and completely still.

The echo of those three little words burrowed inside him and wrapped themselves around his heart. He closed his eyes against the warmth suddenly spreading through him. He couldn't remember ever hearing those words directed at him before. And now that they had been, he didn't know what to say. Or do.

Slowly, carefully, he disengaged himself from her and gently set her back on her feet. In these first awkward moments, a strained silence slammed down between them and he was grateful she didn't say anything more.

This was his own fault. He'd let himself get too close. Let *her* get too close. And now there was no way to leave her without hurting her.

"Davis," she said, and he knew the temporary silence was finished. Now he'd have to talk and say the things he knew would tear at her heart and soul. He had to refuse the gift she'd offered him. Have to tell her that there was no future for her with a man who had no past.

"Marie," he said quickly, wanting to stop her before she said those words again. "I'm not looking for anything permanent."

"I didn't say you were," she said.

His gaze snapped to her. "But you said—"

She actually smiled at him. It was sad, regretful, but still a smile. "I said I love you. I do."

He flinched. He'd never expected to hear those words. Had never put himself in the position where he *might* hear them. Hell, he didn't know squat about love. About loving. Now, if she wanted to know how to pull together a recon mission in less than twenty-four hours, he was her man. He could field-strip a machine gun and have it back together again in less time than it took to think about it. He could do a hundred push-ups without breaking a sweat, and if the corps demanded it, he could find a way to walk on water.

But damn it, when it came to love, *she* was the expert and he was as blind and stupid as any first-week grunt in boot camp.

"You and I, what we have together is…*good*," he finished with feeling, even knowing that "good" was a major understatement. What he'd found with her was more than he'd ever thought existed.

"It's more than good," she said, as if reading his thoughts, "but I think you know that."

His back teeth ground together and every cell in his body stiffened. Why was she being so damned *nice?* Any other woman would be dragging him over hot coals about now. But then, no other woman before Marie had ever claimed to love him. Of course she'd react differently than he'd expect. "Don't make this harder on both of us," he said.

"Don't worry," she said, and hooked the last of the buckles on her overalls.

He just stared at her. She hadn't bothered to put her top back on, so the overalls barely covered her breasts. Her black hair was mussed, her eyes were overly bright and her mouth swollen from his kisses. And Davis wanted her more than life itself.

Which is what had gotten him into this mess in the first place. Curling his hands into helpless fists at his sides, he waited for her to go on. Waited to give her the time to work up to telling him off. As he deserved.

"I didn't mean to say the words out loud," she continued. "It just sort of…slipped out."

She was *apologizing* to him? "Damn it, Marie," he said tightly, "*yell* at me. Throw something. Jeez, at least tell me what a bastard I am!"

She shook her head and chuckled humorlessly. "It wouldn't help."

It'd sure as hell help him, he wanted to say. It would relieve some of the overwhelming guilt that had settled in the pit of his stomach, making him feel cold all over. But then, he didn't have the right to feel better, did he? This wasn't about him. It was about her.

"Marie," he said, "I don't want to hurt you."

"I know that."

"Don't expect more from me than I can give."

"I don't expect anything from you, Davis." She said it sadly, with a slow shake of her head.

"You should," he said.

"Why? So I can be disappointed?" She shook her head again and walked past him to the sofa. There she sat down and curled her feet up under her. "No, thanks. But I won't make this any easier on you, either, Davis. I can't pretend I don't love you. I do."

Davis winced inwardly and fought his instinct to run. Hell. What kind of marine was he that three little words could make him turn tail like this? And what kind of man was he that he could face down armed-to-the-teeth enemies but a woman declaring her love brought him to his knees?

"I understand you don't love me back," she said quietly. "I guess it just happens that way sometimes," she added, her voice getting smaller, quieter. "Fate playing little jokes."

"Marie…"

"It's okay, Davis," she said, and folded her arms across her chest. "It really is. Some people you love. Some you don't."

It wasn't okay. Nothing about this was okay.

"Marie, I care for you," he said, and knew it wasn't enough. Would never be enough for her.

A tiny, almost-not-there smile touched her mouth briefly. "I'm sure you do, Davis. But caring isn't loving, is it?"

"No." He squeezed that word past the knot in his throat and watched it hit her like a bullet. A prize bastard, that's what he was. But even knowing that didn't change a damn thing.

"Davis…if you don't mind, I'm kind of tired, so…"

She wanted him to leave.

Not so surprising, he told himself. Why wouldn't she? She confesses her love and he shuts down like an unplugged computer. Emptiness welled up inside him, and it felt as though a black hole had opened wide to swallow his heart and the barren thing most people would call his soul.

He should have been better prepared for tonight. He'd known all along his time with Marie would end. Davis didn't have relationships. He had encounters. Brief, fiery, encounters. This was the first time he'd actually gotten to know a woman. Like her. And though it was illogical and irrational, he couldn't help feeling disappointed that she hadn't even *asked* him to stay. It didn't make any sense at all, but he wanted her to want him to stay even if he couldn't.

No one had *ever* asked him not to leave.

And in this, at least, Marie was no different from the rest.

"All right," he said quietly. "I'll go." Then, remembering, he added, "But until we know for sure about whether or not there's a baby, I won't go far."

"Oh, Davis," she said, and her voice was barely above a whisper. "You're already so far away, I can't reach you."

She was right. And he could only hope that a benevolent God would have the good sense to *not* sentence an innocent baby to a life with him as its father.

He inhaled sharply, took one last look at her, opened the door and stepped outside. It didn't surprise him at all when the skies burst like a popped water balloon and drenched him with a wall of rain.

He deserved nothing less.

A cold wind raced through the tiny forest of perfectly sculpted pine trees. The fresh clean scent of the Christmas tree lot filled the air, and the thick layer of sawdust covering the bare earth behind their feet muffled their footsteps. Dozens of people wandered up and down the aisles, admiring, then dismissing the pines in the quest for the perfect Christmas tree.

From a small wooden snack stand near the office came the aromas of hot chocolate, hot dogs and popcorn. The sky overhead was cloudy, but the sun continued to peek in and out, giving the lot a dappled, shady look that only fed into the feeling that Christmas was just around the corner.

And in the midst of happy families and professional carolers, two people stood uneasily, staring at each other.

"You didn't have to do this," Marie said for the third time in five minutes.

Davis looked down at her, shoved his hands into his jeans pockets and nodded. "Yes, I did," he said. "I promised."

He'd promised. That's what he'd said when he'd turned up at the Santini house a half an hour ago. Marie hadn't actually expected him to show up. Not after what had happened the night before. But apparently, she'd underestimated Sergeant Davis Garvey's sense of duty.

At least Jeremy was happy, she thought, her eyes skimming the crowds for her nephew. But the boy had disappeared again. He'd spent the last fifteen minutes darting in and out of the trees like a young Daniel Boone. In fact, he was having the time of his life, completely unaware of any discomfort between the adults accompanying him.

"Look, Marie," Davis said, and something inside her cringed. She didn't want to talk about last night again. She didn't want to remember, as she had all during the sleepless hours of the longest night of her life, the look on his face when she'd blurted, "I love you."

"Jeremy's having a good time," she said in an effort to keep their conversation centered on the hunt for a Christmas tree. Darn it. Why hadn't Gina or Angela come along for the ride? Why had they left her alone with the man who was breaking her heart by inches?

"Yeah, he is," Davis said, never taking his gaze from her.

Tugging the cowl-necked collar of her sky-blue sweater a bit higher, Marie said only, "He would have understood though, if you hadn't shown up. I could have explained."

He snorted a choked laugh. "Explain what? That

a marine was too scared to face his aunt, so instead he broke his word to a kid?"

"I could have come up with something," she insisted. And it would have been far easier than this. A dull, throbbing ache started up around her heart and it seemed as though it grew with every pulse beat. How hard it was to stand so close and yet so far from him. To remember the feel of his arms around her and the soft brush of his breath on her flesh and to know that she'd never experience that again.

"No reason for you to," Davis argued, dragging her attention away from her lovely self-pity party. "Kids have a right to expect an adult to keep his word."

Something flickered in his blue eyes, and she thought she caught a flash of remembered pain in his expression. It's not just Jeremy he's talking about, she told herself, and wondered what broken promises Davis had weathered as a boy. And if they'd had anything to do with shaping the man he was now.

"There he is," Davis said suddenly, and pointed off down the aisle on the right.

"Guess we'd better catch up to him." Marie started walking and tried not to enjoy it too much when Davis fell into step beside her.

"This is nice," he said, glancing around him at the lot and the strings of colored lights hanging overhead.

"Yes," she said, willing to talk about anything other than last night. How difficult could it be? They'd spend an hour together and then he'd be gone, leaving her to lick her wounds in private. "We've never been here before, though Jeremy's always wanted to."

"Grocery store lots," he said.

She laughed quietly. "He told you."

"Of course."

Marie searched for something else to say and finally came up with "Actually, to me, these are not really Christmas trees."

"Could have fooled me," he said, shrugging his shoulders.

Was it her imagination or did his shoulders look even broader in that plain black sweatshirt? Immediately she pushed that thought aside and grasped at the dangling thread of conversation.

"Nope," she went on firmly. "A nice Douglas fir. That's my kind of tree. It's tradition. What we've always had."

He nodded vaguely.

"What about you?" she asked, determined to have a nice, civilized conversation, even if she had to drag words from him. If she was dying inside, she didn't have to let him know it. "What kind of tree did your family go in for?"

He reached out a hand and dragged it through the long needled boughs of the trees they passed. "Plastic."

"Fake trees?" she asked, and couldn't hide the dismay in her voice. "Oh, no."

"Oh, yeah." Davis shook his head and stuffed his hand back into his pocket. "One place I remember had a pink plastic tree and they had a colored light wheel they used to shine on it every night. Looked hideous."

One place? she thought.

"And then another time, there was no tree at all. But I remember thinking the menorah was kind of pretty."

Menorahs and pink trees?

"Where did you grow up, Davis?" she asked.

"St. Louis," he answered stiffly, then slowly turned his head until he was looking at her. "In a series of foster homes."

How sad, she thought, and instantly ached for the child he'd been. "What about your parents?"

He shrugged as if trying to rid himself of a years-old burden. "My mother died when I was about Jeremy's age."

She couldn't imagine anything worse than not being able to grow up as she had, safe in the knowledge of her parents' love. "I'm so sorry, Davis."

"Long time ago." He inhaled sharply, deeply.

"What about your father?"

"My father put me up for adoption a few months later."

He sounded so cold, so matter of fact, his voice, as much as what he'd said, tore at her. What a horrible way to grow up. Never knowing a place to call your own. Never having a family to depend on. *Knowing* that your only living parent gave you away.

Maybe, she thought, this was part of the reason behind Davis's wariness about love. Maybe being denied something for most of your life left you unable to accept it when it was finally offered.

"Davis, I don't know what to say."

"Nothin' to say," he told her. He pulled one hand free of his pocket and shoved it along the side of his head. Mind spinning, Davis wondered why in the hell he'd chosen to tell her the story of his childhood. He never talked about the past. Tried not to think about it.

"It must have been awful for you," she said softly.

He stiffened at the sympathy in her tone. He didn't want pity. Didn't need it. A big woman pushing a screaming kid in a stroller passed them and Davis waited until she was a few steps farther away before saying, "Don't feel sorry for me, Marie. I don't need your sympathy."

"Don't you?" she asked, and her green eyes became warm and liquid.

He steeled himself against that soft expression of hers and reminded both of them, "It was a long time ago. I'm not that lonely kid anymore."

"I think you're wrong, Davis," she said, and reached out to lay one hand on his forearm. Even through the thick fabric of his sweatshirt, he felt a trickle of her warmth seep into his bones, swirl into his bloodstream.

And for one brief, incredible moment, he felt alive again. As alive as he felt every time he joined his body to hers. Then she spoke again and the moment was gone.

"I think there's still some of that boy in you, Davis." She looked up at him, silently daring him to look away. He didn't. "A boy who didn't have a family, so he told himself he didn't need one. A boy without love who convinced himself love wasn't necessary."

Every word she uttered chipped away at the hard, protective shell he'd erected around his heart so many years ago. Every glance, every touch, warmed a soul that had been cold ever since he could remember.

And still he fought her.

If he admitted, even to himself, just how much Marie and even her family had come to mean to him, then he'd have to acknowledge just how much he'd missed in his life. And how much he would go on missing because he couldn't bring himself to tear down the wall he'd built up around himself.

"I can't change what happened to you when you were a child, Davis," she said. "And only you can change the way you live your life now."

Could he? he wondered. Or was it far too late for him to be anything more than he already was? Could a man who knew nothing about love really learn to give and accept it? A part of him wanted badly to believe it was possible.

"Hey, you guys!" Jeremy shouted at them, and his voice arrived a split second before he slid to a stop beside Davis, kicking sawdust up into the air.

"What's up, kiddo?" Marie asked, giving the boy a forced, too-hearty smile.

"I found it," he said with a grin. "The perfect tree." He grabbed Marie's hand and started pulling her after him. "C'mon, before somebody else gets it!"

She threw an over-the-shoulder glance at Davis, and the emotions churning in her eyes nearly staggered him. She loved him. Marie Santini actually loved him. Now the question was, was he man enough to do something about that?

Grumbling to himself, Davis followed after Jeremy and Marie. He was grateful the kid had found the tree he wanted, because at the moment there was nothing Davis would like more than to chop at something with an ax.

Chapter Twelve

"All I'm saying is that you could at least *fight* for him."

Marie glared at her younger sister. Between college break and only working part-time, Gina was around far too much lately. Gina had been saying the same blasted thing for three days now, and it was getting old. As if Marie didn't want to fight for him. As if she didn't want to have him here, with her. But damn it, she had *some* pride, didn't she?

She'd told Davis she loved him. She'd told him it was up to him to decide how he wanted to spend the rest of his life…with her or alone. What more could she do?

Gina answered that question for her.

"You ought to go down to that base, look Davis dead in the eye and tell him you love him."

She choked out a strained laugh. "Gee, what a keen idea. Too bad it won't work."

"How do you know unless you try?"

"What makes you think I didn't?"

Gina sat down hard on a stool by the workbench. "You're kidding. You told him you love him and he left anyway?"

"Amazing, huh?" Marie retorted, then bent over the engine of Laura's Honda again. The darn thing was back in the shop. Her mind wasn't on work. It was, as it had been, on Davis. Still, a part of her realized that she'd have to find a cheap used car for her friend. No way was this poor Honda going to keep running for another year.

"Jeez, honey, I'm sorry."

Marie winced beneath Gina's sympathy and understood just what Davis had meant when he'd told her he didn't want her pity.

"Why didn't you tell me to shut up or something?"

Marie straightened briefly, pinned the other woman with a look and reminded her, "I have been telling you that for three days."

Gina shrugged and gave her an "oops" look. "So I don't listen as well as I talk."

"Now there's a news flash."

"Hey, I'm on your side, remember?"

"How can I forget?" Marie asked, turning her attention back to the dirty spark plugs. "You, Angela and Mama keep reminding me of that while you're all telling me how to fix my life."

"Well, somebody has to," Gina snapped.

One eyebrow lifted. "Like your life is so perfect."

Gina jumped off the stool, marched across the concrete floor, leaned both hands on the Honda's fender, looked at her sister and said, "Look, if you don't want my help, just say so. There's no reason to be insulting."

"Good." Marie glanced at her. "I don't want your help."

"Man," Gina huffed, "who would have thought a man could make you so crabby? I thought sex was supposed to improve your outlook, not ruin it." Stepping back and away from the car, she turned for the set of open double doors. "Since I'm not needed, I'll just go home."

"Good plan." Finally. Peace.

But the minute Gina left, the silence in Santini's crowded in on Marie. A twinge of guilt poked at her. She shouldn't have come down so hard on her sister. It wasn't as if it were Gina's fault Marie was so miserable.

Sighing, she straightened up again, gave the Honda's tire a good kick and resigned herself to the fact that she wouldn't be getting any work done today, either. The garage seemed too empty. Her own breath practically echoed in the quiet. She'd thought she wanted to be alone. But now that she was, alone didn't sound so great.

She tossed the wrench she held on to the rolling mechanic's bench and walked to the doorway. Gray skies and a sullen, cold wind did nothing for her mood. Stuffing her hands into the pockets of her overalls, she tried not to remember the last time she'd worn them. She fought to keep at a distance the memory of her overalls dropping to her living room floor. She didn't want to recall the feel of the cold door pressing against her back as Davis took her wildly, passionately to a world she'd never hoped to enter.

But despite her best efforts, the memories came, flooding into her mind, one after the other, never pausing, never giving her a chance to catch her breath. His eyes, his hands, his mouth, his voice. All these things and more she remembered in vivid detail and wondered hopelessly how long the memories could last. What? Twenty, thirty years, tops?

"Oh, man…"

"Marie?"

She jumped, startled and half turned to look at her mother. Maryann Santini stood watching her, a worried expression stamped on her familiar features.

"Mama?" Marie said past a sudden, tight knot lodged in her throat. "What are you doing here?"

The older woman shook her graying head. "What? I can't stop by to say hello?"

"Sure, it's just—" Understanding shone in Mama's eyes and Marie felt her resolution to be strong, crumbling. The tears she'd been holding at bay for three long days and even longer nights quickly pooled in her eyes, blurring her vision. She gulped hard and gave in to the misery aching inside. "Mama...why doesn't he love me?"

Mama held her arms out and Marie stepped into them, just as she had when she was a child. And just like then, she felt the strong net of Mama's love surround her.

"What do you mean you don't have the reports finished yet?" Davis practically snarled into the telephone. The corporal on the other end of the line stammered some half-witted excuse and Davis cut him off. "Save the stories and get the damn work done by this afternoon. Understood?"

He dropped the receiver into its cradle and stared at the black phone as if it was behind all of his problems. Hell, he knew he was overreacting. A month ago, he wouldn't have cared if the corporal was a little late.

Now, though, it seemed the smallest things could set him off. He'd noticed that his fellow marines were walking a wide berth around him, and he couldn't blame them. Hell, if he could have figured a way to do it, *he* wouldn't spend any time with him, either.

The last three days without Marie had been the longest of his life. His apartment seemed lonelier, his world emptier and his future…too damned depressing to think about.

Marie. It all came back to Marie. He'd walked away, leaving everything unresolved between them. For some idiotic reason, he'd convinced himself that he *could* walk away, as he had done so many times before. But it had been impossible. Not seeing her didn't help any; his mind just conjured up memories of her face, her hands, her voice, her laugh.

He'd told her that he wouldn't go far until they knew if they'd made a baby or not. But what would he use for an excuse to stay close once that information was in? And what if there *was* a baby?

At that thought, a tiny flicker of light flashed for an instant, deep within him. Was it *hope?*

Jumping up from his chair, he paced the office. Back and forth he went, his combat boots smacking into the worn linoleum floor with an even regularity that pounded in his head like a second heartbeat. On his third time around the room, he paused briefly at a small window and stared down at the base stretching out below him.

Marines, going about their business, hustled across the tarmac. From a distance, he heard the muted roar of the helicopters as the chopper pilots flew training exercises. Trucks loaded with supplies rolled past his building and everything looked as it should.

For more years than he wanted to remember, this base and others like it had been his world. It had always been enough, too. The corps had given him what he'd been cheated out of as a boy. Family. A place to belong. A sense of pride and accomplishment. Honor and duty.

It was who he was, he told himself as he stared down at the faceless marines going about their work. This place, this life was all he had. All he'd ever had.

Turning around slowly, he stared at his desk across the room and his gaze landed on a certain sheaf of papers. His reenlistment was due. If he didn't re-up, he'd be out of the corps within six months.

He caught himself at the thought. *"If?"* he said softly. He always signed the papers. Never considered *not* signing them.

Until now.

Suddenly his future opened up in front of him. Davis saw himself moving from one base to the next, always packing and unpacking in strange apartments. Always alone. Always starting over. Never belonging. Never having ties to anyone or anything beyond his stretch in the corps.

And when he faced mandatory retirement, he wondered, what then? Who would he be? What would he have to show for his life? A string of commendations? A few more ribbons on a uniform he could no longer wear?

Davis reached up and laid one hand against the window jamb. His vision blurred as he stared past today and into the years ahead. He would be alone, as he always had been. He would have lived his life on the edges of real life. He would have spent years, closed up on himself. Not touching or being touched. Not loving or being loved.

His fingers curled tight around the wooden molding and his back teeth ground together.

For the first time, he realized that the years ahead looked as empty as those behind him. An instant later, in a blinding flash of insight, Davis acknowledged that sort of future didn't fit him anymore. He'd tasted belonging. He'd seen what being loved could be like. And he couldn't go back to being the way he was. A future without Marie in it was just too bleak to consider.

The image of her face swam to the surface of his mind and he started thinking again, as he had for the last three days, about everything she'd said to him that day at the Christmas tree lot. Started thinking about a lot of things.

When he was a kid, he could remember lying in the dark, wishing things were different. Wishing he had a place to call home. Now he was finally being given a chance at that gift and he, like an idiot, was running from it. Afraid he'd be found lacking somehow. Afraid he'd mess it up and have nothing.

"A helluva thing," he muttered grimly as he slammed a fist into the wall. "A *marine* running scared."

"You having a nightmare?" a deep voice startled him and Davis looked up as Gunner Sergeant Nick Peretti strolled into their shared office.

"Nightmare?"

"Yeah," Nick said on a laugh. "A marine, scared?"

Davis laughed, too, but there was no humor in it.

Nick noticed. Sympathetically he said, "It's a woman, isn't it?"

"Not just any woman," Davis told him. "*My* woman. If I haven't blown it all to hell."

The other man's eyebrows went straight up. "Is there something you'd like to share with the class?"

Davis laughed aloud, crossed the room and slapped Nick on the back heartily enough to stagger him. "Not just yet, Teacher. I'll let you know."

As he headed for the door, Nick shouted, "Good luck!"

"I'll need it," he called back, and hoped to God he hadn't come to his senses too late.

"All right now. Dry your eyes," Mama said sternly, handing Marie a tissue.

She did as she was told, and when she was through, she shook her head. "I don't know what to do, Mama. I mean, I knew he'd leave eventually. I just didn't expect it to hurt this badly."

Mama caught her daughter's chin in her hand and turned her face up. "What do you mean, you knew he'd leave?"

"Every other guy I've ever liked has."

"And you think you know why?"

"Sure," Marie told her. "I'm not pretty and perky like Gina or Angela. I'm a mechanic, for Pete's sake."

"So what's wrong with that?" Mama's voice took on a fighting edge.

"Nothing," Marie said quickly. "I like what I do. It's just not very…girlie."

"And do you think Davis liked Gina or Angela better than you?"

"No," she said with a half smile, remembering how tense Davis got while waiting for Gina to be quiet for a while.

"So, he doesn't mind you're a mechanic?"

"No." she said, thinking about it as she said it. "But that's not the only problem, Mama. He's never had a family. He doesn't think he knows how to belong. How to love."

"Piffle."

"What?" Marie laughed and looked at her mother.

"So he's never had a family. So what? He was never in the marines until he joined, was he?" Mama patted Marie's cheek and leaned in to say, "A person can learn, Marie, honey. With enough love, anything is possible."

That was the problem though, wasn't it? He didn't love her. Or if he did, he didn't love her enough.

"It's up to you, what you want to do," Mama said as she stood up and smoothed out the fall of her dress. "But if it was me, I wouldn't be so quick to give up."

"I don't know…." She wanted to think there was a chance, but wouldn't that just be keeping her hopes up for another crash landing?

"You think about it," Mama said. "Maybe," she added, "if you expect him to stay, he will. Meanwhile, I'm going home to get Jeremy ready for his Christmas pageant. You coming home to change?"

"No. I brought my things here. I'll just meet you guys at the school."

"Okay. Don't be late, though. Those kids're so excited, the play is bound to be entertaining."

She waved and walked off down the sidewalk toward home. It was a long walk, but Mama insisted she liked the exercise. Marie watched her go, her mind racing with thoughts, hopes, dreams.

* * *

Two hours later, Marie looked into the bathroom mirror and fluffed her hair one last time. She gave herself a quick once-over and decided she looked pretty good, considering she'd been crying her eyes out only a couple of hours ago.

There was a new determination in her eyes and a firm set to her chin, too. She'd thought about what Mama said and had made up her mind to go see Davis in the morning. She'd face him down on his own turf and *order* him to admit to loving her. No way was she going to give up on him—*them*—this easily.

If he thought the marines were a tough outfit, he just hadn't seen the Santinis in high gear.

Grinning at her reflection, Marie put her holly wreath earrings on, affixed the holly pin Jeremy had made for her to the left shoulder of her lemon-yellow sweater, then left. She'd already locked the service bay doors, so she walked through the office and out the door, locking it behind her.

It wasn't until she turned around that she saw him.

Standing alongside the Mustang parked in her driveway, Davis, in full uniform, stood watching her. It was the first time she'd ever seen him in his marine uniform and she had to admit, he made quite a picture. Tall, muscular and so handsome, he took her breath away, he looked like a recruiting poster for the corps.

And she was reading a lot of hope into his coming to see her.

She walked down the driveway and stopped a few feet from him. "Hi," she said, "I didn't expect to see you here."

"I know." He nodded abruptly, then turned toward his car. "I have something for you."

Confused, Marie watched as he dragged a live Christmas tree—a two-foot pine in a terra-cotta pot—from the back seat of the Mustang. A huge red bow was attached to its tip and the ends of the ribbon fluttered wildly in the breeze. Davis staggered under the potted tree's weight as he carried it up the driveway. He set it down in front of her and Marie looked from the pine to him.

"What's this about?" She fought to slow down the rapid beat of her heart, but lost the battle. Just being close to him was enough to send her system into overdrive, and she'd just have to accept it.

He braced his feet wide apart, folded his arms across his broad chest and said simply, "It's a Scotch pine."

"I can see that," she said with a small smile. "Why is it here?"

A slightly disgusted look crossed his face briefly as he admitted. "It's here because I couldn't find a

Douglas fir." He shook his head in frustration. "Went to three nurseries before I settled for this one."

He had gone looking for a Douglas fir? Why? she wondered, even as a ribbon of hope began to stream through her insides.

"Uh-huh," she said softly. "And you're bringing me a tree because…"

He unfolded his arms and scraped one palm across his face as he searched for the words he needed so desperately. "Because I thought the blasted thing could be like a visual aid."

"For what?" She hoped he knew where he was going with this, but Marie wanted to hear him say it.

"To show you that I'm ready for roots."

A bubble of excitement blossomed in her chest. She took a hard grip on it and said, "You are?"

"Yeah." He looked deeply into her eyes and she read so many wonderful things in those familiar blue depths, Marie wanted to shout. But she kept still as he went on. "I want to plant this tree with you and decorate it every year."

"Every year?"

"Yes."

Afraid to believe, afraid not to, Marie stared at him and realized all of her dreams were hanging right there, within reach. "I…don't know what to say," she admitted.

"Don't say anything, Marie," Davis said, and

felt his hopes rise as her features softened into the incredibly loving expression he'd missed seeing so much. "Just listen. The last three days I've been a miserable bastard." He paced off a few steps, then walked right back to her. "I've shouted at everyone and made everyone's life hell all because I'm an idiot."

She didn't argue the point. Was that a good sign or a bad one?

He didn't wait to find out. Rushing on with everything he wanted—needed—to tell her, Davis kept talking. "You'd probably be a hell of a lot better off without me, but I'd be in damn poor shape without you."

She smiled. Okay, that was definitely a good sign.

"The last few days without you have been terrible, but they made me realize something. Something I've known all along but was too damn scared to admit."

"What's that, Davis?"

He reached out and laid both hands on her shoulders. Her soft yellow sweater caressed his palms as he looked down into her incredible eyes. "I'm tired of being alone, Marie. I'm tired of pretending it's enough. I want to belong. I want a family." He paused, searched her features for a long moment, then added, "I want *you*."

She didn't say anything. She just blinked at him as her throat knotted.

Say it all, he told himself. Take a risk. Take a chance.

"My enlistment is nearly up," he said, his words tumbling over each other in his hurry to tell her everything he'd been thinking about—planning—the last couple of hours. "I don't want to sign up again. I want to leave the corps and stay here, in Bayside. With you."

Her mouth dropped open. "You do?"

"Yeah," he said on a smile. "I do. I'd like us to expand your shop. Do the restorations we talked about. Be partners. In everything."

"Davis…"

"I know we haven't known each other long, Marie," he said quickly, "but I feel like I've known you forever."

She reached out and laid one palm on his chest. He accepted it like a benediction, feeling her warmth spiral through him in such a tide of love that he knew he'd never feel the cold again. "I feel that, too," she said softly, and Davis's whole being was swept by relief. He wasn't too late.

His fingers tightened on her shoulders, then he released her and reached into one of his pants pockets for the small, dark blue box he'd brought with him in hope. Opening it up, he held it out to her and said, "I want to marry you, Marie."

She looked at the diamond-and-emerald ring for what seemed forever before she lifted her gaze to his again. "Davis, if this is because you're worried about the possibility of a baby—"

"No!" He interrupted her quickly, as vehemently as he could. "No, this is about us. He grabbed her left hand and held it tightly. "If there is a baby, that's a bonus. What I want—what I *need* is you."

"Oh, Davis," she said on a soft sigh, "I want to believe you."

"I love you, Marie."

She blinked, clearly surprised.

He smiled. "I'm not afraid to say it anymore. The only thing that scares me is the thought of living without you."

Marie curled her fingers around his and squeezed. "You don't have to, Davis. I love you, too."

He released a pent-up breath and grinned, feeling the power and strength of that smile right down to his soul. "Then you will marry me?" he asked as he took the ring from the box and held it just at her fingertip.

"I will," she said, and he slid the ring home, feeling a sense of satisfaction like nothing he'd ever known before.

Pulling her into his arms, he held her tightly to him, resting his chin on top of her head. Burrowed in close, Marie said, "You know, if you hadn't come here today, I'd already planned on going to the base tomorrow to hunt you down."

He pulled back slightly and smiled down at her. "A recon mission?"

"You bet," she said, and slid her arms around his waist. "And you know the saying… I Always Get My Man."

Davis laughed and shook his head. "That's the mounties, not the marines."

"Who cares?" she asked, going up on her toes.

"Not me, lady," he said and kissed her, promising them both a lifetime of love. And Davis knew the moment his lips touched hers that he had, at long last, found home.

Epilogue

Christmas Eve, afternoon

Davis sat on the floor of Marie's living room, surrounded by what looked to be ten thousand numbered pieces of plastic. And somehow, in the next few hours, he'd have to fit them all together into the space station that Jeremy expected to find beneath the tree tomorrow morning.

"What's the matter, Sarg?" Marie asked from the bedroom doorway. "Giving up already?"

He grinned at her and shook his head. "Marines don't quit."

"Yeah," she said as she walked across the room to him, "but you won't be a marine much longer, will you?"

When she was close enough, he pulled her down onto his lap and gave her a squeeze. "Nope," he said, and didn't feel the least bit sorry about his decision.

One part of his life was over, but a new and even more interesting part was about to begin.

Marie reached up and cupped his cheek. Smoothing her thumb across his skin, she marveled again that they had found each other. She was happier than she'd ever been, and come New Year's Eve, she'd be a bride. And to top that, she had a very special Christmas present for her soon-to-be husband.

"Davis," she said softly, "there's something I want to tell you—"

Footsteps pounding up the stairs outside the apartment interrupted her and they both turned as one when the front door opened and Gina stormed inside. Marie tried to scoot off Davis's lap, but he held her in place.

"What's wrong with you?" Marie asked, settling into the curve of Davis's arms.

"I'm so mad, I could spit," Gina snapped, flashing an angry look at Davis. "This guy in my ballroom dance class? Today he practically dragged me across the floor, and when I told him he was doing everything all wrong, he told me I should just shut up and let the man lead."

"So?" Not that Marie wasn't sympathetic, but she had some plans of her own here.

"*So* I told him that if he had the slightest idea of

how to lead, I wouldn't mind at all. And he called me a waste of valuable space." She jammed both fists on her hips and tapped the toe of her shoe against the floor. "Do you believe that? I mean, I'm paying for those lessons. He shouldn't get to insult me like that."

Davis snickered. Marie heard him.

"What do you want us to do about it?" she asked her sister.

"He's a marine, just like *him!*" Gina waved one hand at Davis. "So I figured maybe Davis could have him shot at dawn or something."

"I'll see what I can do," he said. "What's his name? Maybe I know him."

"Nick Peretti," Gina snapped. "He's some kind of sergeant or something."

"Gunnery Sergeant," Davis provided.

"That's it! So you *do* know him." Gina's eyes flashed with sparks of vengeance.

"I've...run into him a time or two," Davis hedged.

"With your car?"

"No."

"Too bad." Then, just as quickly as she'd arrived, Gina turned for the door again. "The next time you see him, you tell him he'd better watch out before ticking off a Santini."

"Oh," Davis said over the slam of the door, "I'll warn him."

In the sudden stillness, Marie shook her head and looked up at him. "Are you absolutely *sure* you want to get involved with this family?"

He laughed.

"I mean it, Davis," she said, one corner of her mouth curving into a smile, "this is your last chance to retreat."

"Marines don't retreat."

"Good," she said, and leaned into him before giving him his present. "In that case, there's something you should know."

"Yeah?" he asked, reaching past her for section A1 of the space station.

"Gina's going to be an aunt again in about eight months or so."

"That's good…." He stopped dead, slowly turned his head to look down at her, and when he saw her smile, he stammered. "Are—are you sure?"

"I'll see the doctor to be sure. But trust me. We're pregnant." Marie told him, reaching up to touch his face, his mouth.

"Then we're going to have a—"

"Baby."

"Baby," he repeated, awestruck. His right hand drifted to her flat abdomen and rested there lightly, reverently. When he looked at her again, Marie was sure she saw the shimmer of dampness in his eyes, and her heart turned over.

"I love you, Davis," she whispered.

"I love you, Marie."

Then, pulling his head down to hers, she said softly, "Merry Christmas."

Just before his lips found hers, he added. "And a happy new life."

* * * * *

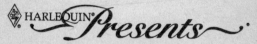

REQUEST YOUR FREE BOOKS!

**2 FREE NOVELS
PLUS 2
FREE GIFTS!**

Passionate, Powerful, Provocative!

YES! Please send me 2 FREE Silhouette Desire® novels and my 2 FREE gifts (gifts are worth about $10). After receiving them, if I don't wish to receive any more books, I can return the shipping statement marked "cancel." If I don't cancel, I will receive 6 brand-new novels every month and be billed just $4.05 per book in the U.S. or $4.74 per book in Canada. That's a saving of at least 15% off the cover price! It's quite a bargain! Shipping and handling is just 50¢ per book.* I understand that accepting the 2 free books and gifts places me under no obligation to buy anything. I can always return a shipment and cancel at any time. Even if I never buy another book, the two free books and gifts are mine to keep forever.

225/326 SDN E5QG

Name	(PLEASE PRINT)

Address		Apt. #

City	State/Prov.	Zip/Postal Code

Signature (if under 18, a parent or guardian must sign)

Mail to the **Silhouette Reader Service:**
IN U.S.A.: P.O. Box 1867, Buffalo, NY 14240-1867
IN CANADA: P.O. Box 609, Fort Erie, Ontario L2A 5X3

Not valid for current subscribers to Silhouette Desire books.

**Want to try two free books from another line?
Call 1-800-873-8635 or visit www.morefreebooks.com.**

* Terms and prices subject to change without notice. Prices do not include applicable taxes. N.Y. residents add applicable sales tax. Canadian residents will be charged applicable provincial taxes and GST. Offer not valid in Quebec. This offer is limited to one order per household. All orders subject to approval. Credit or debit balances in a customer's account(s) may be offset by any other outstanding balance owed by or to the customer. Please allow 4 to 6 weeks for delivery. Offer available while quantities last.

Your Privacy: Silhouette Books is committed to protecting your privacy. Our Privacy Policy is available online at www.eHarlequin.com or upon request from the Reader Service. From time to time we make our lists of customers available to reputable third parties who may have a product or service of interest to you. If you would prefer we not share your name and address, please check here. ☐

Help us get it right—We strive for accurate, respectful and relevant communications. To clarify or modify your communication preferences, visit us at www.ReaderService.com/consumerschoice.

SDES10R